D0456697

MARVEL UNIVERSE ALL-NEW AVENGERS ASSEMBLE VOL. 3. Contains material originally published in magazine form as MARVEL UNIVERSE AVENGERS ASSEMBLE SEASON TWO #9-12. First printing 2015. ISBN# 978-0-7851-9360-9. Published by MARVEL WORLDWIDE, INC., a subsidiary of MARVEL ENTERTAINMENT, LLC. OFFICE OF PUBLICATION: 135 West 50th Street, New York, NY 10020. Copyright © 2015 MARVEL No similarity between any of the names, characters, persons, and/or institutions in this magazine with those of any living or dead person or institution is intended, and any such similarity which may exist is purely coincidental. **Printed in the U.S.A.** ALAN FINE, President, Marvel Entertainment; DAN BUCKLEY, President, TV, Publishing and Brand Management; JOE QUESADA, Chief Creative Officer; TOM BREVOORT, SVP of Publishing; DAVID BOGART, SVP of Operations & Procurement, Publishing; C.B. CEBULSKI, VP of International Development & Brand Management; DAVID GABRIEL, SVP Print, Sales & Marketing; JIM O'KEEFE, VP of Operations & Logistics; DAN CARR, Executive Director of Publishing Technology; SUSAN CRESPI, Editorial Operations Manager; ALEX MORALES, Publishing Operations Manager; STAN LEE, Chairman Emeritus. For information regarding advertising in Marvel Comics or on Marvel.com, please contact Jonathan Rheingold, VP of Custom Solutions & Ad Sales, at jrheingold@marvel.com. For Marvel subscription inquiries, please call 800-217-9158. **Manufactured between 9/18/2015 and 10/26/2015 by SHERIDAN BOOKS, INC., CHELSEA, MI, USA.**

10 9 8 7 6 5 4 3 2 1

MARVEL
AVENGERS ASSEMBLE

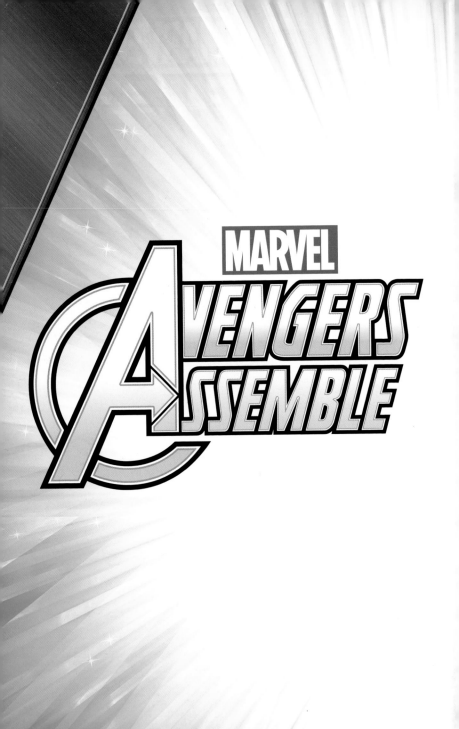

Based on the TV series written by
CHARLOTTE FULLERTON & **KEVIN RUBIO; LEN WEIN;**
EUGENE SON; AND **KEVIN BURKE** & **CHRIS "DOC" WYATT**

Directed by
TIM ELDRED & **PHIL PIGNOTTI**

Art by
MARVEL ANIMATION

Adapted by
JOE CARAMAGNA

Special Thanks to Henry Ong, Hannah MacDonald & Product Factory

Editor
SEBASTIAN GIRNER

Consulting Editor
JON MOISAN

Senior Editor
MARK PANICCIA

Collection Editor
ALEX STARBUCK

Assistant Editor
SARAH BRUNSTAD

Editors, Special Projects
JENNIFER GRÜNWALD & **MARK D. BEAZLEY**

Senior Editor, Special Projects
JEFF YOUNGQUIST

SVP Print, Sales & Marketing
DAVID GABRIEL

Head of Marvel Television
JEPH LOEB

Book Designer
ADAM DEL RE

Editor In Chief
AXEL ALONSO

Chief Creative Officer
JOE QUESADA

Publisher
DAN BUCKLEY

Executive Producer
ALAN FINE

HERE COMES ANT-MAN!

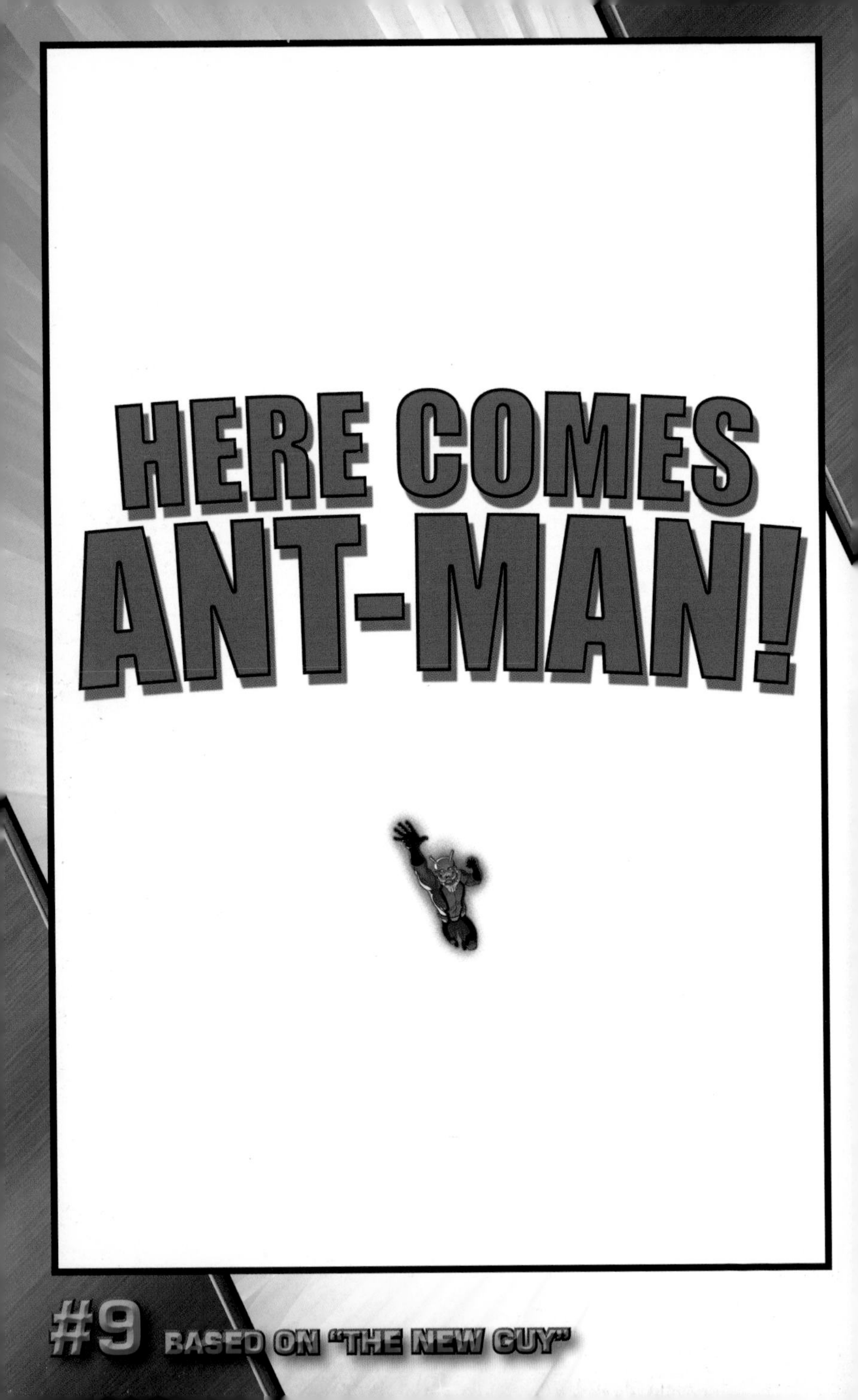

#9 BASED ON "THE NEW GUY"

MARVEL

AVENGERS ASSEMBLE

SEASON 2

The Ave...
welco...
new mer...
Scott Lan...
astoni...
ANT-...

B...
eve...
is b...
abo...

IRON MAN

CAPTAIN AMERICA

THOR

BLACK WIDOW

HULK

FALCON

HAWKEYE

ANT-MAN

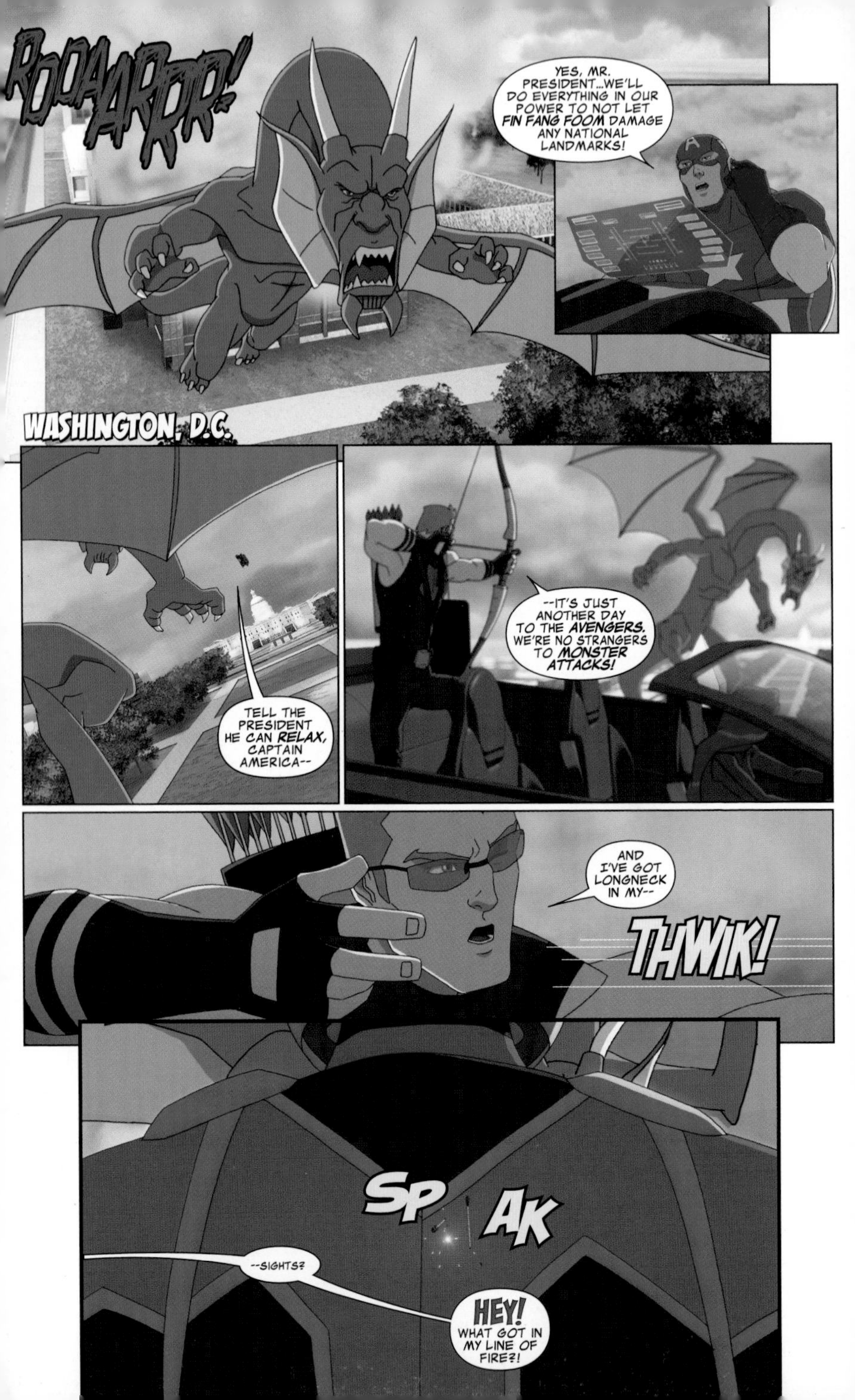
ROOAARRR!
YES, MR. PRESIDENT...WE'LL DO EVERYTHING IN OUR POWER TO NOT LET FIN FANG FOOM DAMAGE ANY NATIONAL LANDMARKS!
WASHINGTON, D.C.
TELL THE PRESIDENT HE CAN RELAX, CAPTAIN AMERICA--
--IT'S JUST ANOTHER DAY TO THE AVENGERS. WE'RE NO STRANGERS TO MONSTER ATTACKS!
AND I'VE GOT LONGNECK IN MY--
THWIK!
SPAK
--SIGHTS?
HEY! WHAT GOT IN MY LINE OF FIRE?!

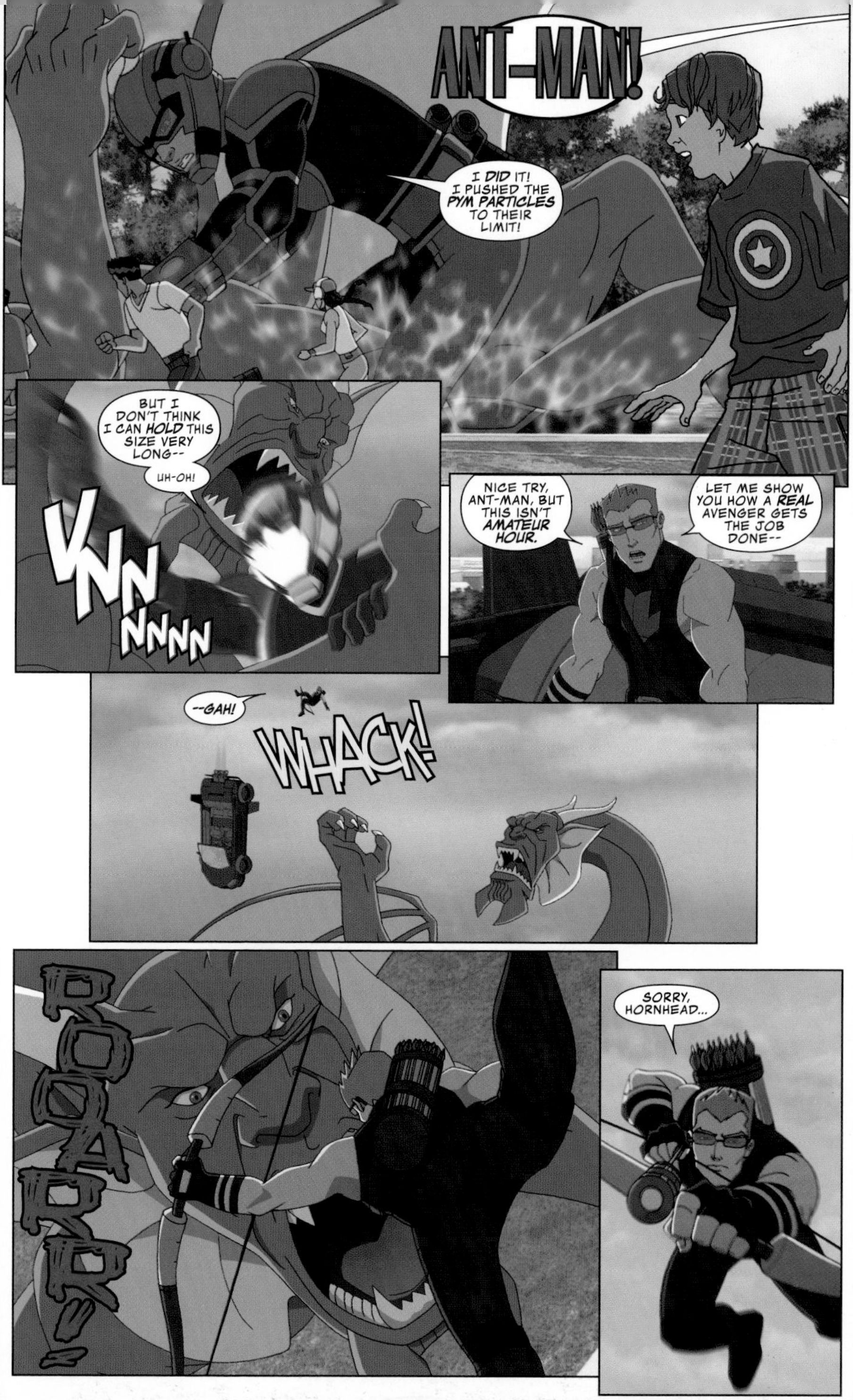
ANT-MAN!
I DID IT! I PUSHED THE PYM PARTICLES TO THEIR LIMIT!
BUT I DON'T THINK I CAN HOLD THIS SIZE VERY LONG--
UH-OH!
VNNNNNN
NICE TRY, ANT-MAN, BUT THIS ISN'T AMATEUR HOUR.
LET ME SHOW YOU HOW A REAL AVENGER GETS THE JOB DONE--
--GAH!
WHACK!
ROOAARR!
SORRY, HORNHEAD...

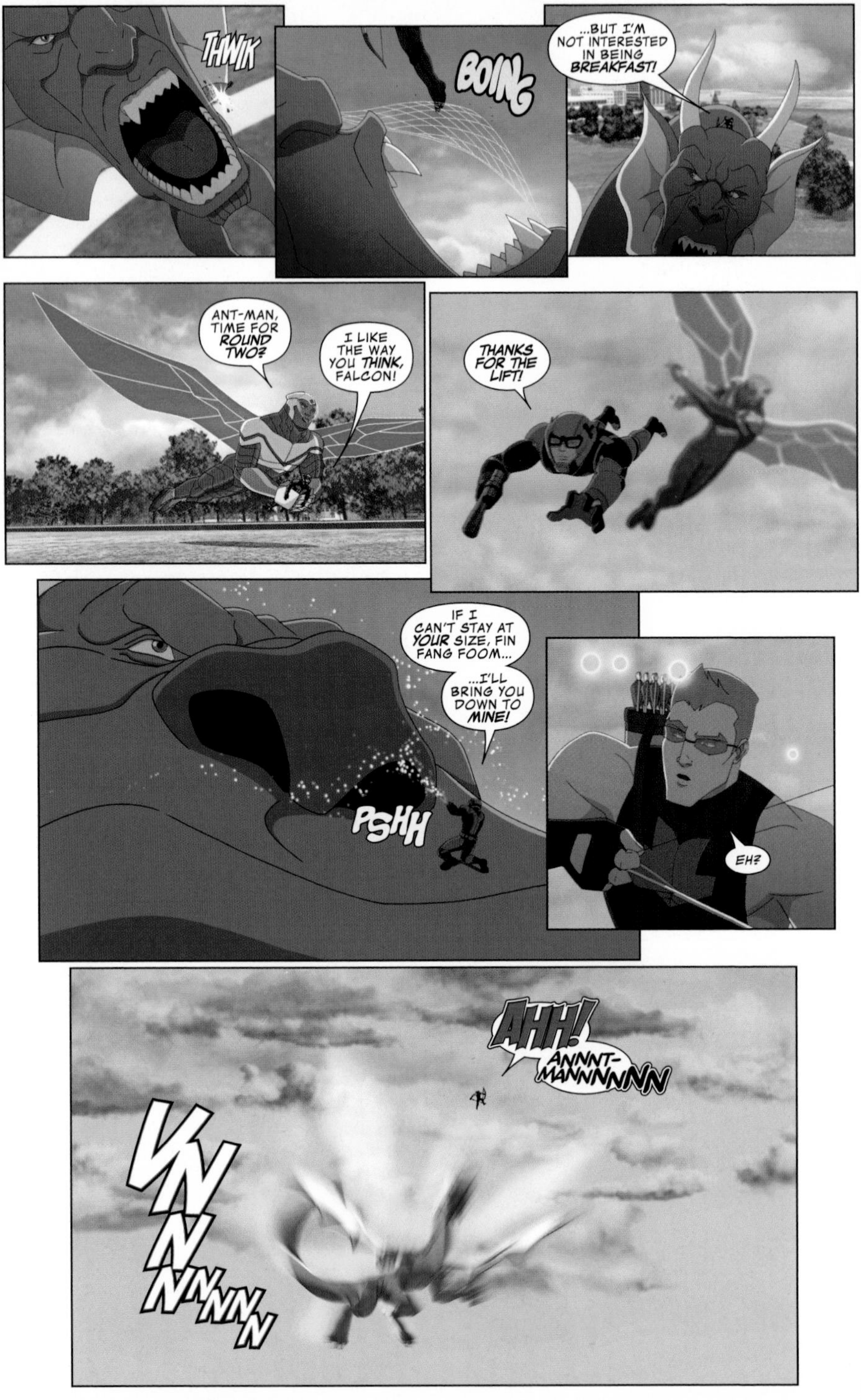
THWIK
BOING
...BUT I'M NOT INTERESTED IN BEING BREAKFAST!
ANT-MAN, TIME FOR ROUND TWO?
I LIKE THE WAY YOU THINK, FALCON!
THANKS FOR THE LIFT!
IF I CAN'T STAY AT YOUR SIZE, FIN FANG FOOM...
...I'LL BRING YOU DOWN TO MINE!
PSHH
EH?
AHH! ANNNT-MANNNNNNN
VNNNNNNNN

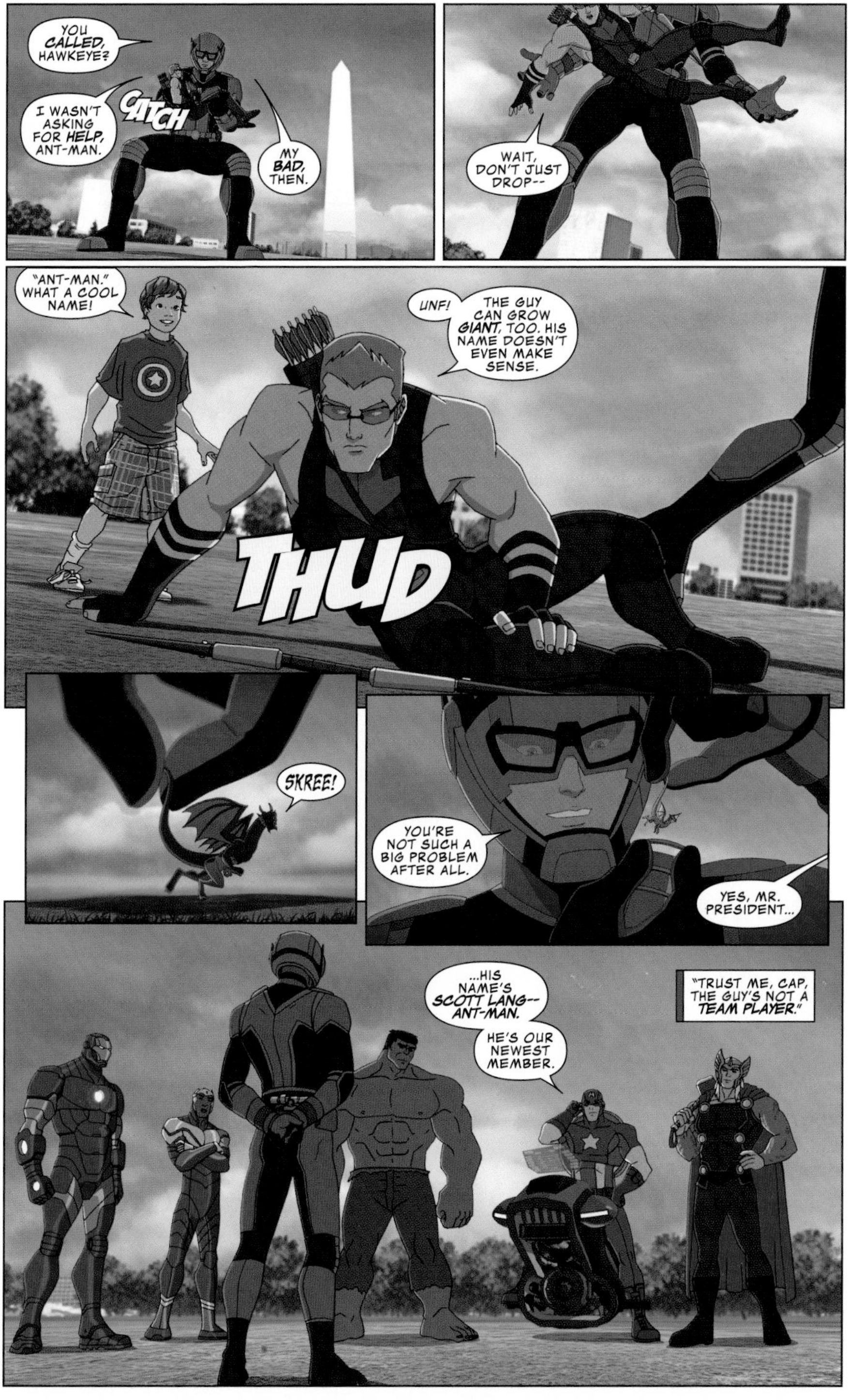
YOU CALLED, HAWKEYE?
I WASN'T ASKING FOR HELP, ANT-MAN.
CATCH
MY BAD, THEN.
WAIT, DON'T JUST DROP--
"ANT-MAN." WHAT A COOL NAME!
UNF!
THE GUY CAN GROW GIANT, TOO. HIS NAME DOESN'T EVEN MAKE SENSE.
THUD
SKREE!
YOU'RE NOT SUCH A BIG PROBLEM AFTER ALL.
YES, MR. PRESIDENT...
"TRUST ME, CAP, THE GUY'S NOT A TEAM PLAYER."
...HIS NAME'S SCOTT LANG-- ANT-MAN.
HE'S OUR NEWEST MEMBER.

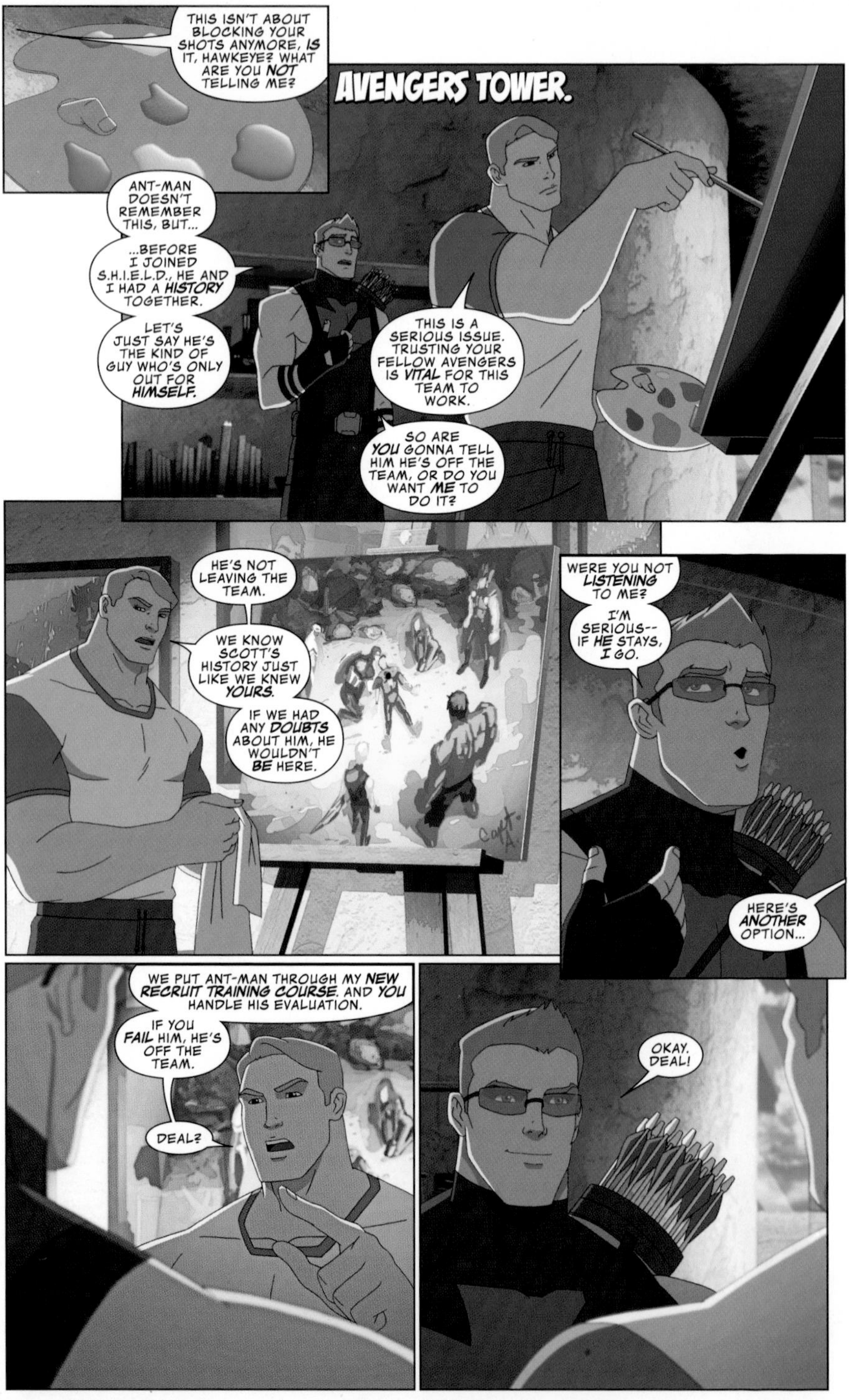

THIS ISN'T ABOUT BLOCKING YOUR SHOTS ANYMORE, IS IT, HAWKEYE? WHAT ARE YOU NOT TELLING ME?
AVENGERS TOWER.
ANT-MAN DOESN'T REMEMBER THIS, BUT...
...BEFORE I JOINED S.H.I.E.L.D., HE AND I HAD A HISTORY TOGETHER.
LET'S JUST SAY HE'S THE KIND OF GUY WHO'S ONLY OUT FOR HIMSELF.
THIS IS A SERIOUS ISSUE. TRUSTING YOUR FELLOW AVENGERS IS VITAL FOR THIS TEAM TO WORK.
SO ARE YOU GONNA TELL HIM HE'S OFF THE TEAM, OR DO YOU WANT ME TO DO IT?
HE'S NOT LEAVING THE TEAM.
WE KNOW SCOTT'S HISTORY JUST LIKE WE KNEW YOURS.
IF WE HAD ANY DOUBTS ABOUT HIM, HE WOULDN'T BE HERE.
WERE YOU NOT LISTENING TO ME?
I'M SERIOUS-- IF HE STAYS, I GO.
HERE'S ANOTHER OPTION...
WE PUT ANT-MAN THROUGH MY NEW RECRUIT TRAINING COURSE. AND YOU HANDLE HIS EVALUATION.
IF YOU FAIL HIM, HE'S OFF THE TEAM.
DEAL?
OKAY. DEAL!

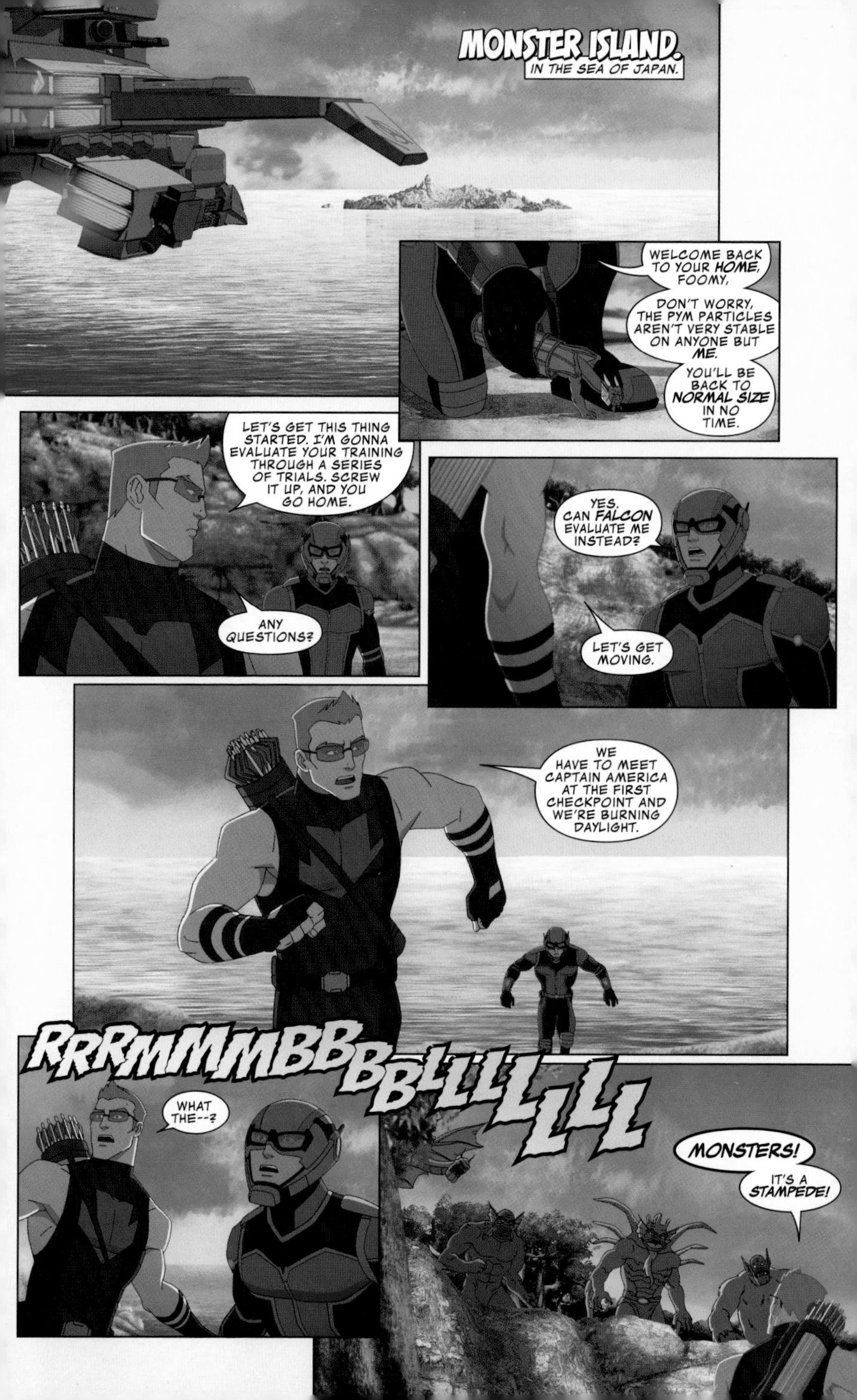
MONSTER ISLAND.
IN THE SEA OF JAPAN.
WELCOME BACK TO YOUR HOME, FOOMY.
DON'T WORRY, THE PYM PARTICLES AREN'T VERY STABLE ON ANYONE BUT ME.
YOU'LL BE BACK TO NORMAL SIZE IN NO TIME.
LET'S GET THIS THING STARTED. I'M GONNA EVALUATE YOUR TRAINING THROUGH A SERIES OF TRIALS. SCREW IT UP, AND YOU GO HOME.
ANY QUESTIONS?
YES. CAN FALCON EVALUATE ME INSTEAD?
LET'S GET MOVING.
WE HAVE TO MEET CAPTAIN AMERICA AT THE FIRST CHECKPOINT AND WE'RE BURNING DAYLIGHT.
RRRMMMMBBBBLLLLLLLL
WHAT THE--?
MONSTERS!
IT'S A STAMPEDE!

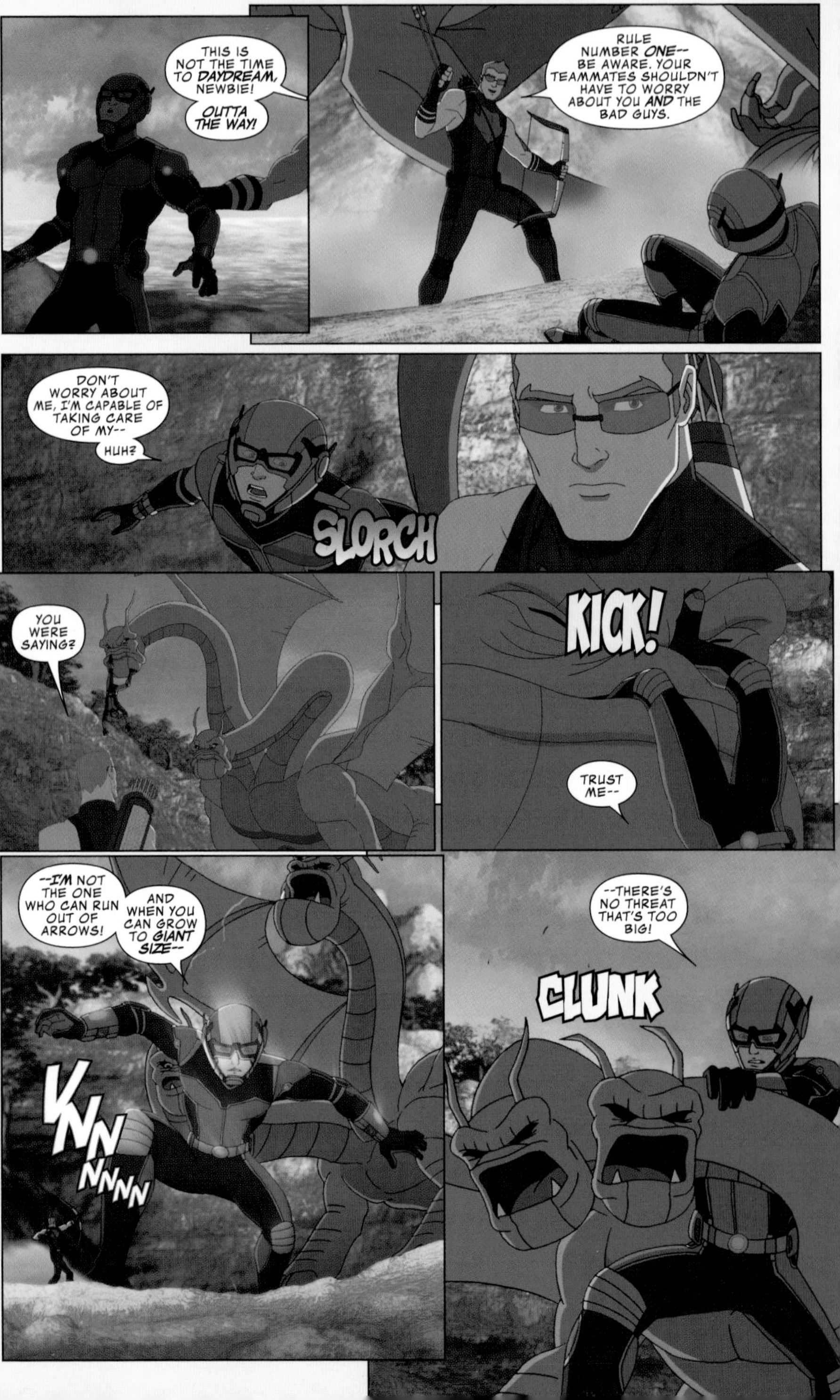
THIS IS NOT THE TIME TO DAYDREAM, NEWBIE!
OUTTA THE WAY!
RULE NUMBER ONE-- BE AWARE. YOUR TEAMMATES SHOULDN'T HAVE TO WORRY ABOUT YOU AND THE BAD GUYS.
DON'T WORRY ABOUT ME, I'M CAPABLE OF TAKING CARE OF MY--
HUH?
SLORCH
YOU WERE SAYING?
KICK!
TRUST ME--
--I'M NOT THE ONE WHO CAN RUN OUT OF ARROWS!
AND WHEN YOU CAN GROW TO GIANT SIZE--
VNNNNNN
--THERE'S NO THREAT THAT'S TOO BIG!
CLUNK

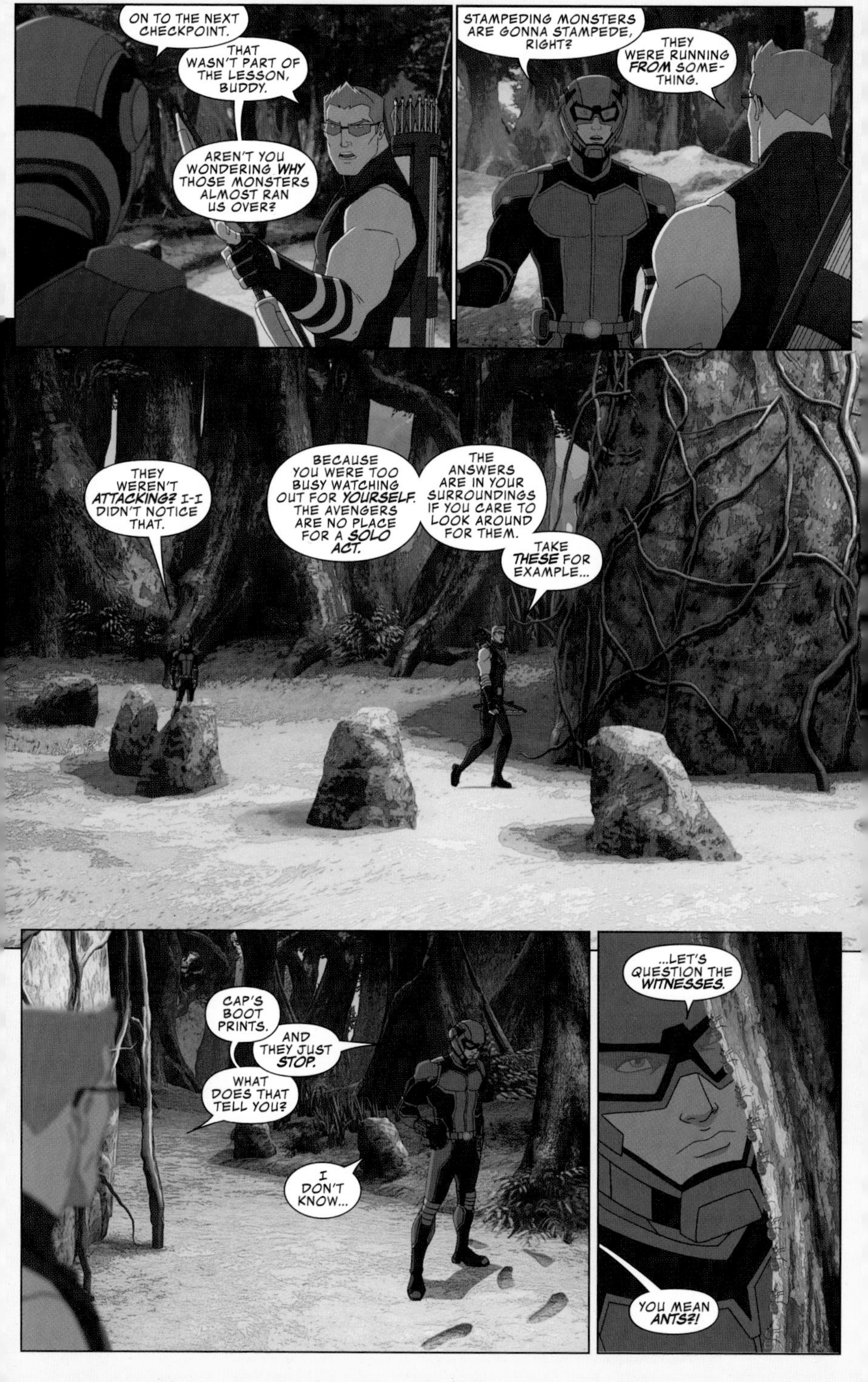

ON TO THE NEXT CHECKPOINT.
THAT WASN'T PART OF THE LESSON, BUDDY.
AREN'T YOU WONDERING WHY THOSE MONSTERS ALMOST RAN US OVER?
STAMPEDING MONSTERS ARE GONNA STAMPEDE, RIGHT?
THEY WERE RUNNING FROM SOMETHING.
THEY WEREN'T ATTACKING? I-I DIDN'T NOTICE THAT.
BECAUSE YOU WERE TOO BUSY WATCHING OUT FOR YOURSELF. THE AVENGERS ARE NO PLACE FOR A SOLO ACT.
THE ANSWERS ARE IN YOUR SURROUNDINGS IF YOU CARE TO LOOK AROUND FOR THEM.
TAKE THESE FOR EXAMPLE...
CAP'S BOOT PRINTS.
AND THEY JUST STOP.
WHAT DOES THAT TELL YOU?
I DON'T KNOW...
...LET'S QUESTION THE WITNESSES.
YOU MEAN ANTS?!

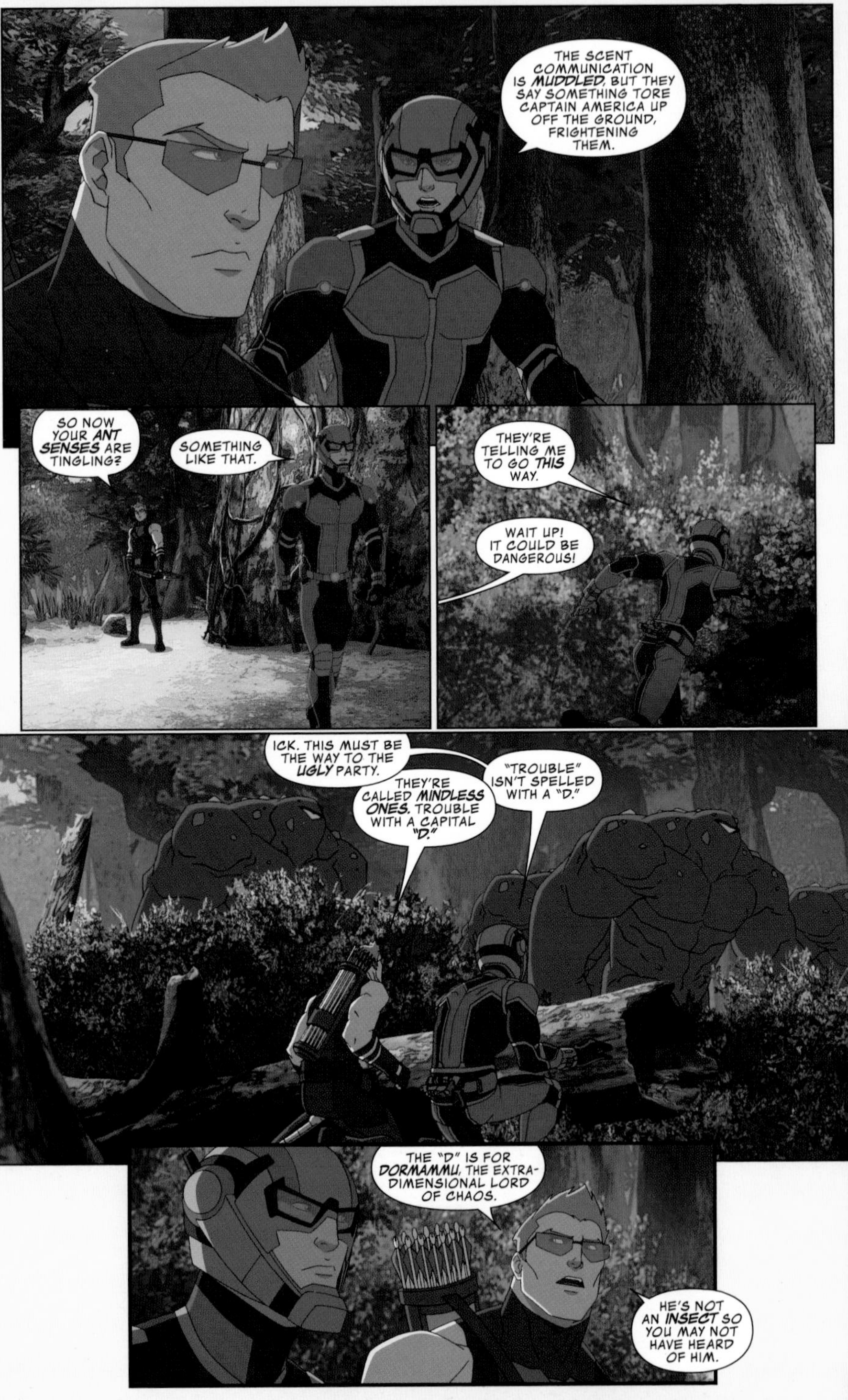
THE SCENT COMMUNICATION IS MUDDLED, BUT THEY SAY SOMETHING TORE CAPTAIN AMERICA UP OFF THE GROUND, FRIGHTENING THEM.
SO NOW YOUR ANT SENSES ARE TINGLING?
SOMETHING LIKE THAT.
THEY'RE TELLING ME TO GO THIS WAY.
WAIT UP! IT COULD BE DANGEROUS!
ICK. THIS MUST BE THE WAY TO THE UGLY PARTY.
THEY'RE CALLED MINDLESS ONES. TROUBLE WITH A CAPITAL "D."
"TROUBLE" ISN'T SPELLED WITH A "D."
THE "D" IS FOR DORMAMMU, THE EXTRA-DIMENSIONAL LORD OF CHAOS.
HE'S NOT AN INSECT SO YOU MAY NOT HAVE HEARD OF HIM.

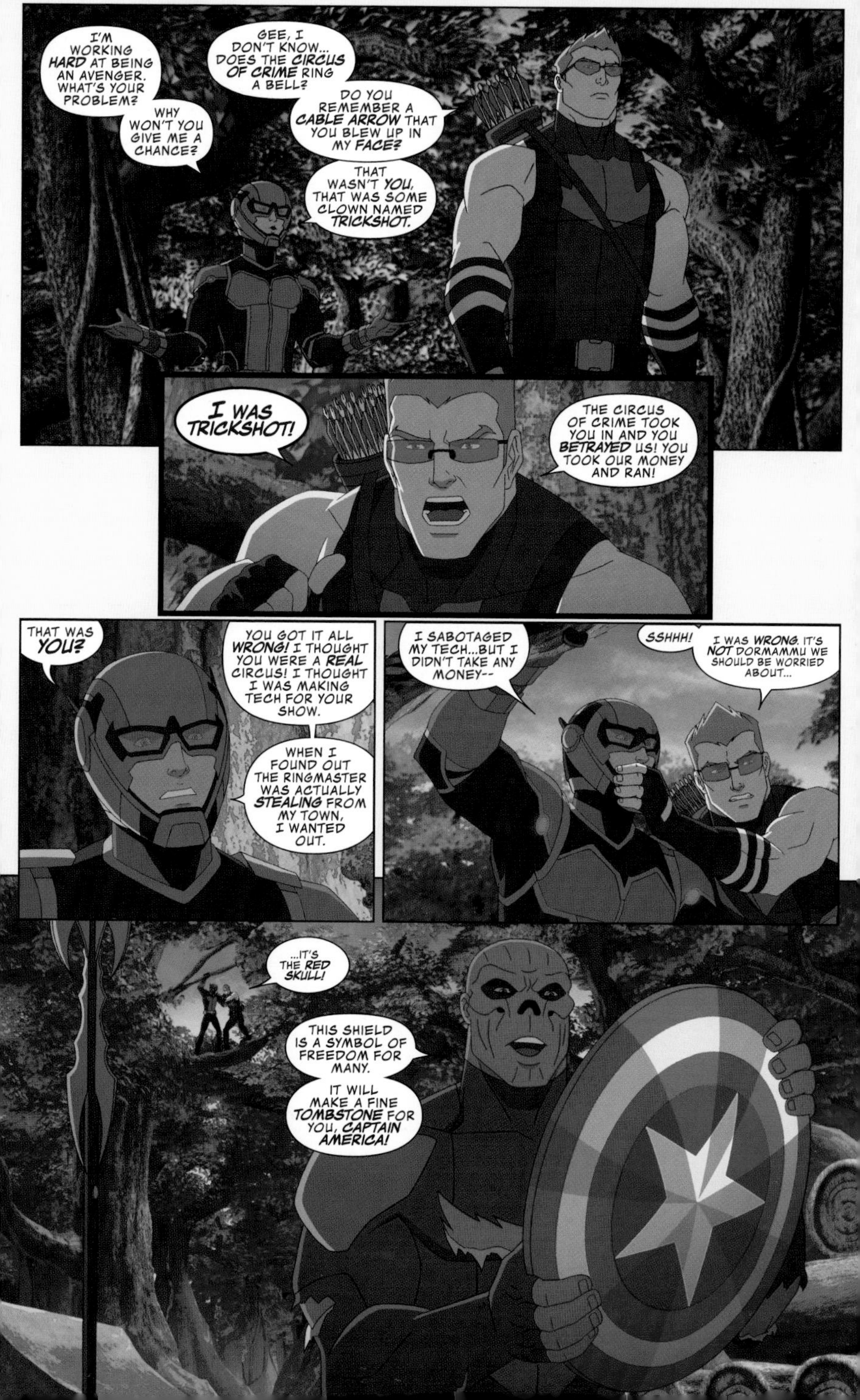

I'M WORKING HARD AT BEING AN AVENGER. WHAT'S YOUR PROBLEM?
WHY WON'T YOU GIVE ME A CHANCE?
GEE, I DON'T KNOW... DOES THE CIRCUS OF CRIME RING A BELL?
DO YOU REMEMBER A CABLE ARROW THAT YOU BLEW UP IN MY FACE?
THAT WASN'T YOU, THAT WAS SOME CLOWN NAMED TRICKSHOT.
I WAS TRICKSHOT!
THE CIRCUS OF CRIME TOOK YOU IN AND YOU BETRAYED US! YOU TOOK OUR MONEY AND RAN!
THAT WAS YOU?
YOU GOT IT ALL WRONG! I THOUGHT YOU WERE A REAL CIRCUS! I THOUGHT I WAS MAKING TECH FOR YOUR SHOW.
WHEN I FOUND OUT THE RINGMASTER WAS ACTUALLY STEALING FROM MY TOWN, I WANTED OUT.
I SABOTAGED MY TECH...BUT I DIDN'T TAKE ANY MONEY--
SSHHH!
I WAS WRONG. IT'S NOT DORMAMMU WE SHOULD BE WORRIED ABOUT...
...IT'S THE RED SKULL!
THIS SHIELD IS A SYMBOL OF FREEDOM FOR MANY.
IT WILL MAKE A FINE TOMBSTONE FOR YOU, CAPTAIN AMERICA!

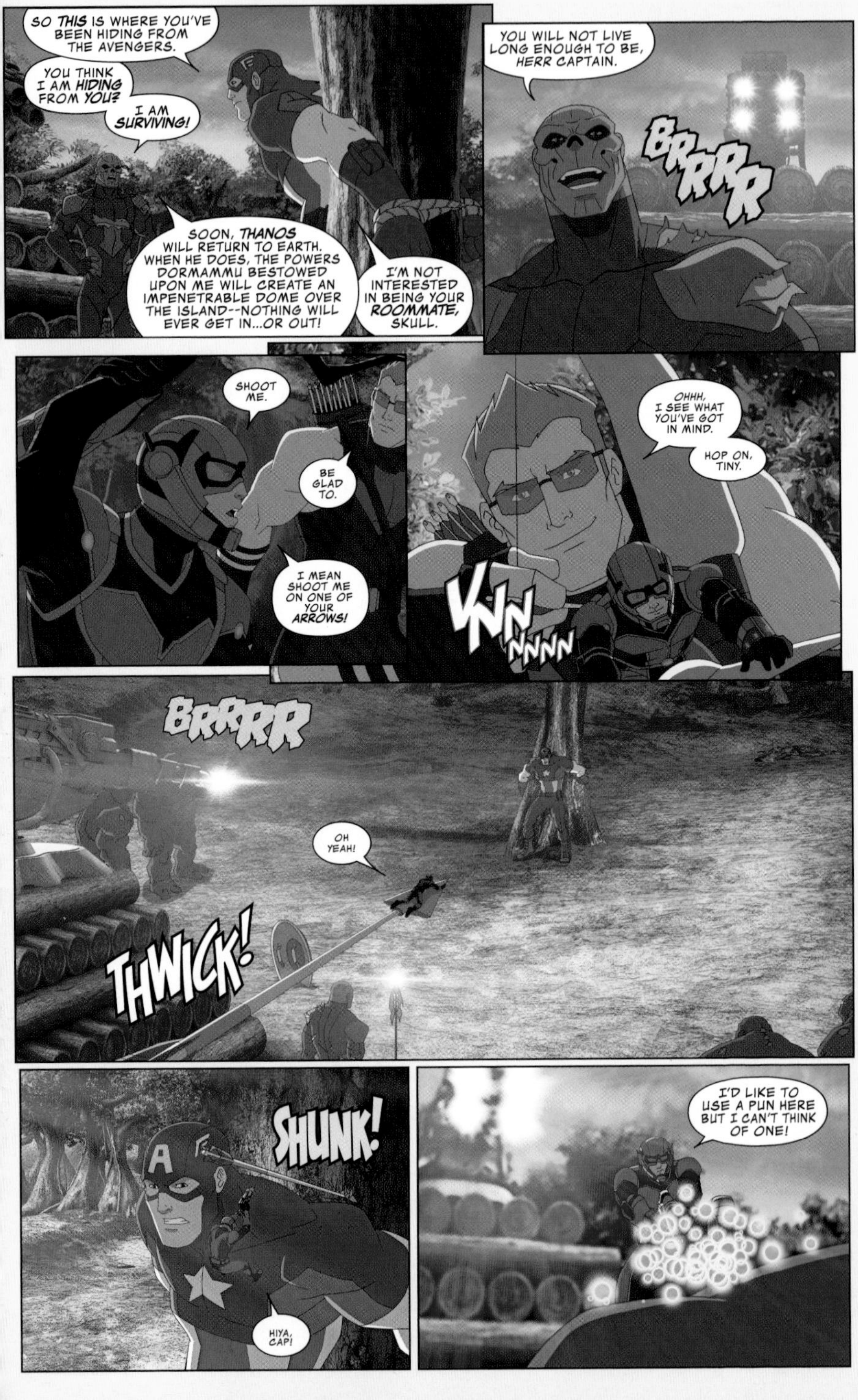
SO THIS IS WHERE YOU'VE BEEN HIDING FROM THE AVENGERS.
YOU THINK I AM HIDING FROM YOU?
I AM SURVIVING!
SOON, THANOS WILL RETURN TO EARTH. WHEN HE DOES, THE POWERS DORMAMMU BESTOWED UPON ME WILL CREATE AN IMPENETRABLE DOME OVER THE ISLAND--NOTHING WILL EVER GET IN...OR OUT!
I'M NOT INTERESTED IN BEING YOUR ROOMMATE, SKULL.
YOU WILL NOT LIVE LONG ENOUGH TO BE, HERR CAPTAIN.
BRRRR
SHOOT ME.
BE GLAD TO.
I MEAN SHOOT ME ON ONE OF YOUR ARROWS!
OHHH, I SEE WHAT YOU'VE GOT IN MIND.
HOP ON, TINY.
VNNNNNN
BRRRR
OH YEAH!
THWICK!
SHUNK!
HIYA, CAP!
I'D LIKE TO USE A PUN HERE BUT I CAN'T THINK OF ONE!

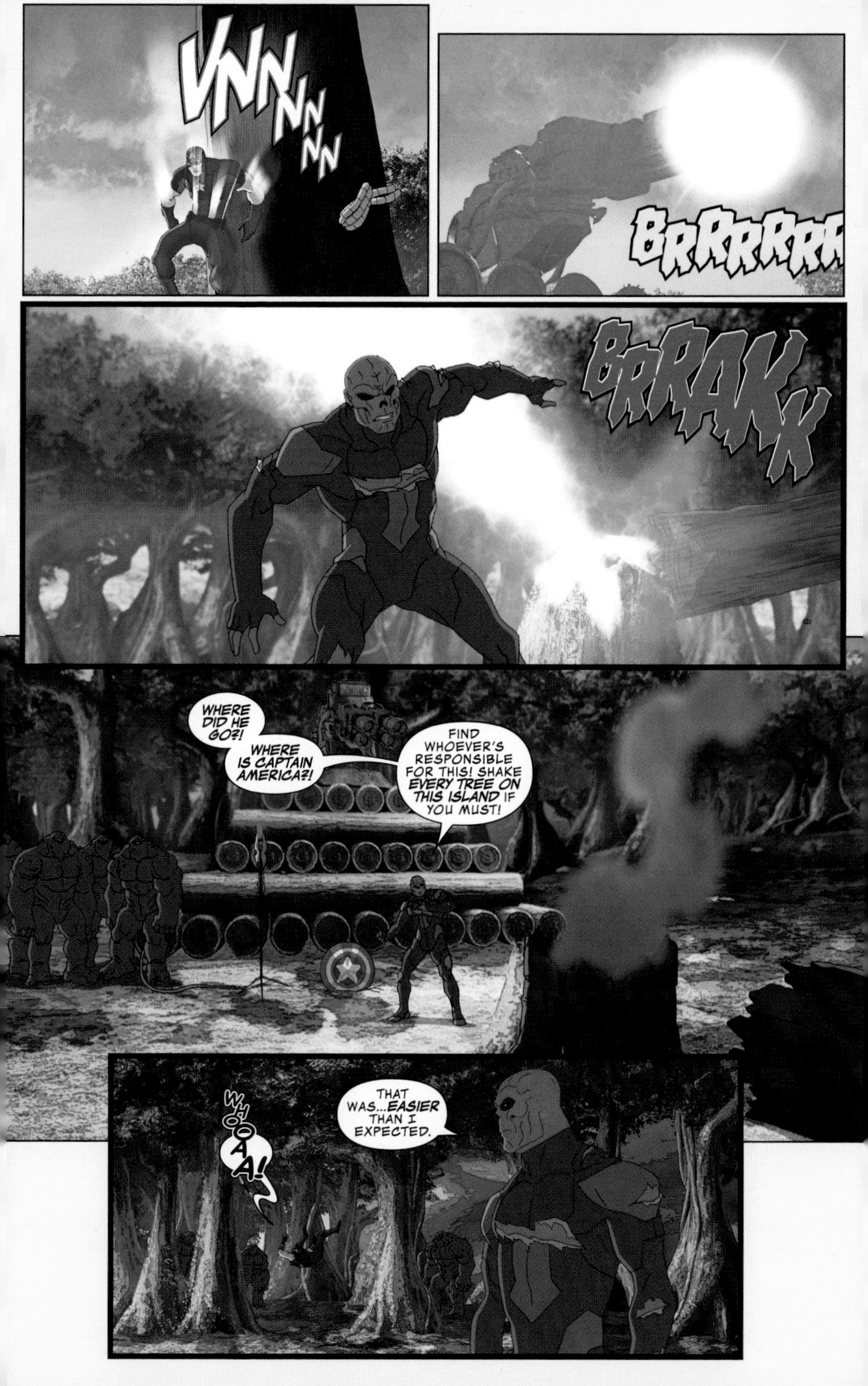
VNNNNNNN
BRRRRRR
BRRAKK
WHERE DID HE GO?! WHERE IS CAPTAIN AMERICA?!
FIND WHOEVER'S RESPONSIBLE FOR THIS! SHAKE EVERY TREE ON THIS ISLAND IF YOU MUST!
WHOOAA!
THAT WAS...EASIER THAN I EXPECTED.

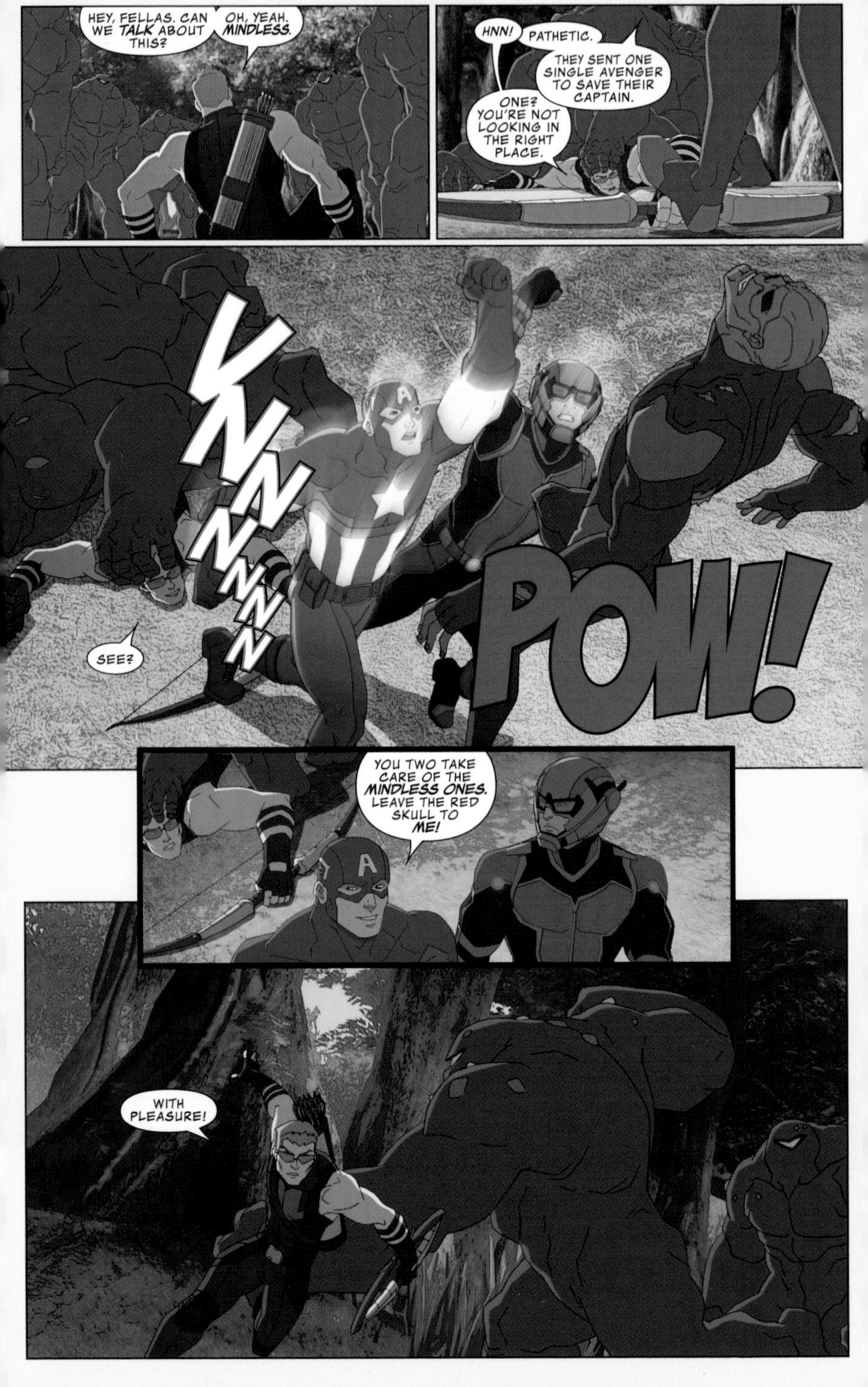
HEY, FELLAS. CAN WE TALK ABOUT THIS?
OH, YEAH. MINDLESS.
HNN!
PATHETIC.
THEY SENT ONE SINGLE AVENGER TO SAVE THEIR CAPTAIN.
ONE? YOU'RE NOT LOOKING IN THE RIGHT PLACE.
VNNNNNN
POW!
SEE?
YOU TWO TAKE CARE OF THE MINDLESS ONES. LEAVE THE RED SKULL TO ME!
WITH PLEASURE!

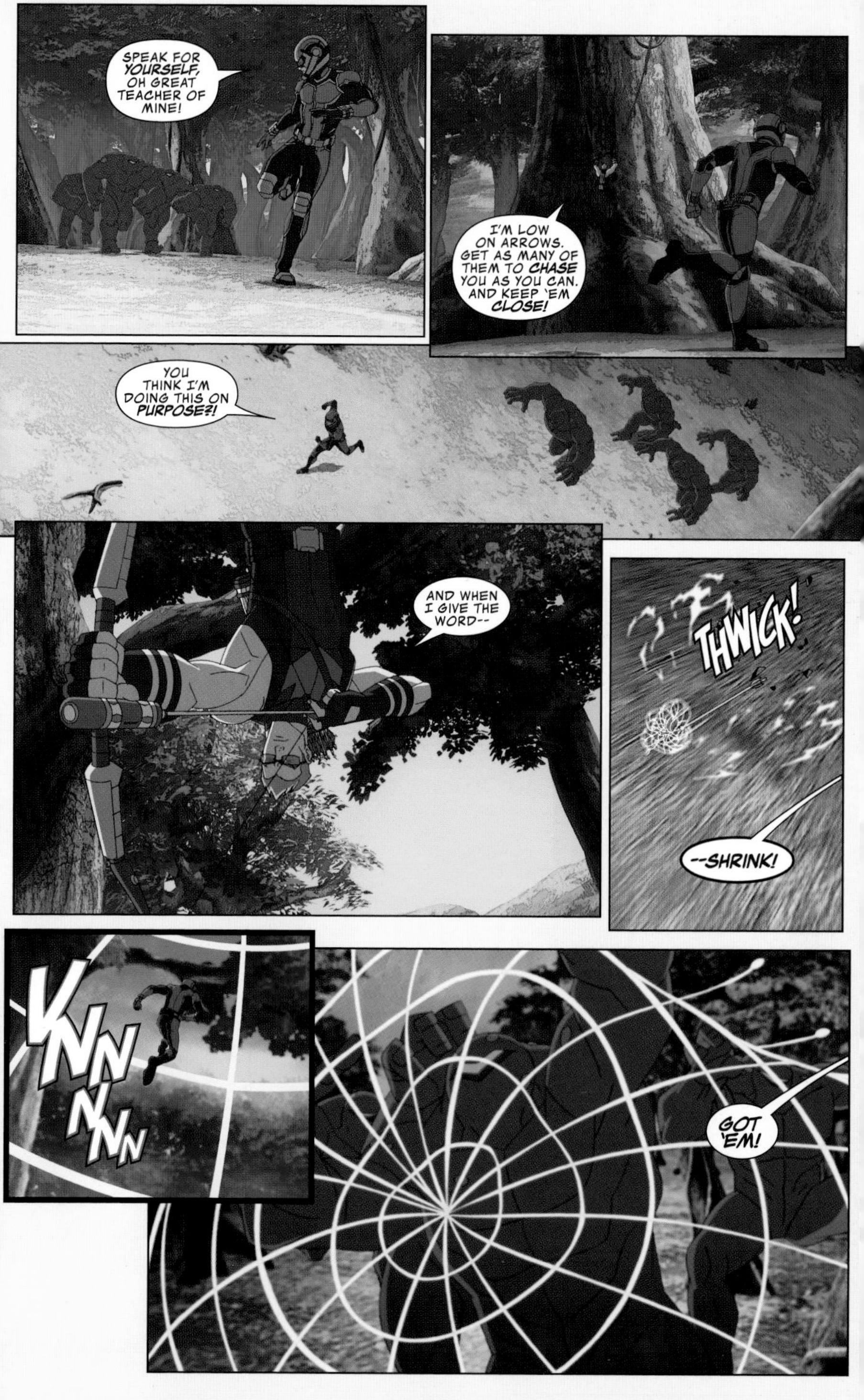
SPEAK FOR YOURSELF, OH GREAT TEACHER OF MINE!
I'M LOW ON ARROWS. GET AS MANY OF THEM TO CHASE YOU AS YOU CAN. AND KEEP 'EM CLOSE!
YOU THINK I'M DOING THIS ON PURPOSE?!
AND WHEN I GIVE THE WORD--
THWICK!
--SHRINK!
KNNNNNN
GOT 'EM!

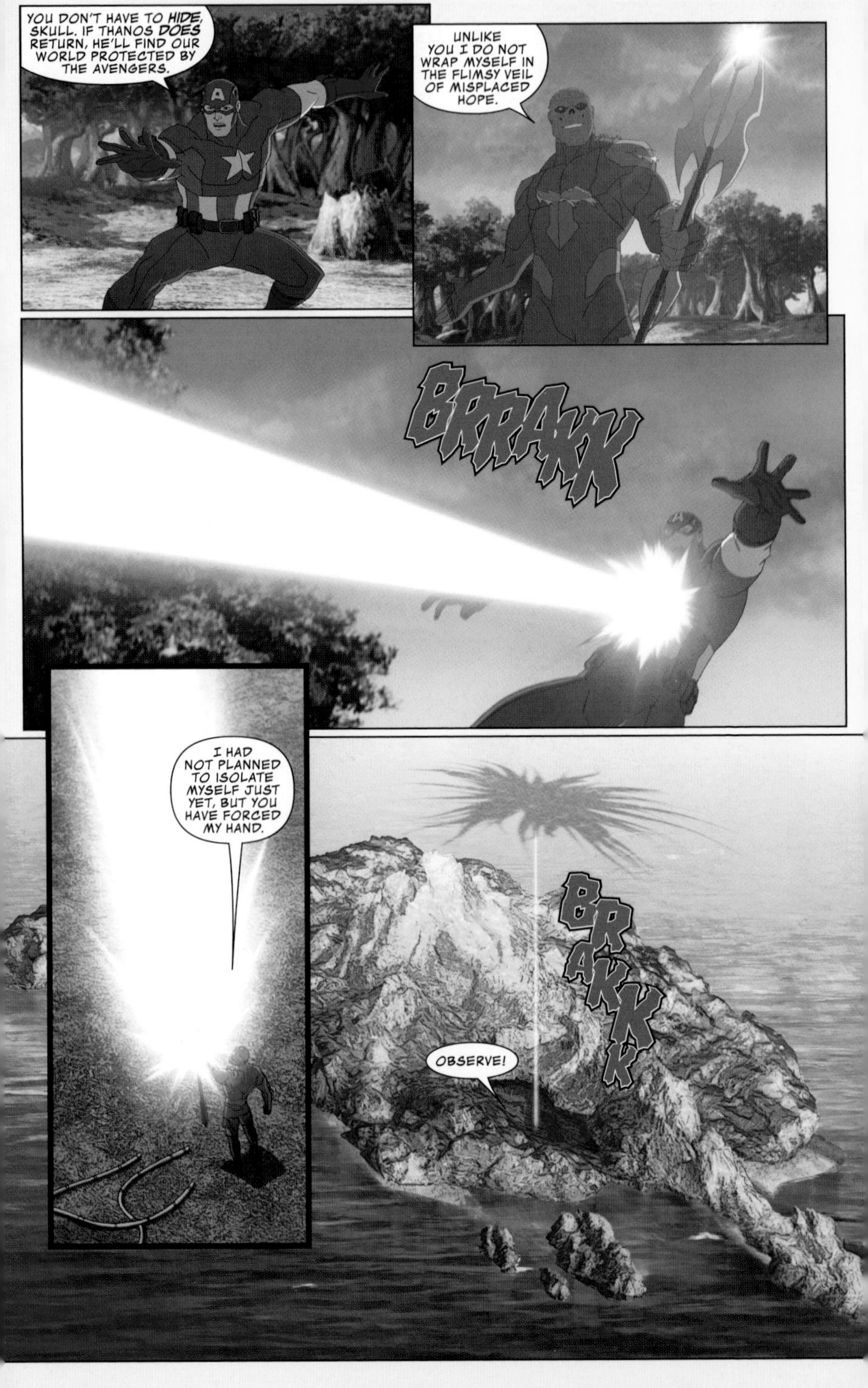
YOU DON'T HAVE TO HIDE, SKULL. IF THANOS DOES RETURN, HE'LL FIND OUR WORLD PROTECTED BY THE AVENGERS.
UNLIKE YOU I DO NOT WRAP MYSELF IN THE FLIMSY VEIL OF MISPLACED HOPE.
BRRAKK
I HAD NOT PLANNED TO ISOLATE MYSELF JUST YET, BUT YOU HAVE FORCED MY HAND.
BRAKKK
OBSERVE!

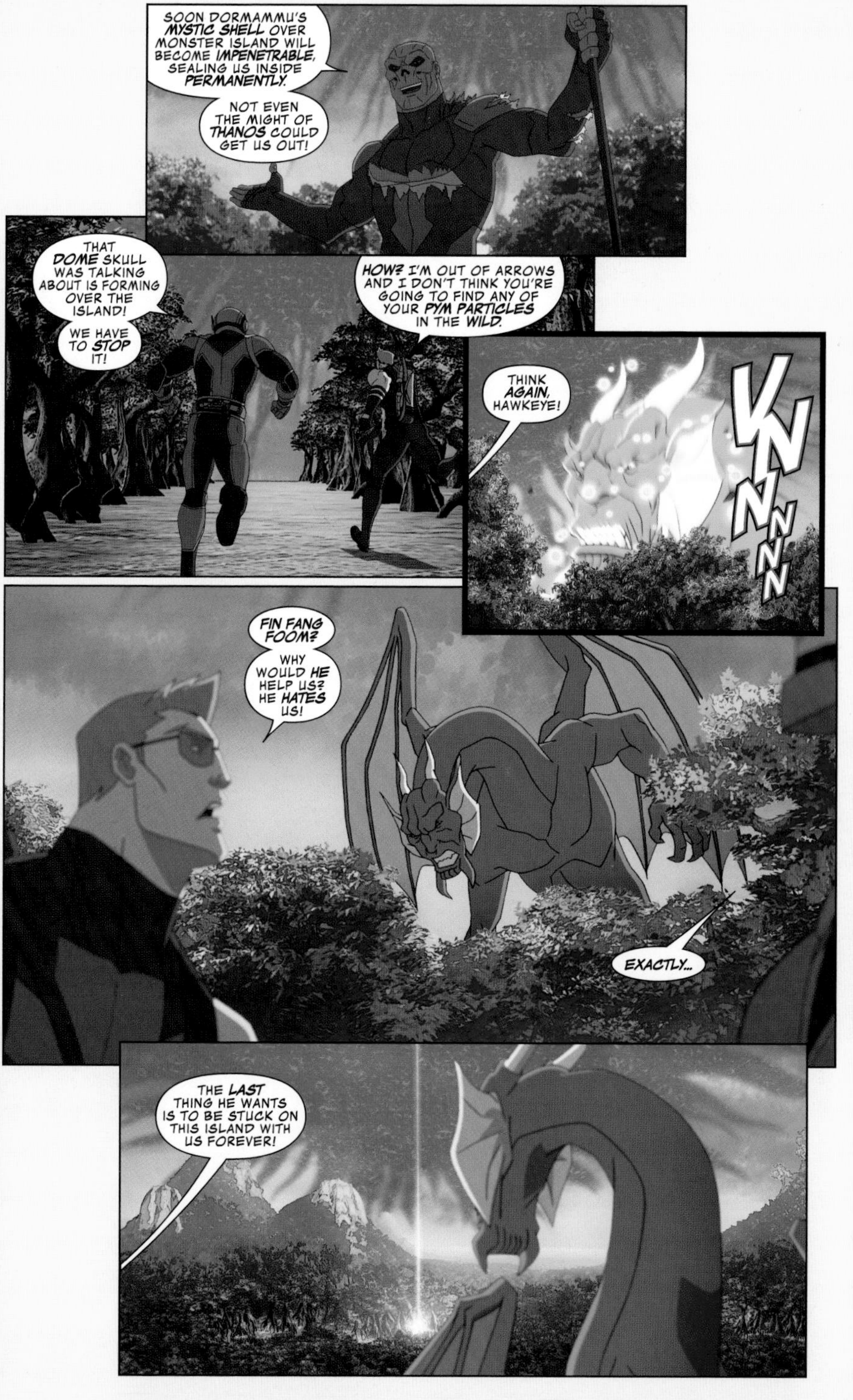
SOON DORMAMMU'S MYSTIC SHELL OVER MONSTER ISLAND WILL BECOME IMPENETRABLE, SEALING US INSIDE PERMANENTLY.
NOT EVEN THE MIGHT OF THANOS COULD GET US OUT!
THAT DOME SKULL WAS TALKING ABOUT IS FORMING OVER THE ISLAND!
WE HAVE TO STOP IT!
HOW? I'M OUT OF ARROWS AND I DON'T THINK YOU'RE GOING TO FIND ANY OF YOUR PYM PARTICLES IN THE WILD.
THINK AGAIN, HAWKEYE!
VNNNNN
FIN FANG FOOM?
WHY WOULD HE HELP US? HE HATES US!
EXACTLY...
THE LAST THING HE WANTS IS TO BE STUCK ON THIS ISLAND WITH US FOREVER!

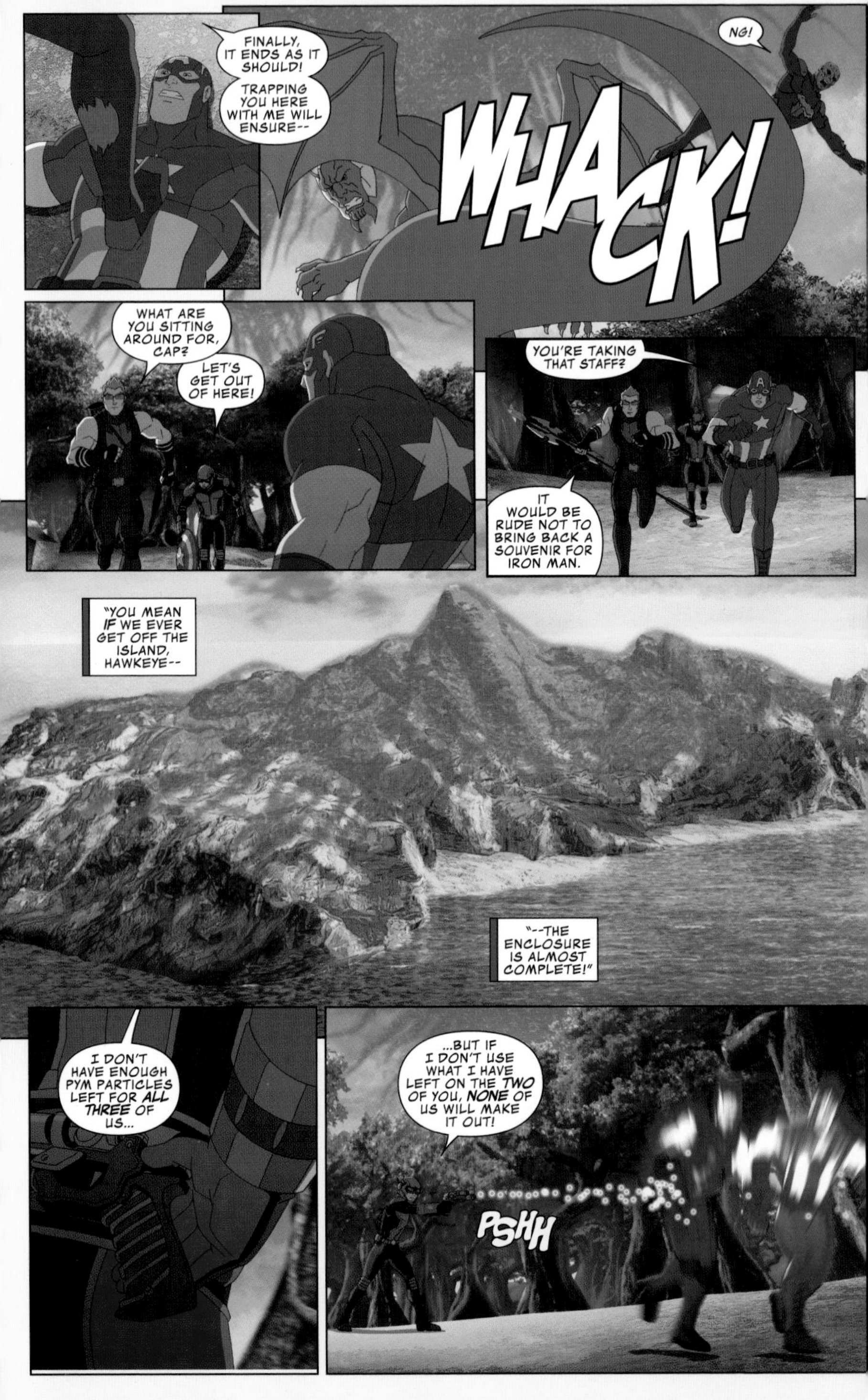
FINALLY, IT ENDS AS IT SHOULD!
TRAPPING YOU HERE WITH ME WILL ENSURE--
NG!
WHACK!
WHAT ARE YOU SITTING AROUND FOR, CAP?
LET'S GET OUT OF HERE!
YOU'RE TAKING THAT STAFF?
IT WOULD BE RUDE NOT TO BRING BACK A SOUVENIR FOR IRON MAN.
"YOU MEAN IF WE EVER GET OFF THE ISLAND, HAWKEYE--
"--THE ENCLOSURE IS ALMOST COMPLETE!"
I DON'T HAVE ENOUGH PYM PARTICLES LEFT FOR ALL THREE OF US...
...BUT IF I DON'T USE WHAT I HAVE LEFT ON THE TWO OF YOU, NONE OF US WILL MAKE IT OUT!
PSHH

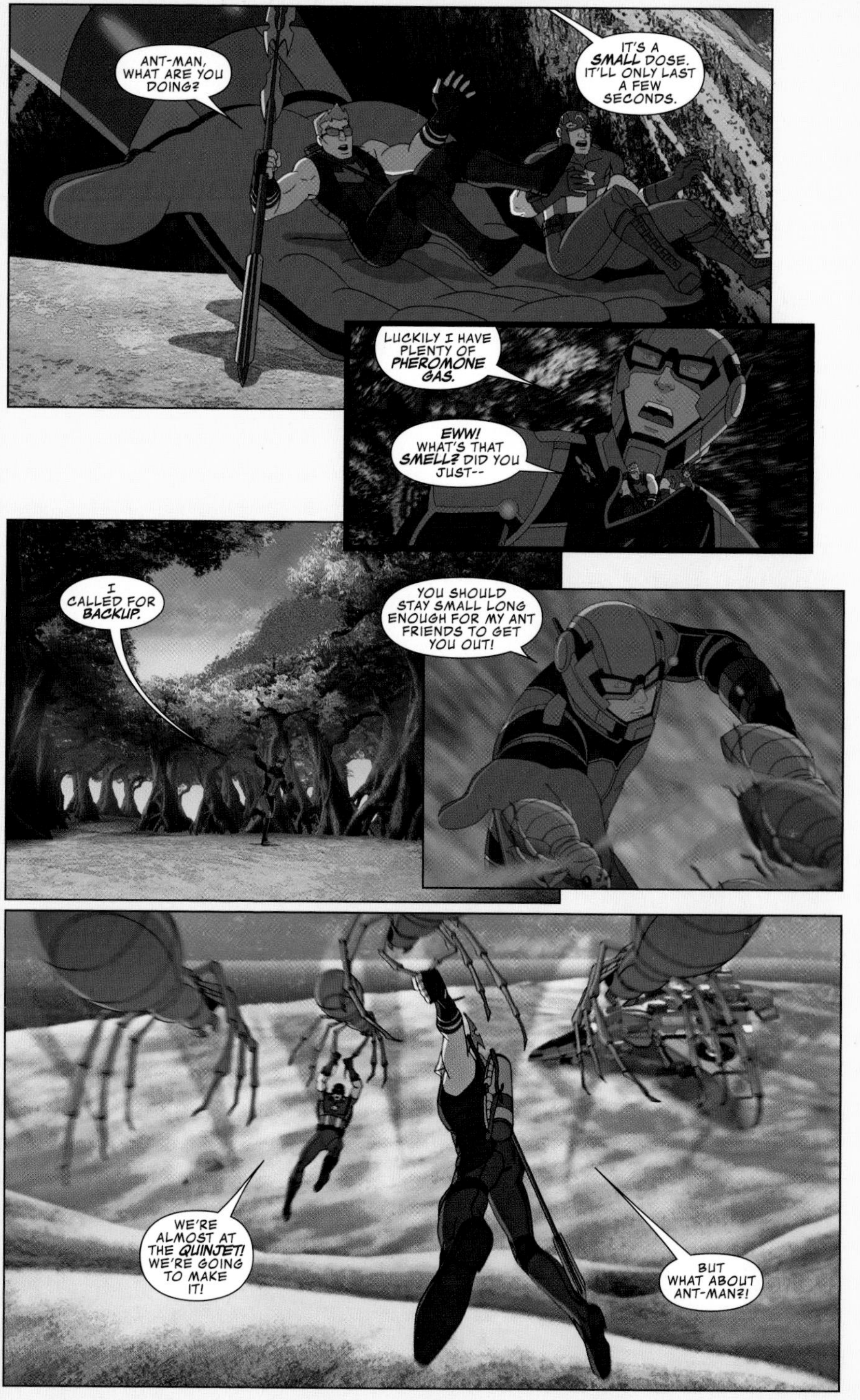
ANT-MAN, WHAT ARE YOU DOING?
IT'S A SMALL DOSE. IT'LL ONLY LAST A FEW SECONDS.
LUCKILY I HAVE PLENTY OF PHEROMONE GAS.
EWW! WHAT'S THAT SMELL? DID YOU JUST--
I CALLED FOR BACKUP.
YOU SHOULD STAY SMALL LONG ENOUGH FOR MY ANT FRIENDS TO GET YOU OUT!
WE'RE ALMOST AT THE QUINJET! WE'RE GOING TO MAKE IT!
BUT WHAT ABOUT ANT-MAN?!

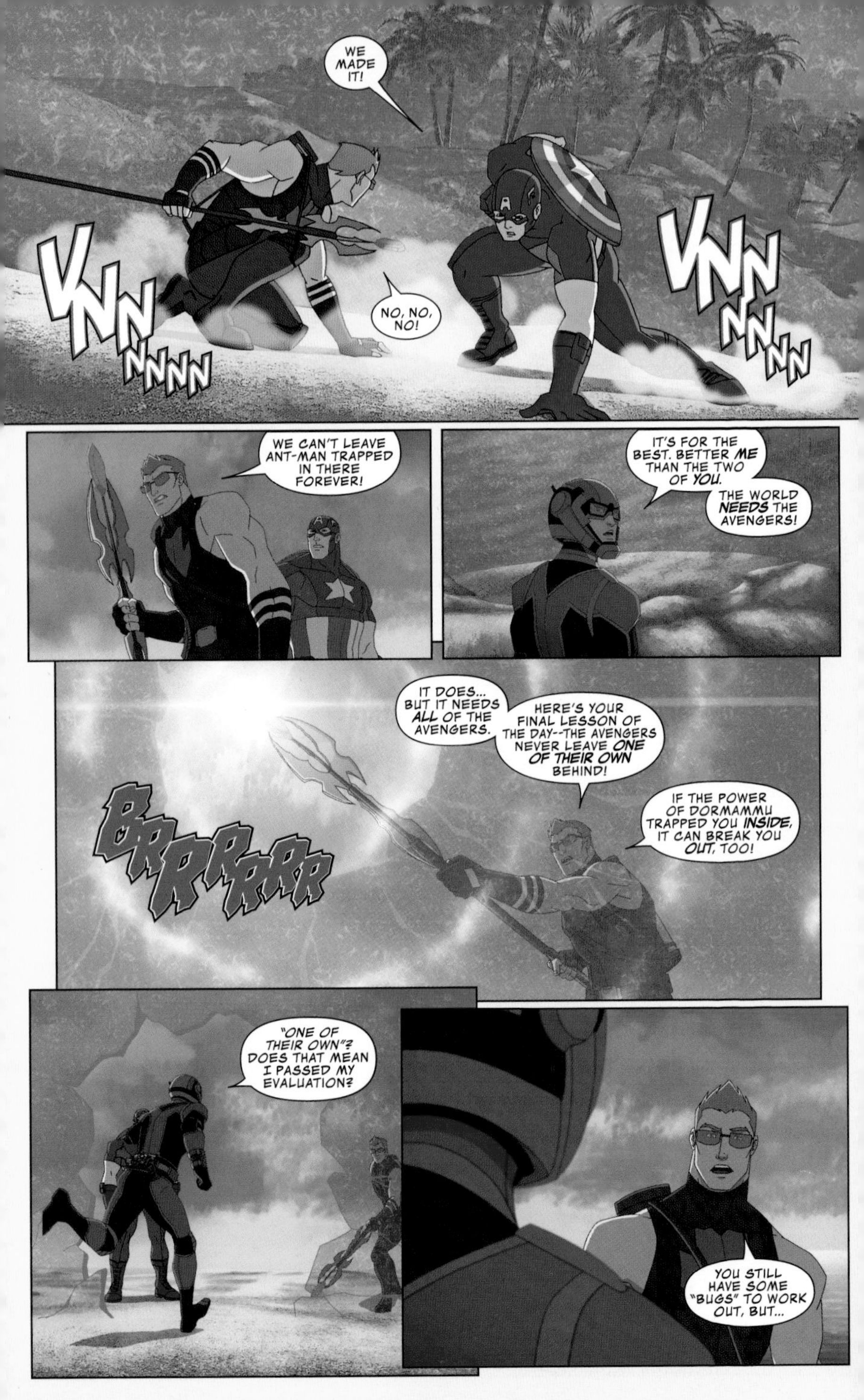
WE MADE IT!
NO, NO, NO!
VNNNNNN
VNNNNNNN
WE CAN'T LEAVE ANT-MAN TRAPPED IN THERE FOREVER!
IT'S FOR THE BEST. BETTER ME THAN THE TWO OF YOU.
THE WORLD NEEDS THE AVENGERS!
IT DOES... BUT IT NEEDS ALL OF THE AVENGERS.
HERE'S YOUR FINAL LESSON OF THE DAY--THE AVENGERS NEVER LEAVE ONE OF THEIR OWN BEHIND!
IF THE POWER OF DORMAMMU TRAPPED YOU INSIDE, IT CAN BREAK YOU OUT, TOO!
BRRRRRRR
"ONE OF THEIR OWN"? DOES THAT MEAN I PASSED MY EVALUATION?
YOU STILL HAVE SOME "BUGS" TO WORK OUT, BUT...

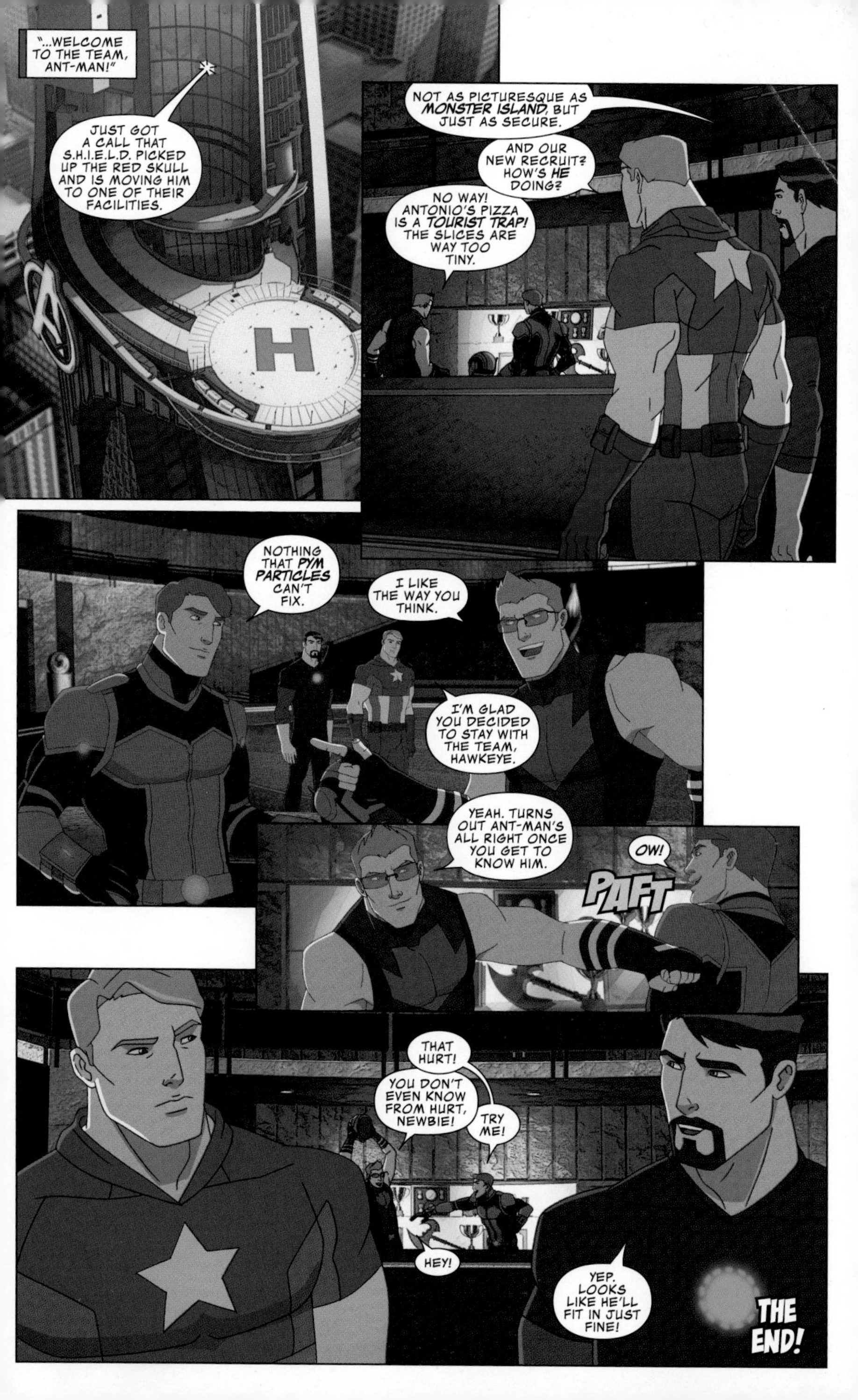
"...WELCOME TO THE TEAM, ANT-MAN!"
JUST GOT A CALL THAT S.H.I.E.L.D. PICKED UP THE RED SKULL AND IS MOVING HIM TO ONE OF THEIR FACILITIES.
NOT AS PICTURESQUE AS MONSTER ISLAND, BUT JUST AS SECURE.
AND OUR NEW RECRUIT? HOW'S HE DOING?
NO WAY! ANTONIO'S PIZZA IS A TOURIST TRAP! THE SLICES ARE WAY TOO TINY.
NOTHING THAT PYM PARTICLES CAN'T FIX.
I LIKE THE WAY YOU THINK.
I'M GLAD YOU DECIDED TO STAY WITH THE TEAM, HAWKEYE.
YEAH. TURNS OUT ANT-MAN'S ALL RIGHT ONCE YOU GET TO KNOW HIM.
PAFT
OW!
THAT HURT!
YOU DON'T EVEN KNOW FROM HURT, NEWBIE!
TRY ME!
HEY!
YEP. LOOKS LIKE HE'LL FIT IN JUST FINE!
THE END!

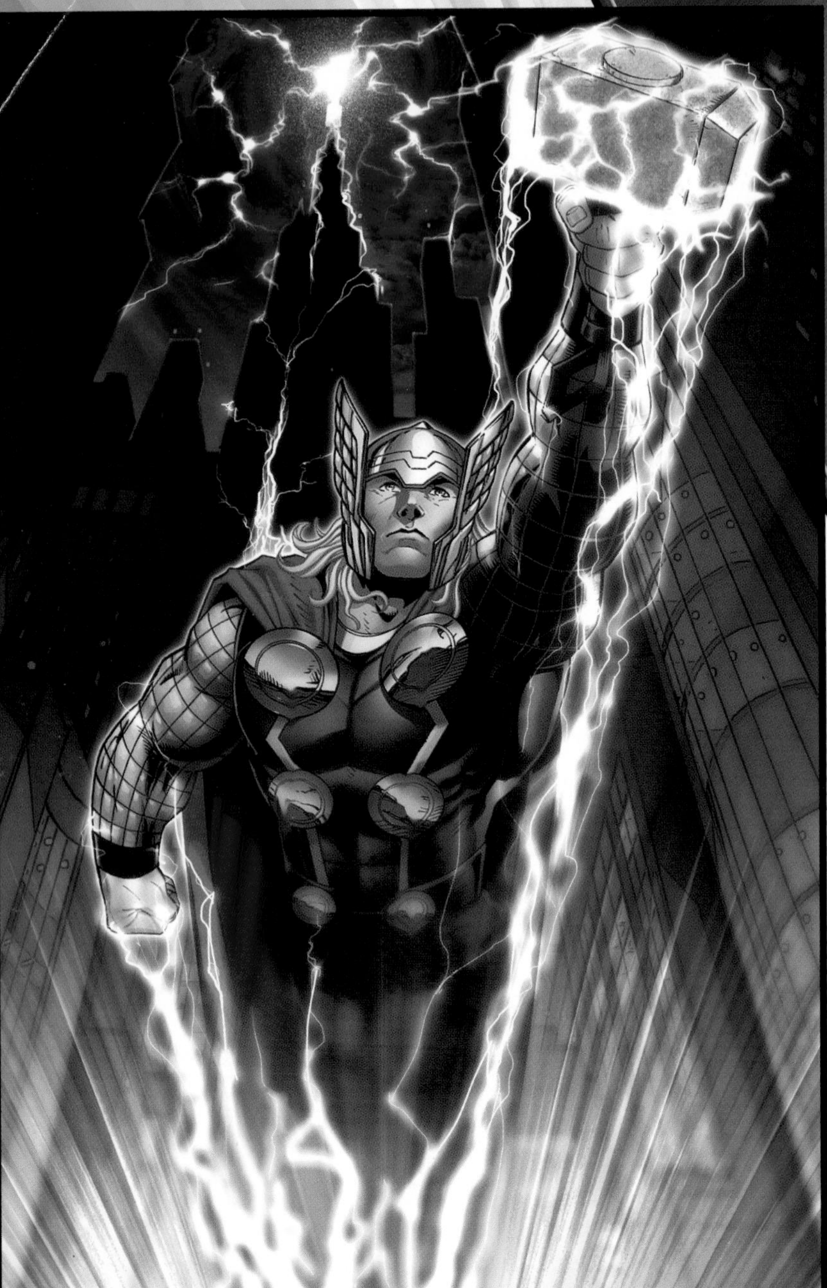

#10 BASED ON "THE DARK AVENGERS"

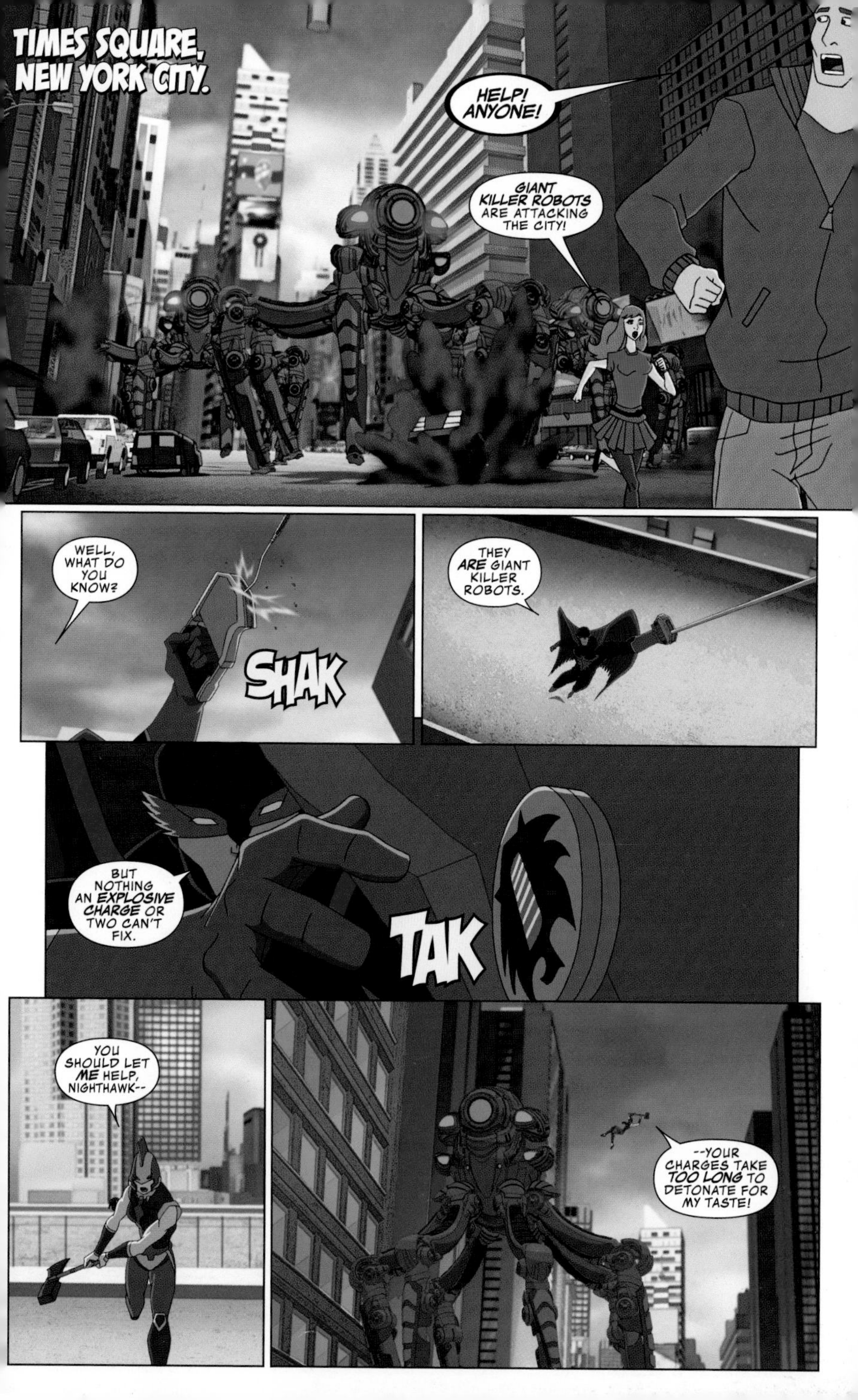
TIMES SQUARE, NEW YORK CITY.
HELP! ANYONE!
GIANT KILLER ROBOTS ARE ATTACKING THE CITY!
WELL, WHAT DO YOU KNOW?
SHAK
THEY ARE GIANT KILLER ROBOTS.
BUT NOTHING AN EXPLOSIVE CHARGE OR TWO CAN'T FIX.
TAK
YOU SHOULD LET ME HELP, NIGHTHAWK--
--YOUR CHARGES TAKE TOO LONG TO DETONATE FOR MY TASTE!

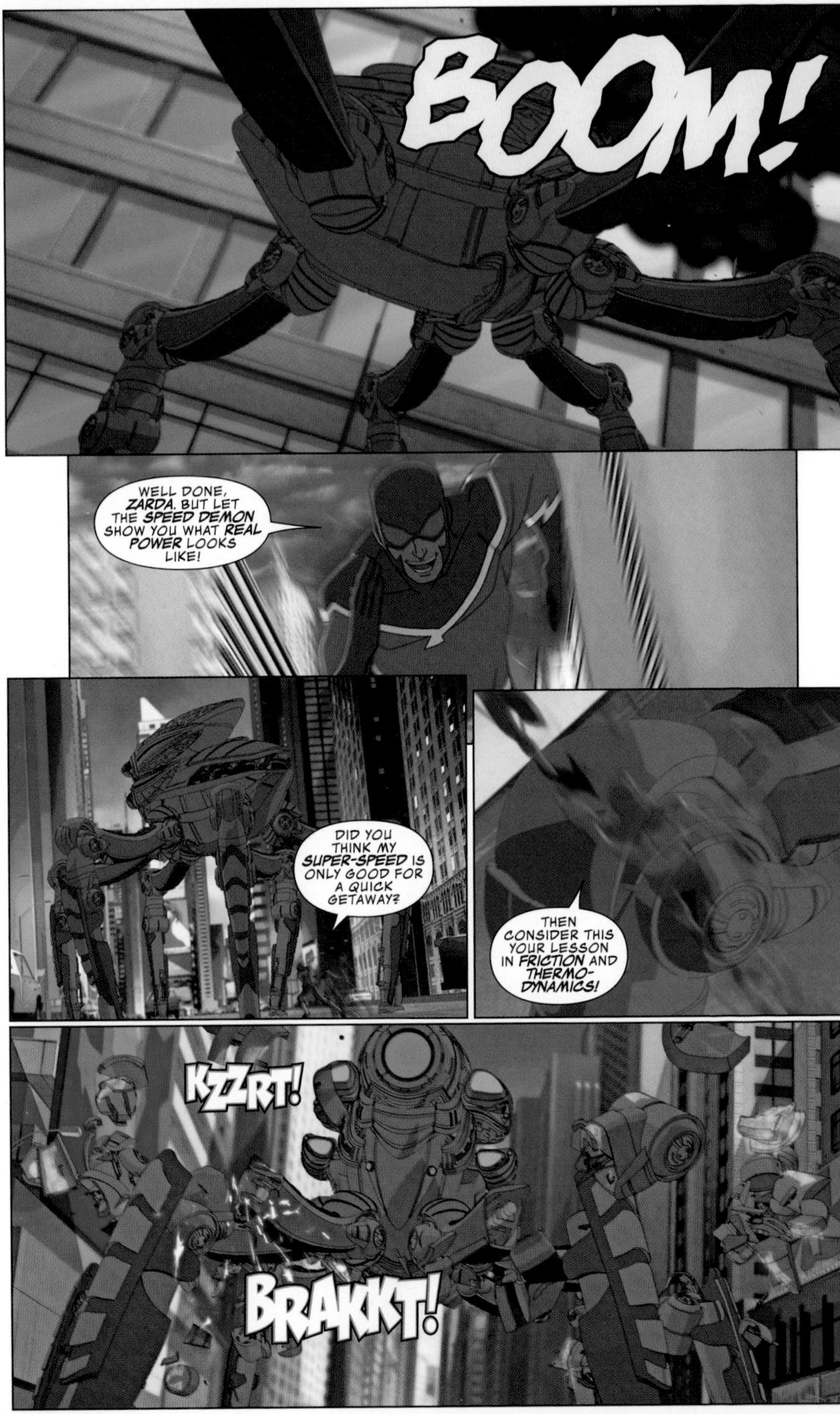
BOOM!
WELL DONE, ZARDA. BUT LET THE SPEED DEMON SHOW YOU WHAT REAL POWER LOOKS LIKE!
DID YOU THINK MY SUPER-SPEED IS ONLY GOOD FOR A QUICK GETAWAY?
THEN CONSIDER THIS YOUR LESSON IN FRICTION AND THERMO-DYNAMICS!
KZZRT!
BRAKKT!

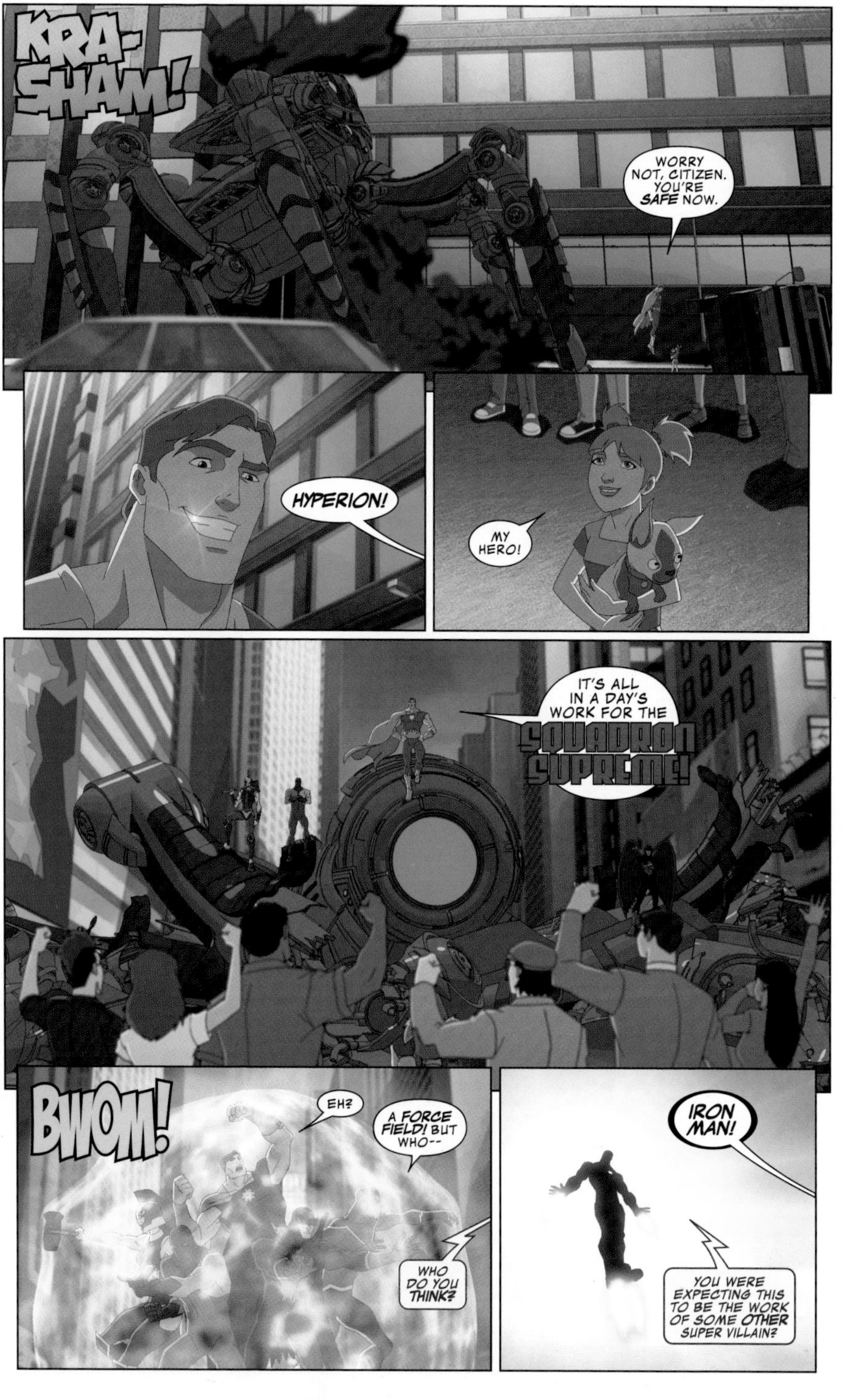
KRA-SHAM!
WORRY NOT, CITIZEN. YOU'RE SAFE NOW.
HYPERION!
MY HERO!
IT'S ALL IN A DAY'S WORK FOR THE SQUADRON SUPREME!
BWOM!
EH?
A FORCE FIELD! BUT WHO--
WHO DO YOU THINK?
IRON MAN!
YOU WERE EXPECTING THIS TO BE THE WORK OF SOME OTHER SUPER VILLAIN?

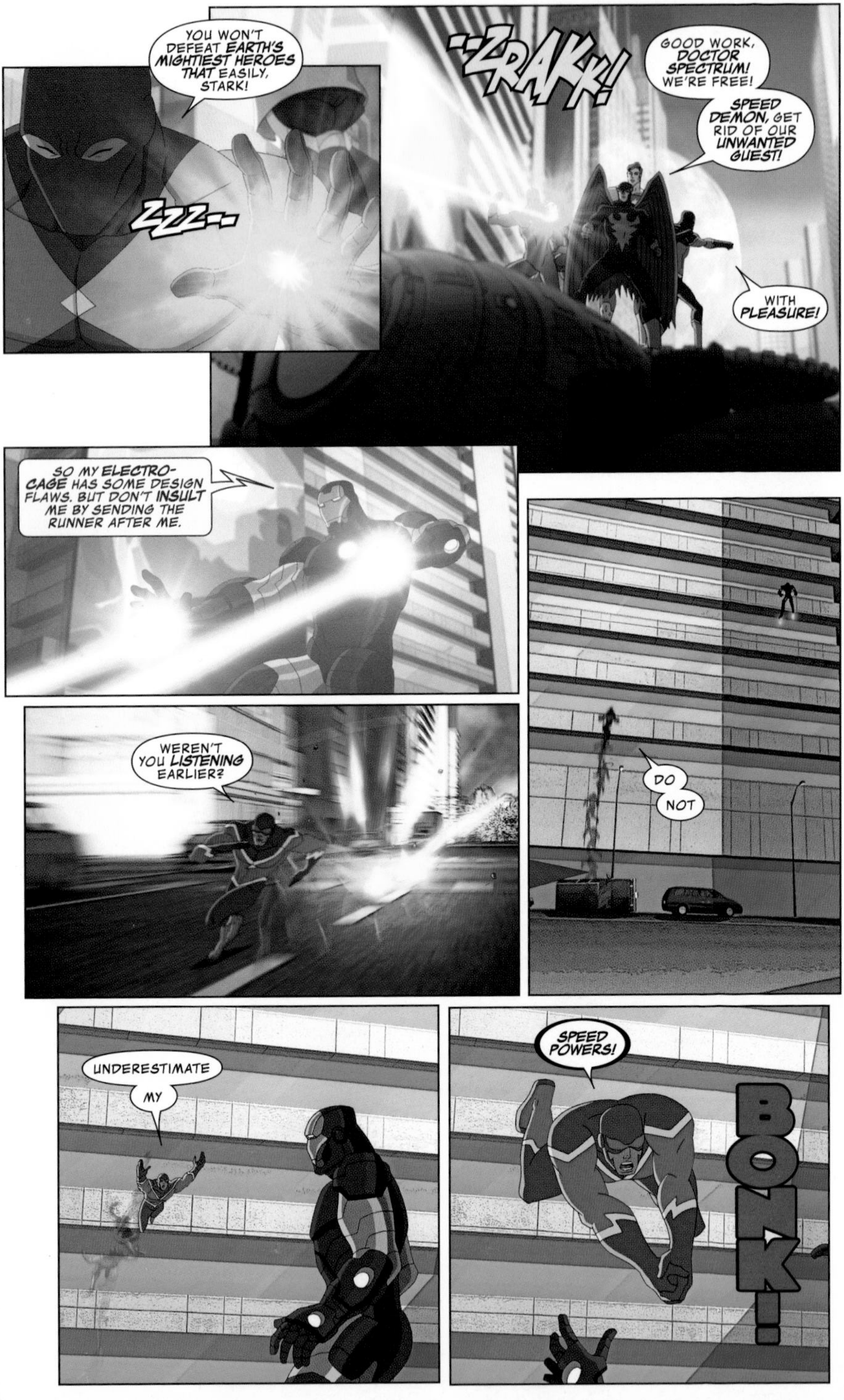
YOU WON'T DEFEAT EARTH'S MIGHTIEST HEROES THAT EASILY, STARK!
ZZZ--
-ZRAKK!
GOOD WORK, DOCTOR SPECTRUM! WE'RE FREE!
SPEED DEMON, GET RID OF OUR UNWANTED GUEST!
WITH PLEASURE!
SO MY ELECTRO-CAGE HAS SOME DESIGN FLAWS. BUT DON'T INSULT ME BY SENDING THE RUNNER AFTER ME.
WEREN'T YOU LISTENING EARLIER?
DO
NOT
UNDERESTIMATE
MY
SPEED POWERS!
BONK!

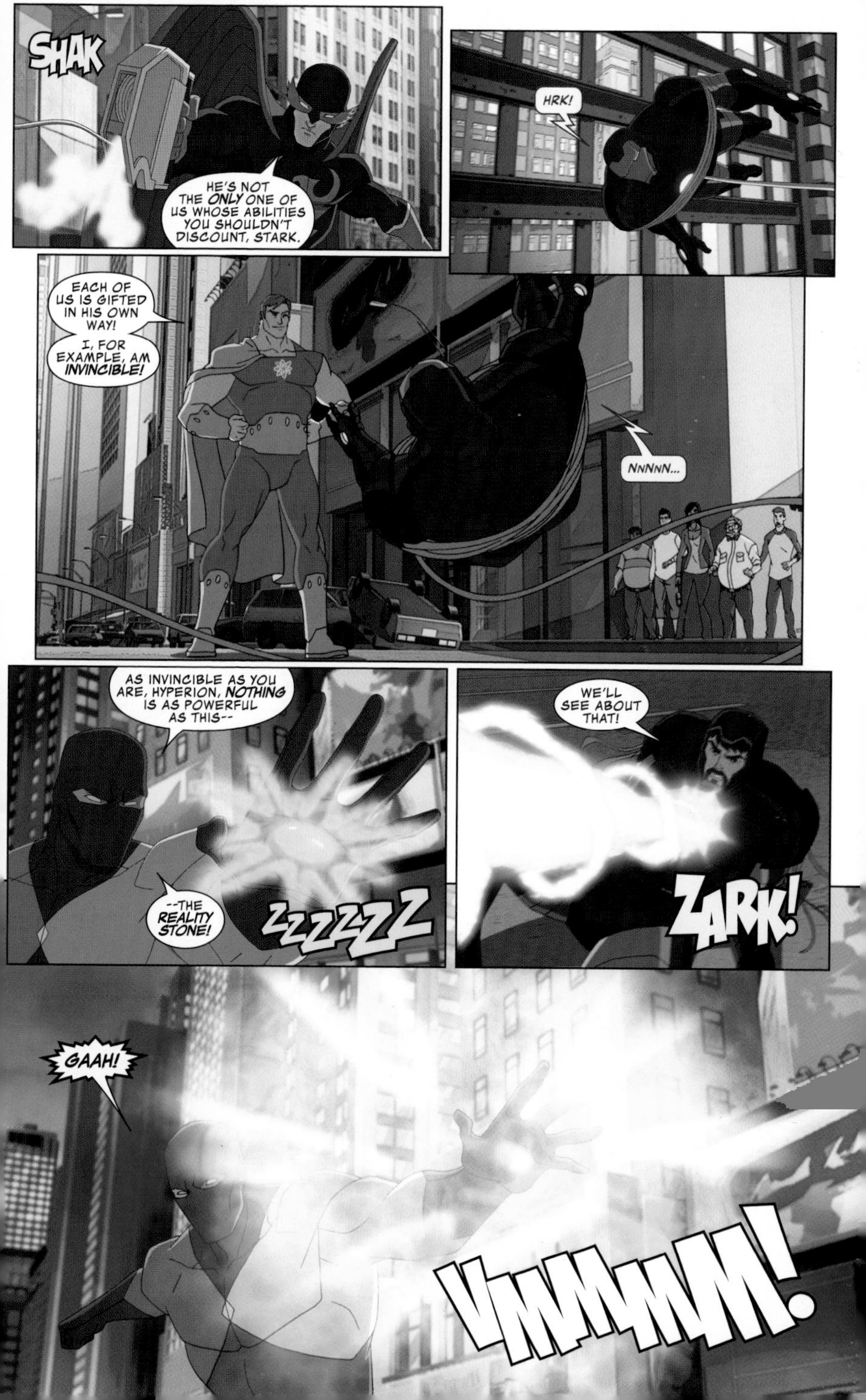
SHAK
HE'S NOT THE ONLY ONE OF US WHOSE ABILITIES YOU SHOULDN'T DISCOUNT, STARK.
HRK!
EACH OF US IS GIFTED IN HIS OWN WAY!
I, FOR EXAMPLE, AM INVINCIBLE!
NNNNN...
AS INVINCIBLE AS YOU ARE, HYPERION, NOTHING IS AS POWERFUL AS THIS--
--THE REALITY STONE!
ZZZZZZ
WE'LL SEE ABOUT THAT!
ZARK!
GAAH!
VMMMMM!

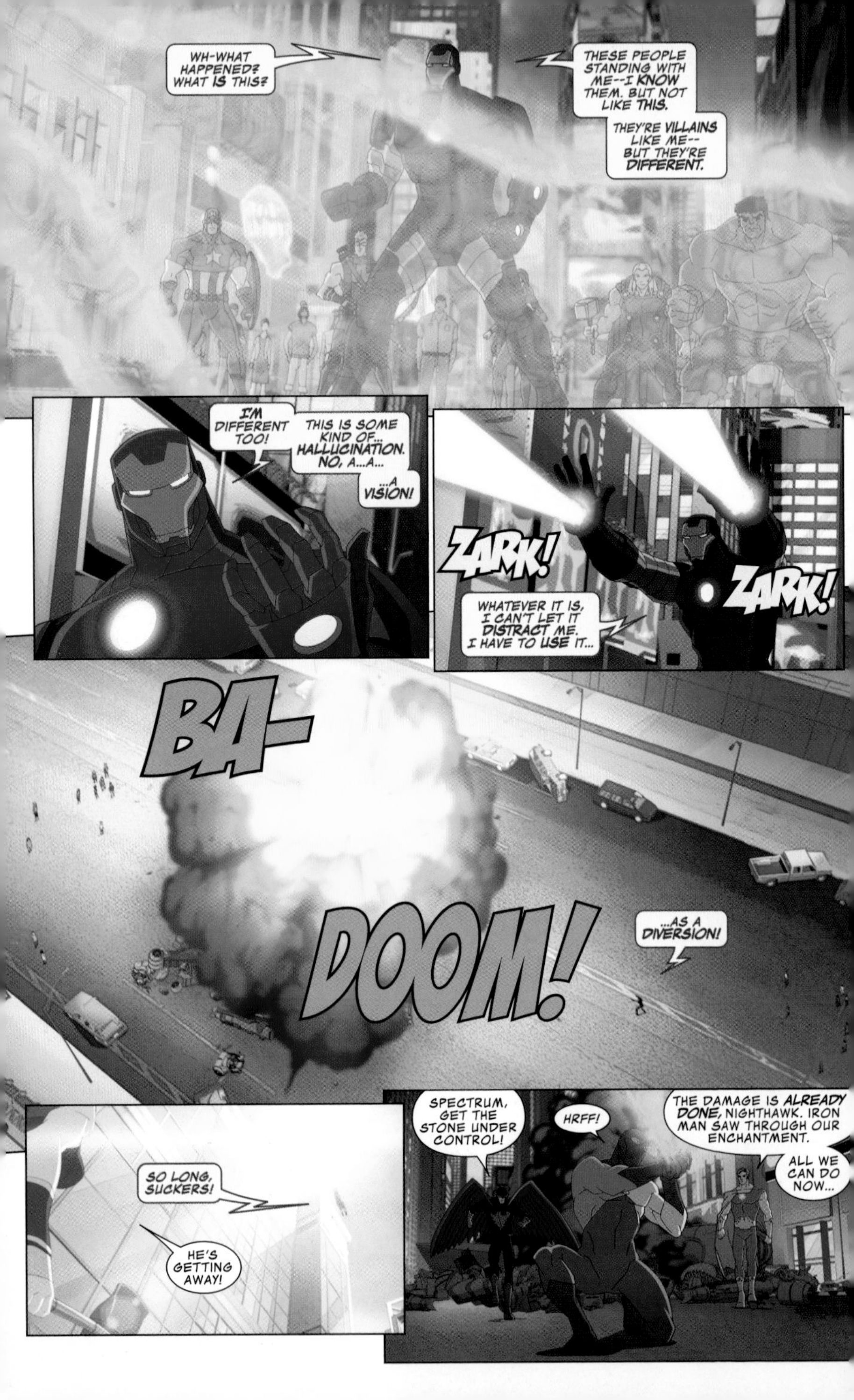
WH-WHAT HAPPENED? WHAT IS THIS?
THESE PEOPLE STANDING WITH ME--I KNOW THEM. BUT NOT LIKE THIS.
THEY'RE VILLAINS LIKE ME-- BUT THEY'RE DIFFERENT.
I'M DIFFERENT TOO!
THIS IS SOME KIND OF... HALLUCINATION. NO, A...A...
...A VISION!
ZARK!
ZARK!
WHATEVER IT IS, I CAN'T LET IT DISTRACT ME. I HAVE TO USE IT...
BA-DOOM!
...AS A DIVERSION!
SO LONG, SUCKERS!
HE'S GETTING AWAY!
SPECTRUM, GET THE STONE UNDER CONTROL!
HRFF!
THE DAMAGE IS ALREADY DONE, NIGHTHAWK. IRON MAN SAW THROUGH OUR ENCHANTMENT.
ALL WE CAN DO NOW...

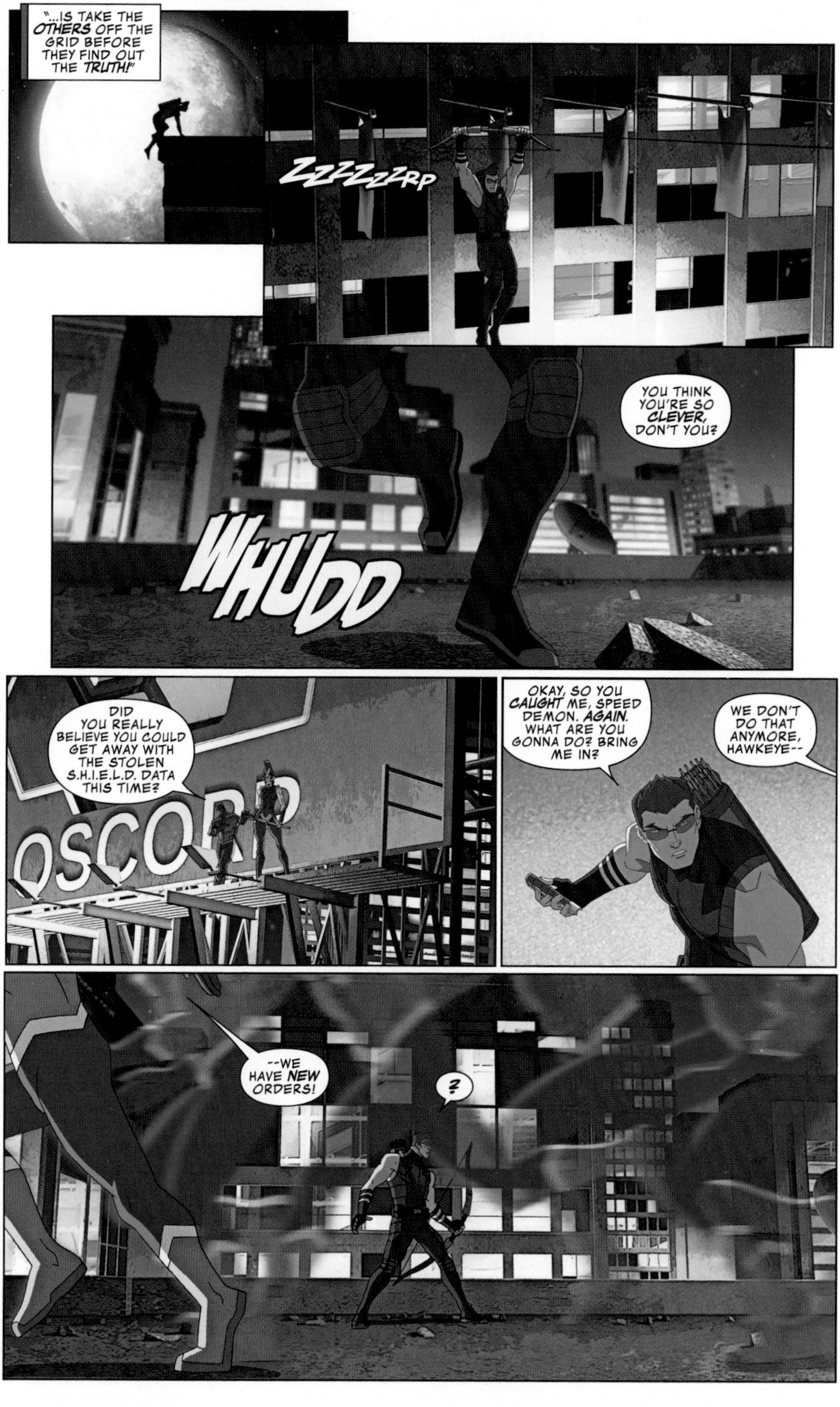
"...IS TAKE THE OTHERS OFF THE GRID BEFORE THEY FIND OUT THE TRUTH!"
ZZZZZZZRP
YOU THINK YOU'RE SO CLEVER, DON'T YOU?
WHUDD
DID YOU REALLY BELIEVE YOU COULD GET AWAY WITH THE STOLEN S.H.I.E.L.D. DATA THIS TIME?
OSCORP
OKAY, SO YOU CAUGHT ME, SPEED DEMON. AGAIN. WHAT ARE YOU GONNA DO? BRING ME IN?
WE DON'T DO THAT ANYMORE, HAWKEYE--
--WE HAVE NEW ORDERS!
?

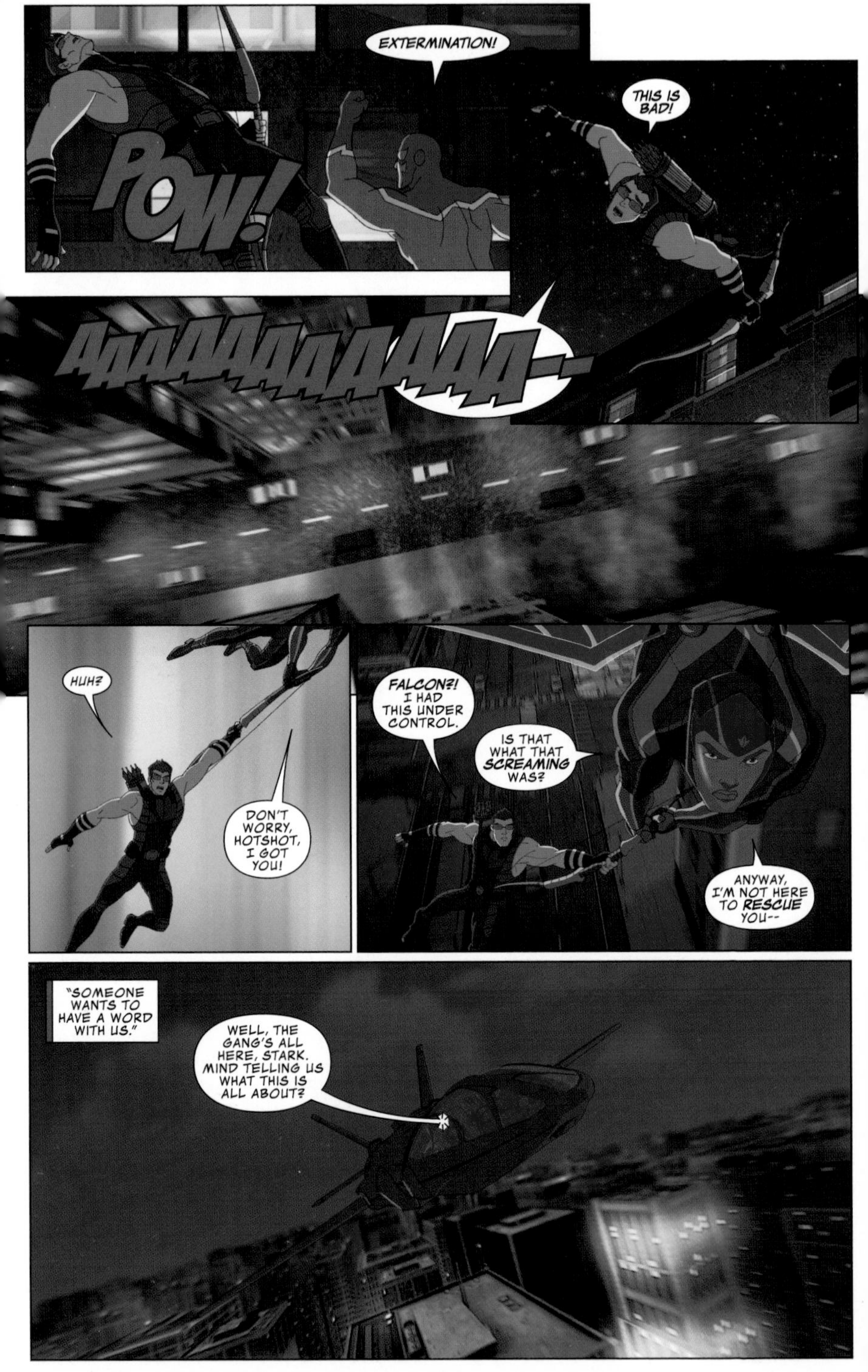
POW!
EXTERMINATION!
THIS IS BAD!
AAAAAAAAAAAA--
HUH?
DON'T WORRY, HOTSHOT, I GOT YOU!
FALCON?! I HAD THIS UNDER CONTROL.
IS THAT WHAT THAT SCREAMING WAS?
ANYWAY, I'M NOT HERE TO RESCUE YOU--
"SOMEONE WANTS TO HAVE A WORD WITH US."
WELL, THE GANG'S ALL HERE, STARK. MIND TELLING US WHAT THIS IS ALL ABOUT?

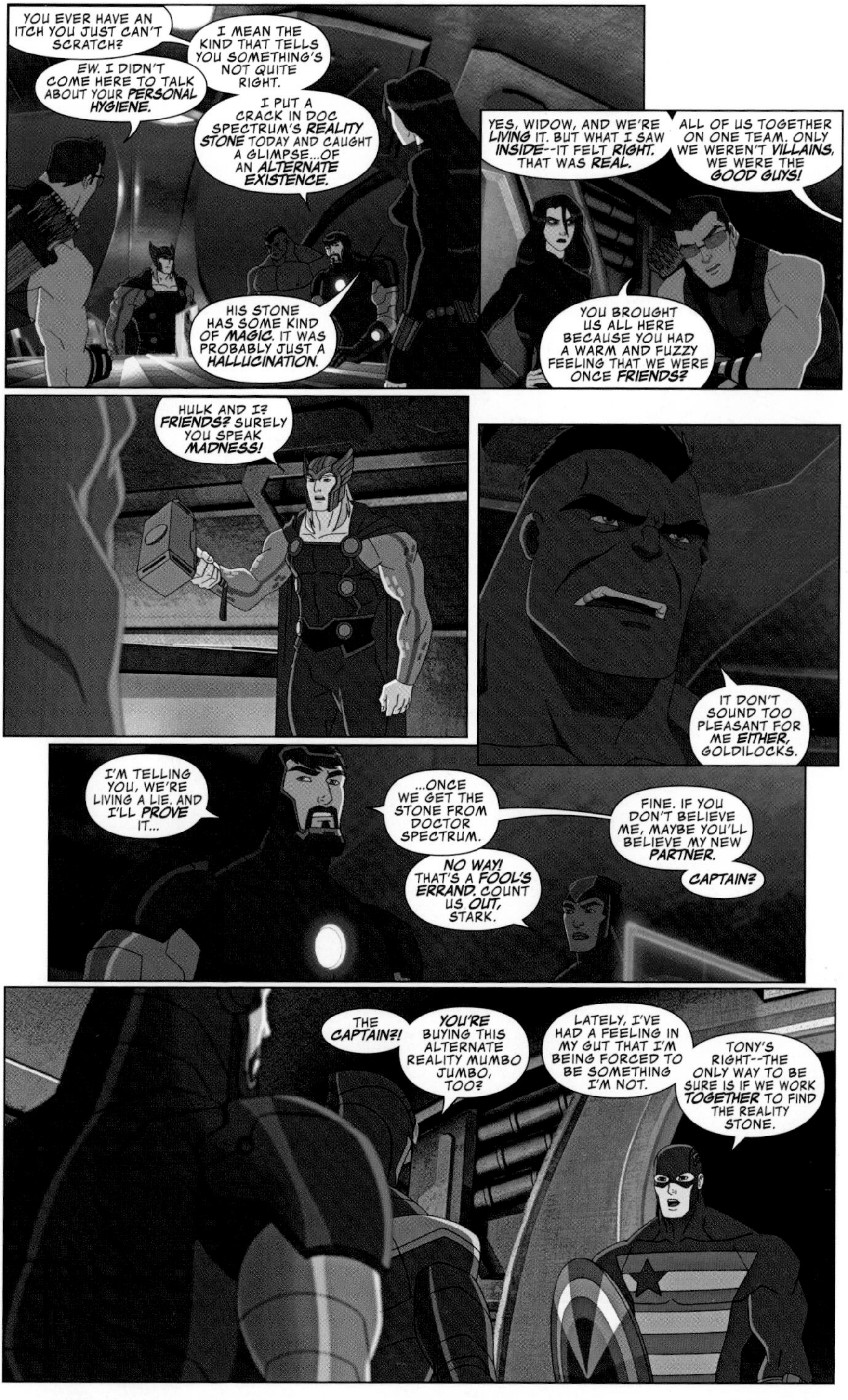
YOU EVER HAVE AN ITCH YOU JUST CAN'T SCRATCH?
I MEAN THE KIND THAT TELLS YOU SOMETHING'S NOT QUITE RIGHT.
EW. I DIDN'T COME HERE TO TALK ABOUT YOUR PERSONAL HYGIENE.
I PUT A CRACK IN DOC SPECTRUM'S REALITY STONE TODAY AND CAUGHT A GLIMPSE...OF AN ALTERNATE EXISTENCE.
HIS STONE HAS SOME KIND OF MAGIC. IT WAS PROBABLY JUST A HALLUCINATION.
YES, WIDOW, AND WE'RE LIVING IT. BUT WHAT I SAW INSIDE--IT FELT RIGHT. THAT WAS REAL.
ALL OF US TOGETHER ON ONE TEAM. ONLY WE WEREN'T VILLAINS, WE WERE THE GOOD GUYS!
YOU BROUGHT US ALL HERE BECAUSE YOU HAD A WARM AND FUZZY FEELING THAT WE WERE ONCE FRIENDS?
HULK AND I? FRIENDS? SURELY YOU SPEAK MADNESS!
IT DON'T SOUND TOO PLEASANT FOR ME EITHER, GOLDILOCKS.
I'M TELLING YOU, WE'RE LIVING A LIE. AND I'LL PROVE IT...
...ONCE WE GET THE STONE FROM DOCTOR SPECTRUM.
NO WAY! THAT'S A FOOL'S ERRAND. COUNT US OUT, STARK.
FINE. IF YOU DON'T BELIEVE ME, MAYBE YOU'LL BELIEVE MY NEW PARTNER.
CAPTAIN?
THE CAPTAIN?!
YOU'RE BUYING THIS ALTERNATE REALITY MUMBO JUMBO, TOO?
LATELY, I'VE HAD A FEELING IN MY GUT THAT I'M BEING FORCED TO BE SOMETHING I'M NOT.
TONY'S RIGHT--THE ONLY WAY TO BE SURE IS IF WE WORK TOGETHER TO FIND THE REALITY STONE.

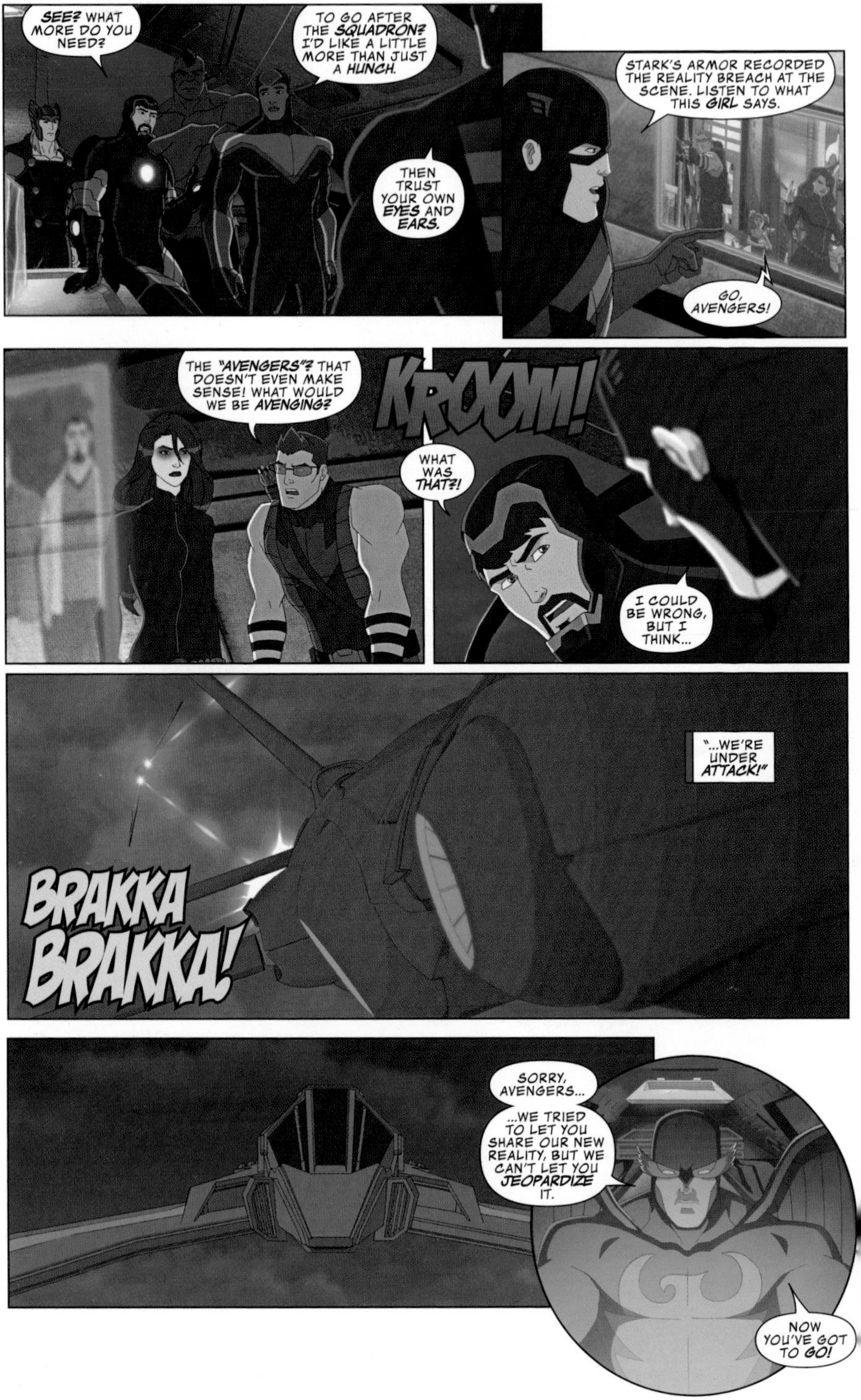
SEE? WHAT MORE DO YOU NEED?
TO GO AFTER THE SQUADRON? I'D LIKE A LITTLE MORE THAN JUST A HUNCH.
THEN TRUST YOUR OWN EYES AND EARS.
STARK'S ARMOR RECORDED THE REALITY BREACH AT THE SCENE. LISTEN TO WHAT THIS GIRL SAYS.
GO, AVENGERS!
THE "AVENGERS"? THAT DOESN'T EVEN MAKE SENSE! WHAT WOULD WE BE AVENGING?
KROOM!
WHAT WAS THAT?!
I COULD BE WRONG, BUT I THINK...
"...WE'RE UNDER ATTACK!"
BRAKKA BRAKKA!
SORRY, AVENGERS...
...WE TRIED TO LET YOU SHARE OUR NEW REALITY, BUT WE CAN'T LET YOU JEOPARDIZE IT.
NOW YOU'VE GOT TO GO!

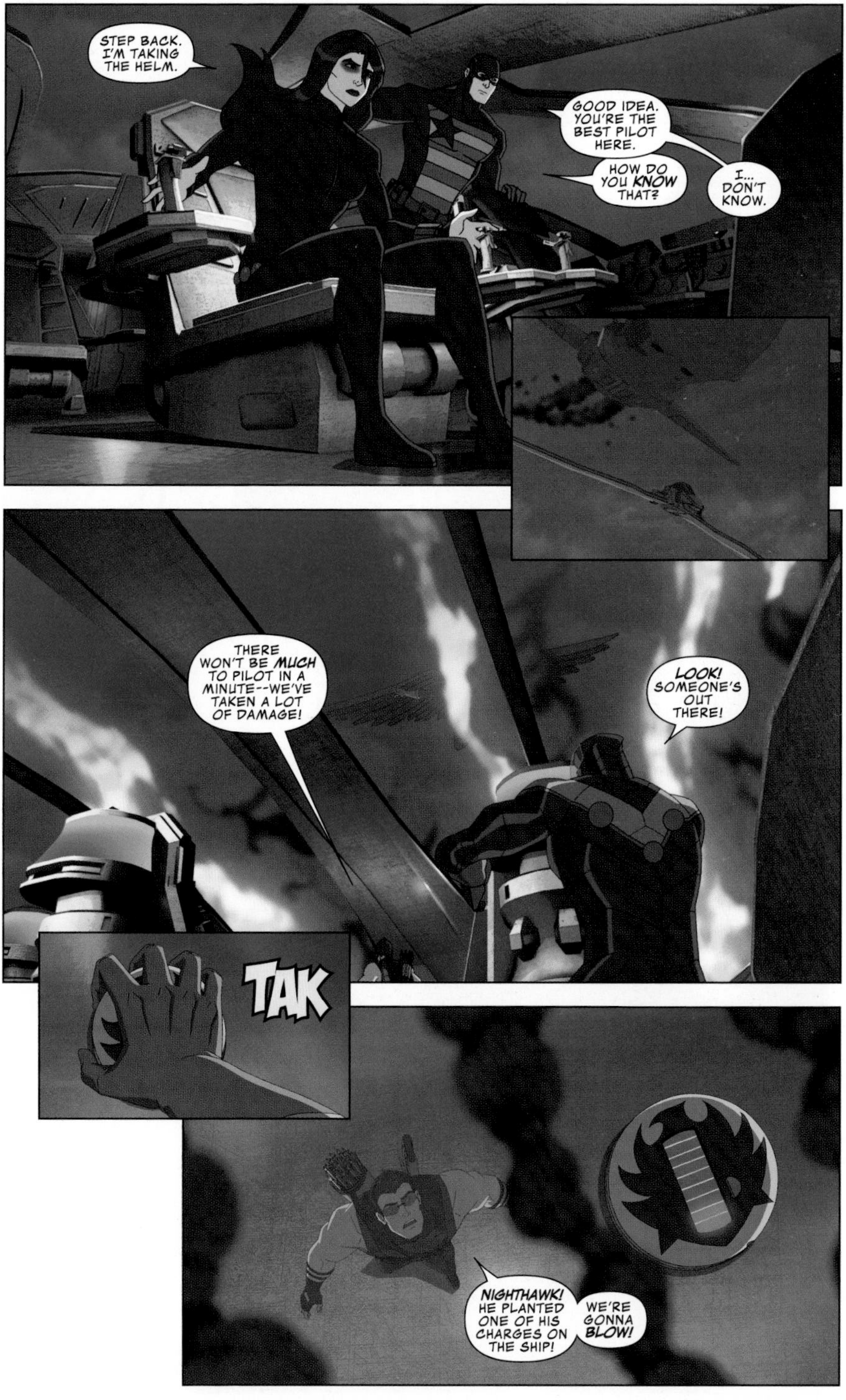
STEP BACK. I'M TAKING THE HELM.
GOOD IDEA. YOU'RE THE BEST PILOT HERE.
HOW DO YOU KNOW THAT?
I... DON'T KNOW.
THERE WON'T BE MUCH TO PILOT IN A MINUTE--WE'VE TAKEN A LOT OF DAMAGE!
LOOK! SOMEONE'S OUT THERE!
TAK
NIGHTHAWK! HE PLANTED ONE OF HIS CHARGES ON THE SHIP!
WE'RE GONNA BLOW!

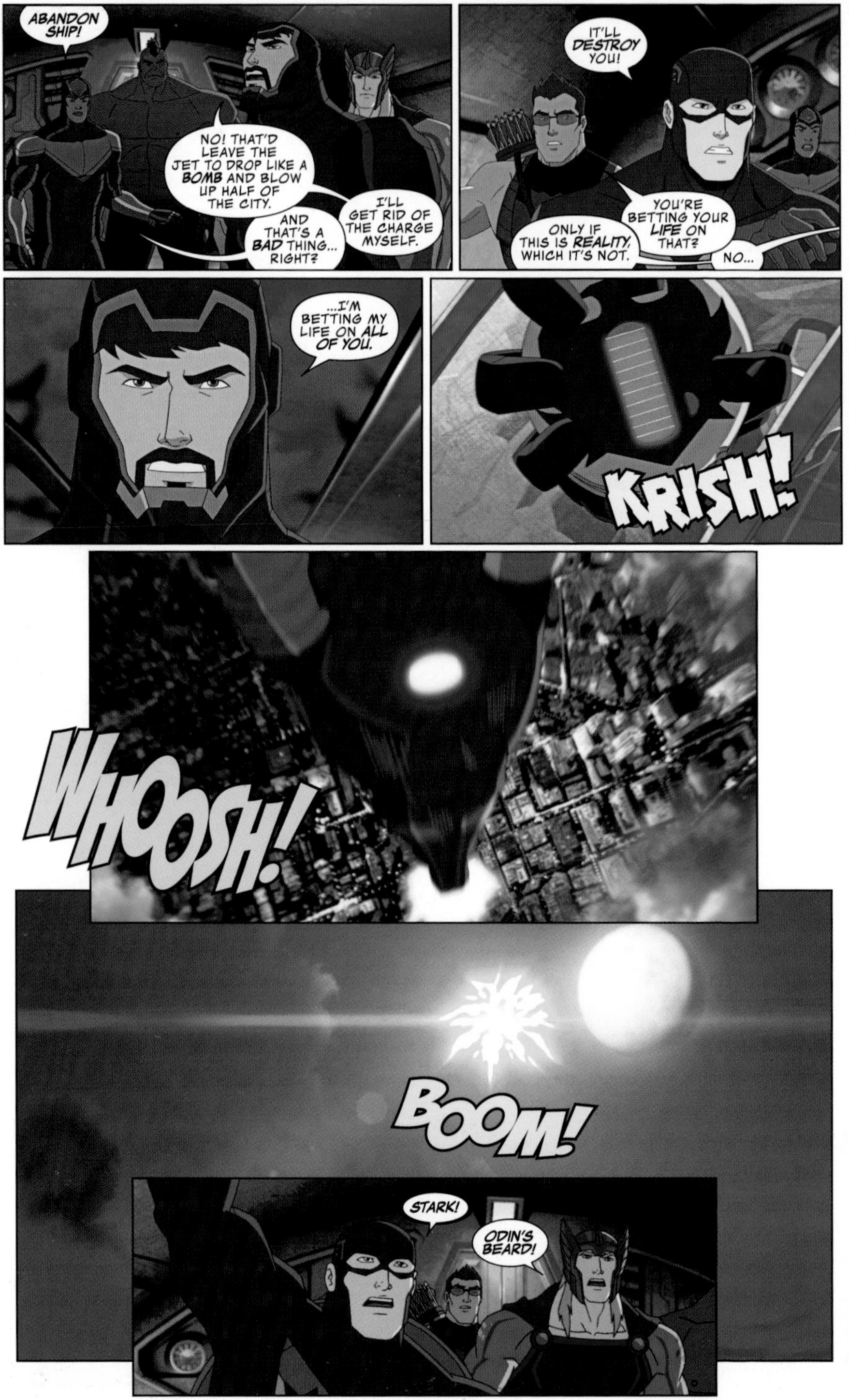
ABANDON SHIP!
NO! THAT'D LEAVE THE JET TO DROP LIKE A BOMB AND BLOW UP HALF OF THE CITY.
AND THAT'S A BAD THING... RIGHT?
I'LL GET RID OF THE CHARGE MYSELF.
IT'LL DESTROY YOU!
ONLY IF THIS IS REALITY, WHICH IT'S NOT.
YOU'RE BETTING YOUR LIFE ON THAT?
NO...
...I'M BETTING MY LIFE ON ALL OF YOU.
KRISH!
WHOOSH!
BOOM!
STARK!
ODIN'S BEARD!

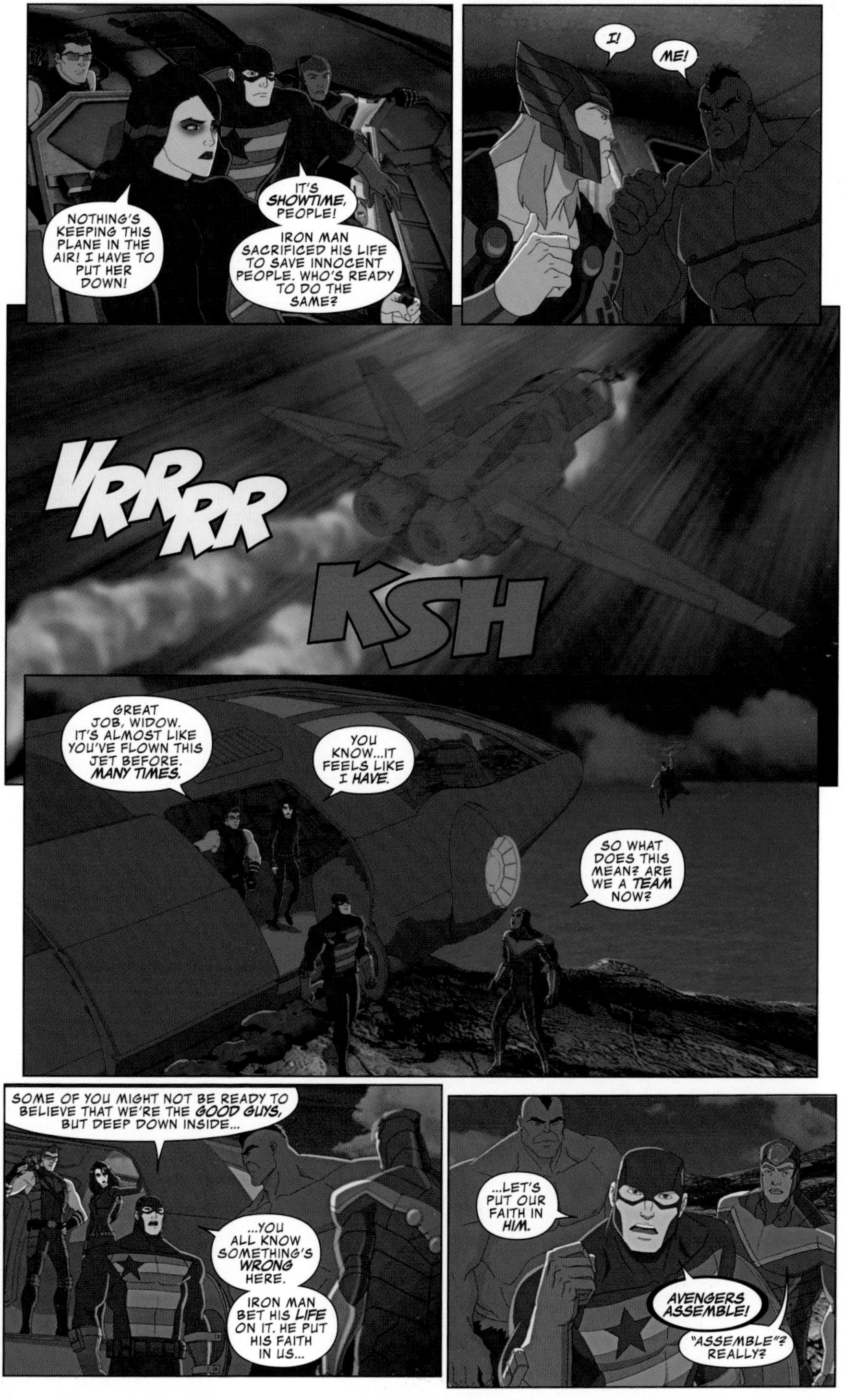
NOTHING'S KEEPING THIS PLANE IN THE AIR! I HAVE TO PUT HER DOWN!
IT'S SHOWTIME, PEOPLE!
IRON MAN SACRIFICED HIS LIFE TO SAVE INNOCENT PEOPLE. WHO'S READY TO DO THE SAME?
I!
ME!
VRRRR
KSH
GREAT JOB, WIDOW. IT'S ALMOST LIKE YOU'VE FLOWN THIS JET BEFORE. MANY TIMES.
YOU KNOW...IT FEELS LIKE I HAVE.
SO WHAT DOES THIS MEAN? ARE WE A TEAM NOW?
SOME OF YOU MIGHT NOT BE READY TO BELIEVE THAT WE'RE THE GOOD GUYS, BUT DEEP DOWN INSIDE...
...YOU ALL KNOW SOMETHING'S WRONG HERE.
IRON MAN BET HIS LIFE ON IT. HE PUT HIS FAITH IN US...
...LET'S PUT OUR FAITH IN HIM.
AVENGERS ASSEMBLE!
"ASSEMBLE"? REALLY?

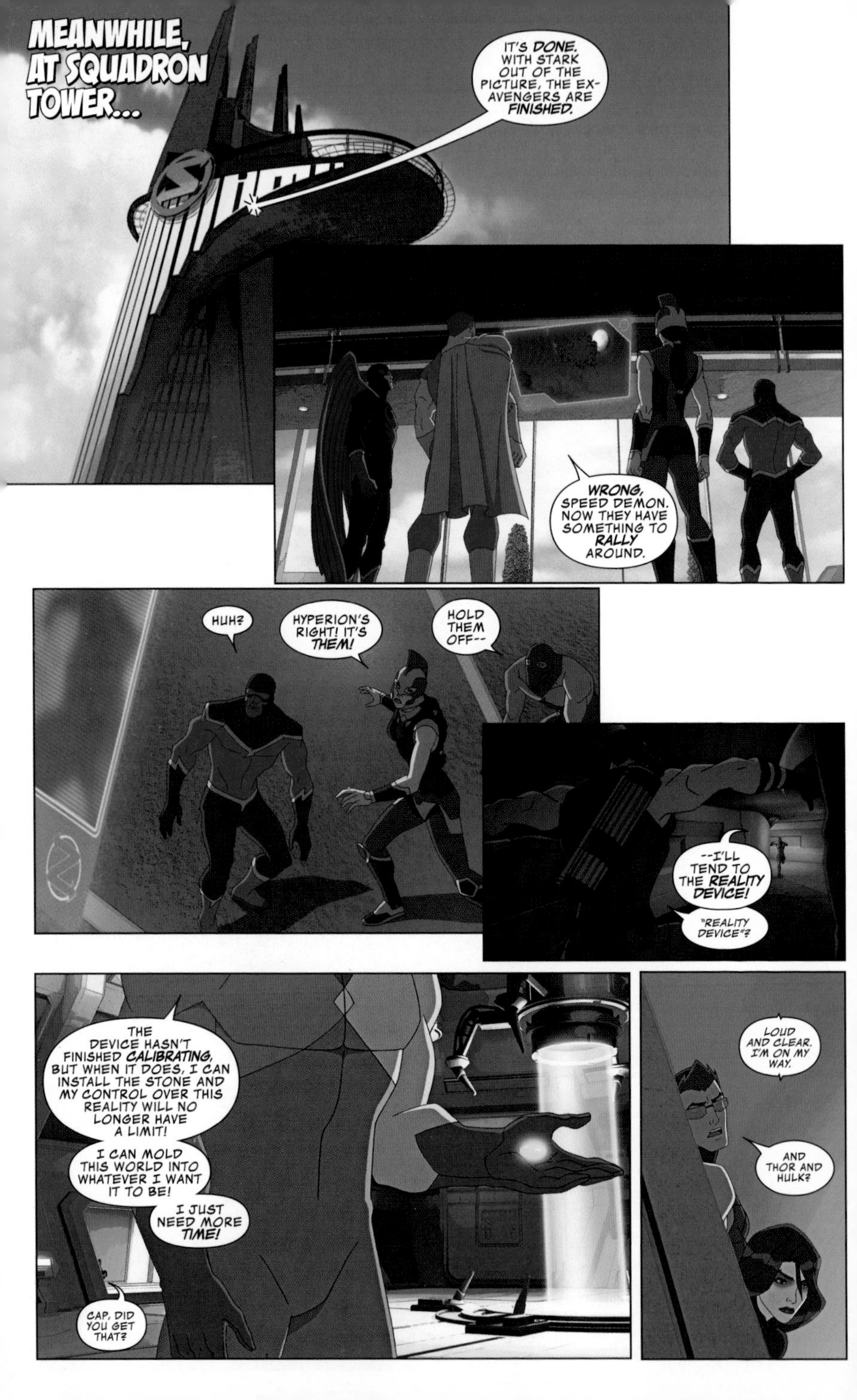

MEANWHILE, AT SQUADRON TOWER...
IT'S DONE. WITH STARK OUT OF THE PICTURE, THE EX-AVENGERS ARE FINISHED.
WRONG, SPEED DEMON. NOW THEY HAVE SOMETHING TO RALLY AROUND.
HUH?
HYPERION'S RIGHT! IT'S THEM!
HOLD THEM OFF--
--I'LL TEND TO THE REALITY DEVICE!
"REALITY DEVICE"?
THE DEVICE HASN'T FINISHED CALIBRATING, BUT WHEN IT DOES, I CAN INSTALL THE STONE AND MY CONTROL OVER THIS REALITY WILL NO LONGER HAVE A LIMIT!
I CAN MOLD THIS WORLD INTO WHATEVER I WANT IT TO BE!
I JUST NEED MORE TIME!
CAP, DID YOU GET THAT?
LOUD AND CLEAR. I'M ON MY WAY.
AND THOR AND HULK?

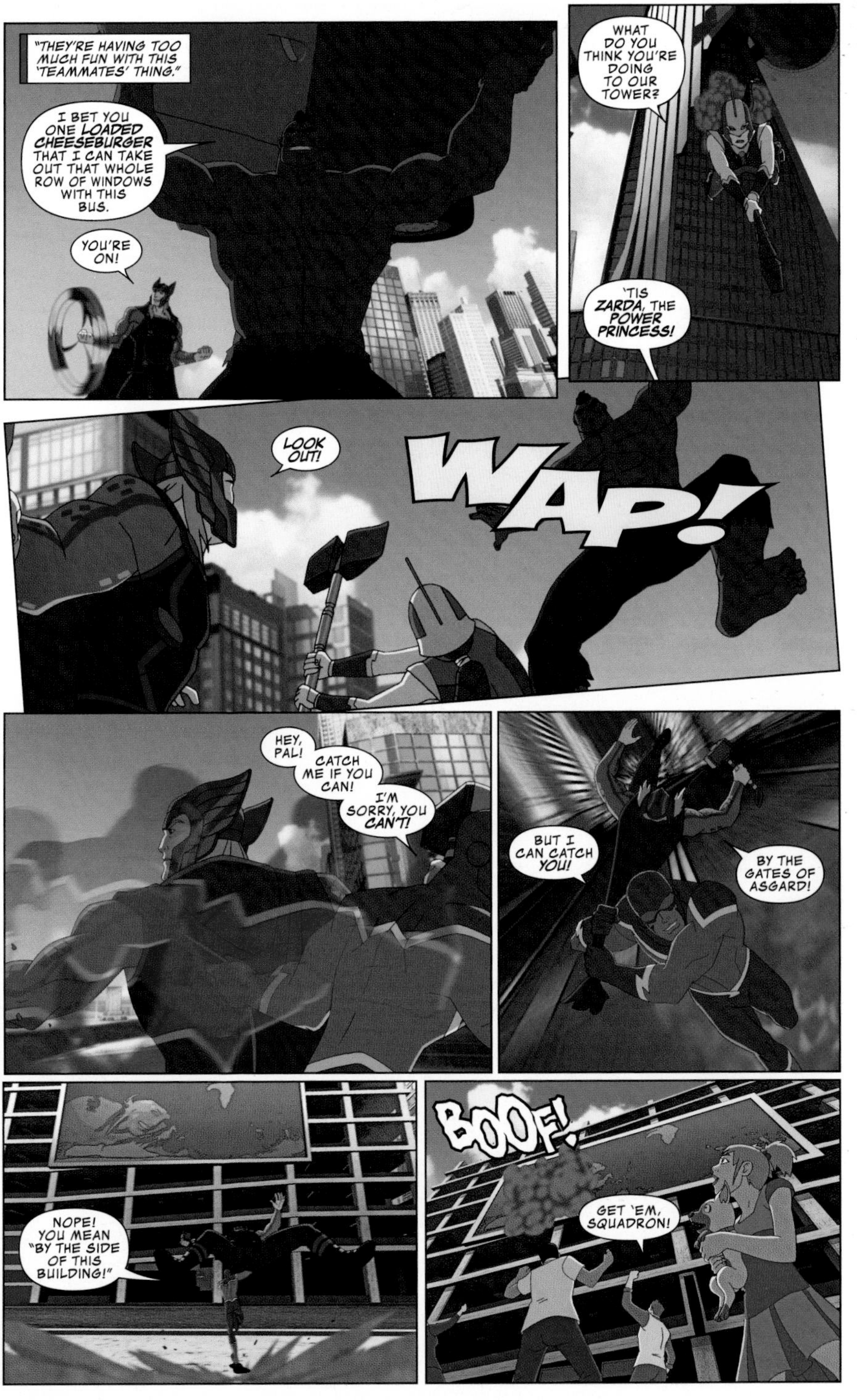
"THEY'RE HAVING TOO MUCH FUN WITH THIS 'TEAMMATES' THING."
I BET YOU ONE LOADED CHEESEBURGER THAT I CAN TAKE OUT THAT WHOLE ROW OF WINDOWS WITH THIS BUS.
YOU'RE ON!
WHAT DO YOU THINK YOU'RE DOING TO OUR TOWER?
'TIS ZARDA, THE POWER PRINCESS!
LOOK OUT!
WAP!
HEY, PAL!
CATCH ME IF YOU CAN!
I'M SORRY, YOU CAN'T!
BUT I CAN CATCH YOU!
BY THE GATES OF ASGARD!
NOPE! YOU MEAN "BY THE SIDE OF THIS BUILDING!"
BOOF!
GET 'EM, SQUADRON!

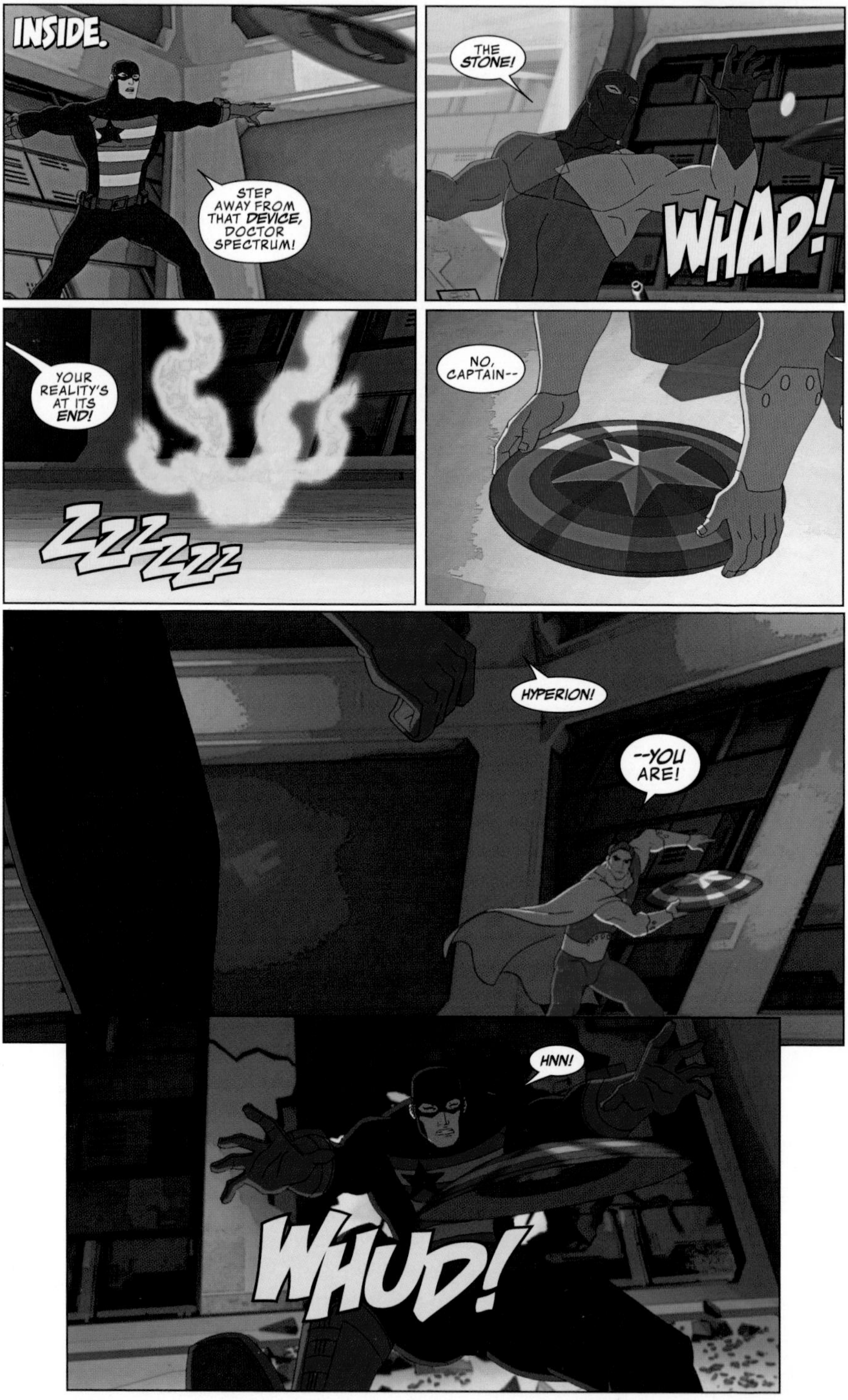
INSIDE.
STEP AWAY FROM THAT DEVICE, DOCTOR SPECTRUM!
THE STONE!
WHAP!
YOUR REALITY'S AT ITS END!
ZZZZZZ
NO, CAPTAIN--
HYPERION!
--YOU ARE!
HNN!
WHUD!

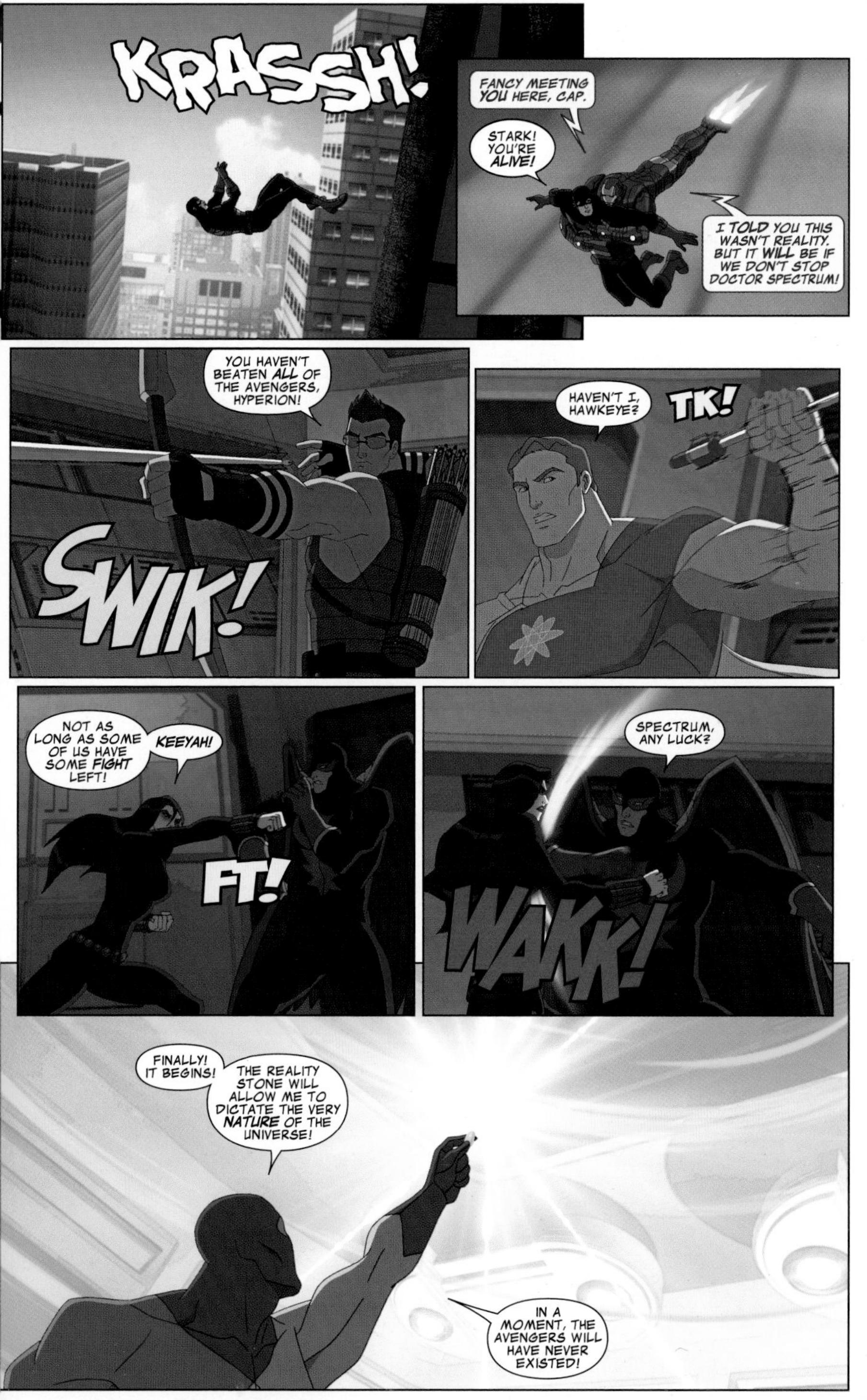

KRASSH!
FANCY MEETING YOU HERE, CAP.
STARK! YOU'RE ALIVE!
I TOLD YOU THIS WASN'T REALITY. BUT IT WILL BE IF WE DON'T STOP DOCTOR SPECTRUM!
YOU HAVEN'T BEATEN ALL OF THE AVENGERS, HYPERION!
SWIK!
HAVEN'T I, HAWKEYE?
TK!
NOT AS LONG AS SOME OF US HAVE SOME FIGHT LEFT!
KEEYAH!
FT!
SPECTRUM, ANY LUCK?
WAKK!
FINALLY! IT BEGINS!
THE REALITY STONE WILL ALLOW ME TO DICTATE THE VERY NATURE OF THE UNIVERSE!
IN A MOMENT, THE AVENGERS WILL HAVE NEVER EXISTED!

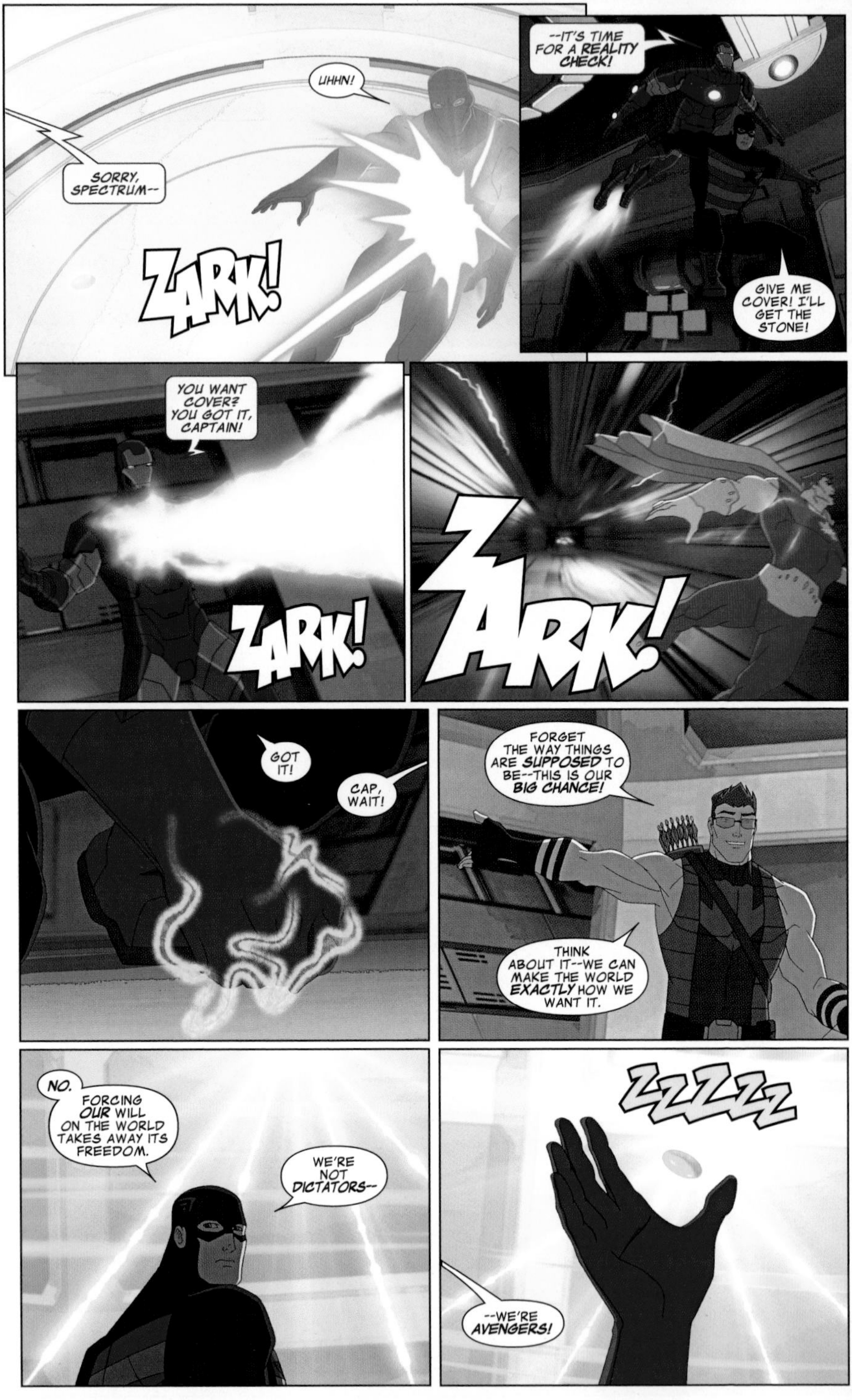
UHHN!
SORRY, SPECTRUM--
ZARK!
--IT'S TIME FOR A REALITY CHECK!
GIVE ME COVER! I'LL GET THE STONE!
YOU WANT COVER? YOU GOT IT, CAPTAIN!
ZARK!
ZARK!
GOT IT!
CAP, WAIT!
FORGET THE WAY THINGS ARE SUPPOSED TO BE--THIS IS OUR BIG CHANCE!
THINK ABOUT IT--WE CAN MAKE THE WORLD EXACTLY HOW WE WANT IT.
NO.
FORCING OUR WILL ON THE WORLD TAKES AWAY ITS FREEDOM.
WE'RE NOT DICTATORS--
ZZZZZ
--WE'RE AVENGERS!

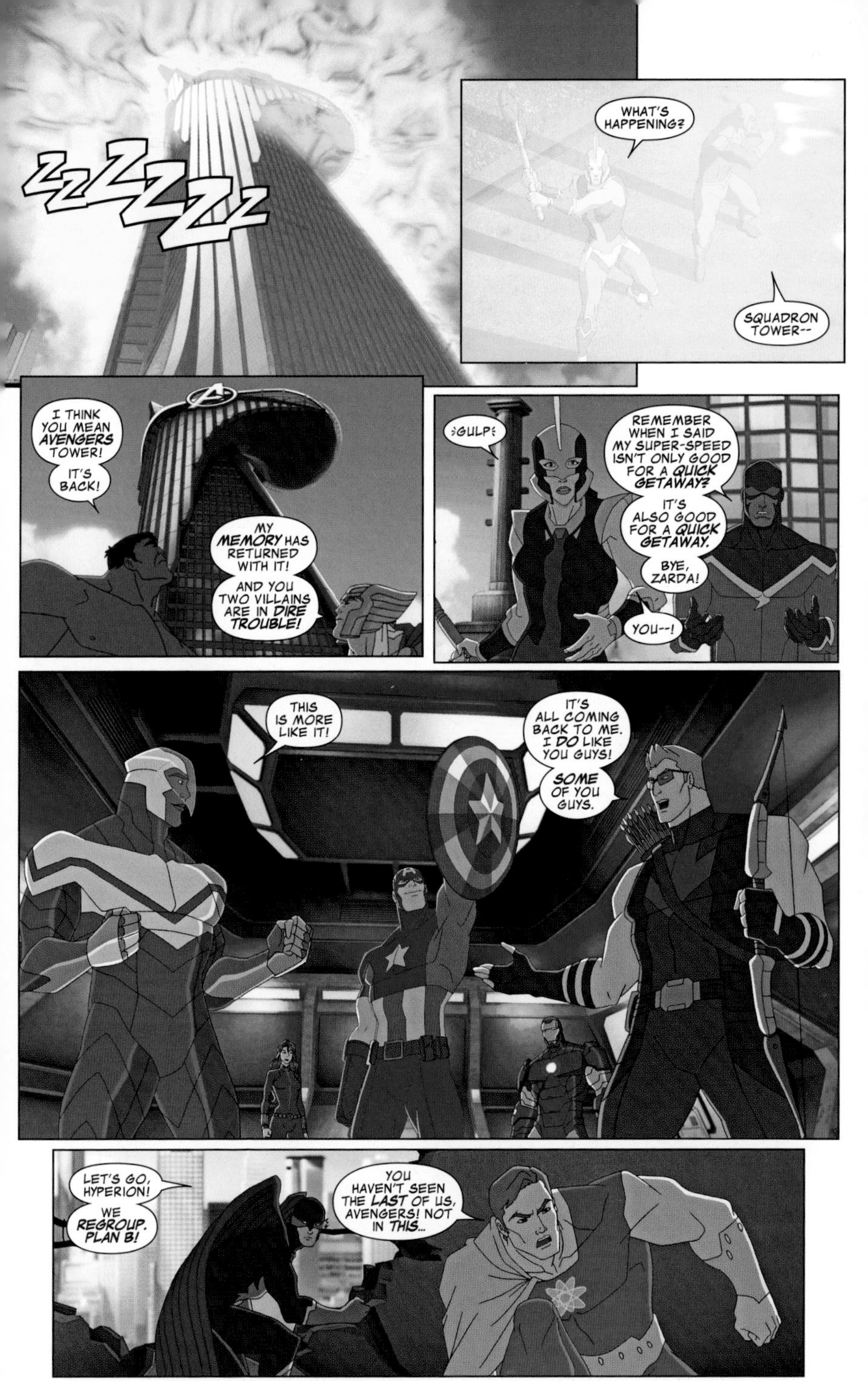
ZZZZZZZ
WHAT'S HAPPENING?
SQUADRON TOWER--
I THINK YOU MEAN AVENGERS TOWER!
IT'S BACK!
MY MEMORY HAS RETURNED WITH IT!
AND YOU TWO VILLAINS ARE IN DIRE TROUBLE!
GULP
REMEMBER WHEN I SAID MY SUPER-SPEED ISN'T ONLY GOOD FOR A QUICK GETAWAY?
IT'S ALSO GOOD FOR A QUICK GETAWAY.
BYE, ZARDA!
YOU--!
THIS IS MORE LIKE IT!
IT'S ALL COMING BACK TO ME. I DO LIKE YOU GUYS!
SOME OF YOU GUYS.
LET'S GO, HYPERION!
WE REGROUP. PLAN B!
YOU HAVEN'T SEEN THE LAST OF US, AVENGERS! NOT IN THIS...

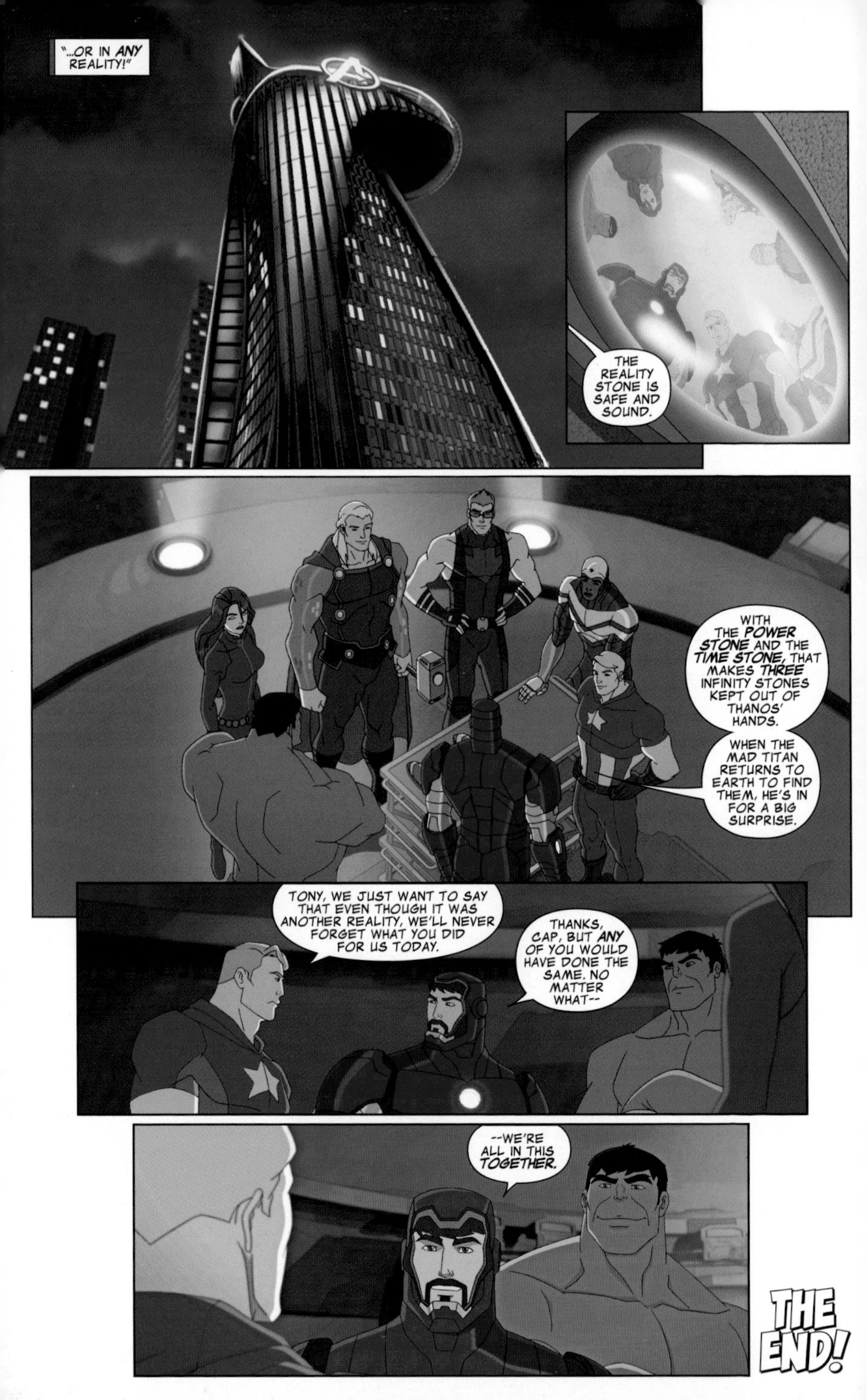
"...OR IN ANY REALITY!"
THE REALITY STONE IS SAFE AND SOUND.
WITH THE POWER STONE AND THE TIME STONE, THAT MAKES THREE INFINITY STONES KEPT OUT OF THANOS' HANDS.
WHEN THE MAD TITAN RETURNS TO EARTH TO FIND THEM, HE'S IN FOR A BIG SURPRISE.
TONY, WE JUST WANT TO SAY THAT EVEN THOUGH IT WAS ANOTHER REALITY, WE'LL NEVER FORGET WHAT YOU DID FOR US TODAY.
THANKS, CAP, BUT ANY OF YOU WOULD HAVE DONE THE SAME. NO MATTER WHAT--
--WE'RE ALL IN THIS TOGETHER.
THE END!

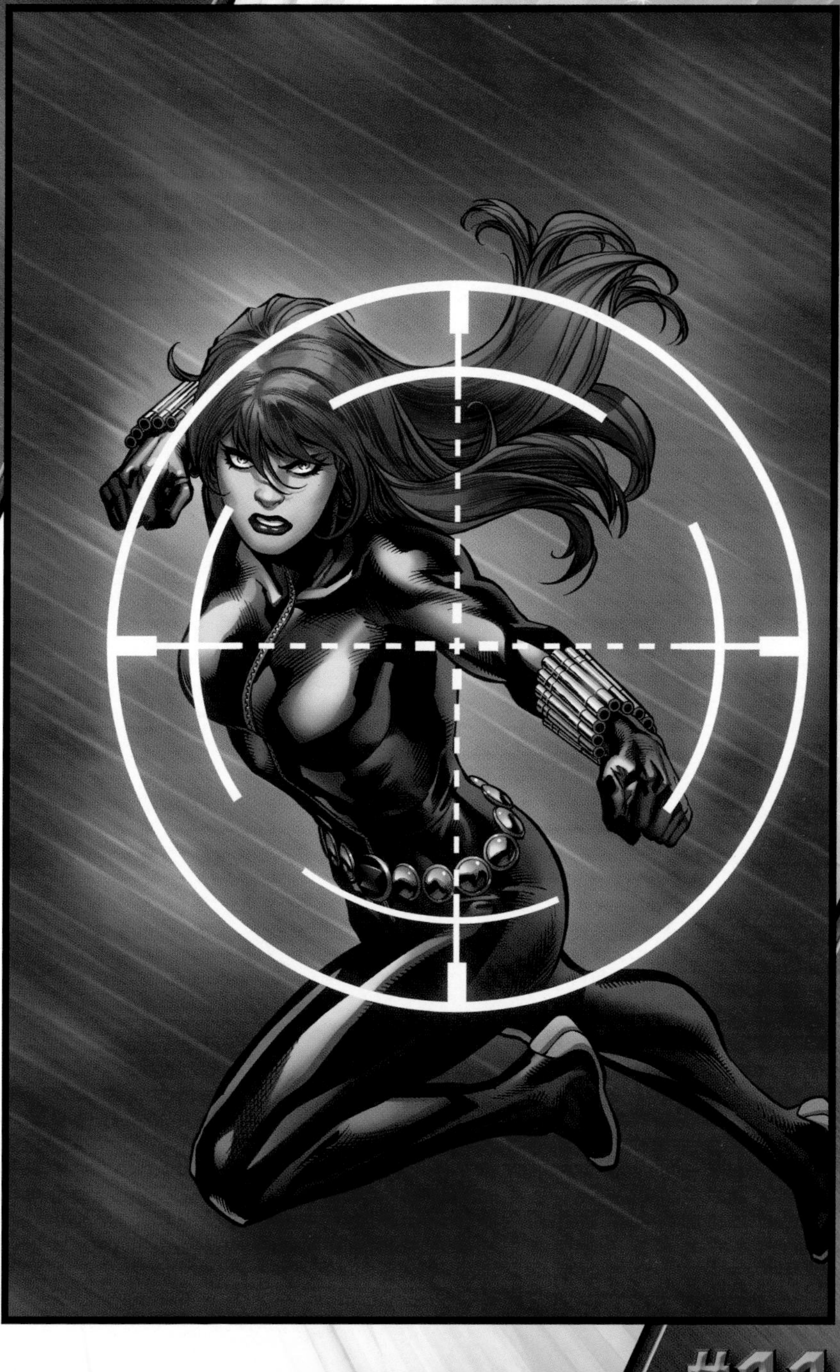

BASED ON "WIDOW'S RUN" #11

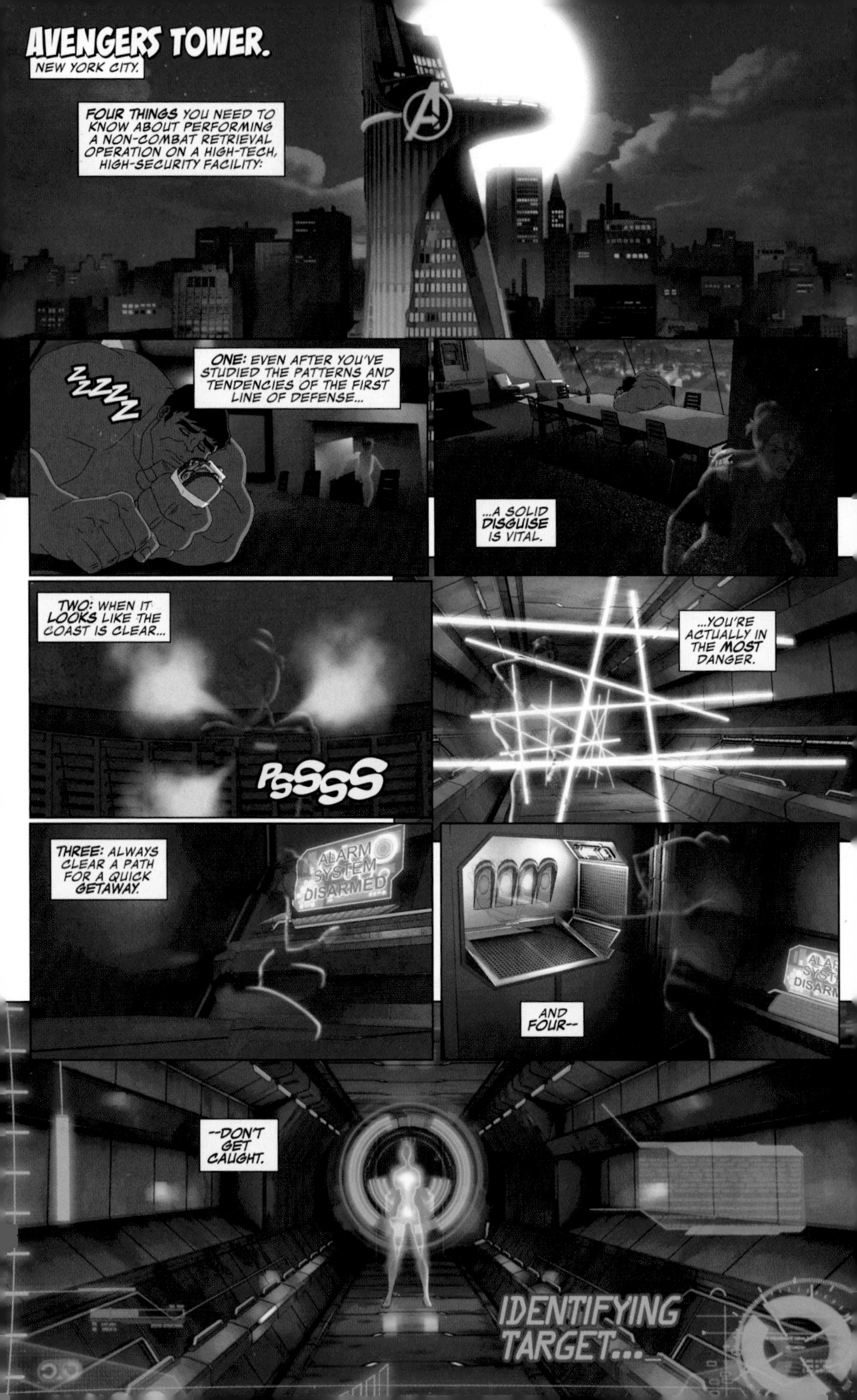
AVENGERS TOWER.
NEW YORK CITY.
FOUR THINGS YOU NEED TO KNOW ABOUT PERFORMING A NON-COMBAT RETRIEVAL OPERATION ON A HIGH-TECH, HIGH-SECURITY FACILITY:
ZZZZZ
ONE: EVEN AFTER YOU'VE STUDIED THE PATTERNS AND TENDENCIES OF THE FIRST LINE OF DEFENSE...
...A SOLID DISGUISE IS VITAL.
TWO: WHEN IT LOOKS LIKE THE COAST IS CLEAR...
PSSSSS
...YOU'RE ACTUALLY IN THE MOST DANGER.
THREE: ALWAYS CLEAR A PATH FOR A QUICK GETAWAY.
ALARM SYSTEM DISARMED
AND FOUR--
--DON'T GET CAUGHT.
IDENTIFYING TARGET...

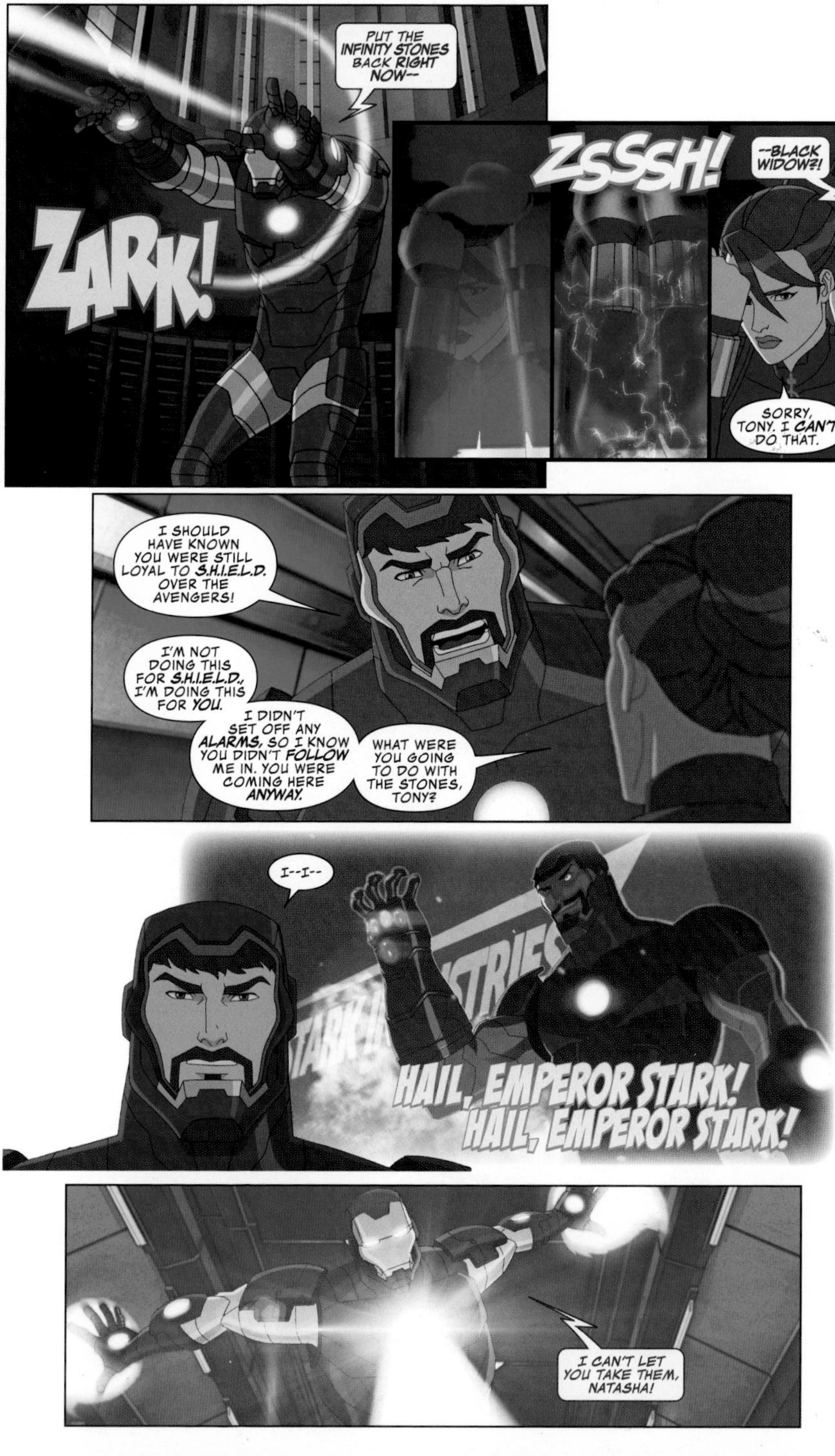
PUT THE INFINITY STONES BACK RIGHT NOW--
ZARK!
ZSSSH!
--BLACK WIDOW?!
SORRY, TONY. I CAN'T DO THAT.
I SHOULD HAVE KNOWN YOU WERE STILL LOYAL TO S.H.I.E.L.D. OVER THE AVENGERS!
I'M NOT DOING THIS FOR S.H.I.E.L.D., I'M DOING THIS FOR YOU.
I DIDN'T SET OFF ANY ALARMS, SO I KNOW YOU DIDN'T FOLLOW ME IN. YOU WERE COMING HERE ANYWAY.
WHAT WERE YOU GOING TO DO WITH THE STONES, TONY?
I--I--
HAIL, EMPEROR STARK! HAIL, EMPEROR STARK!
I CAN'T LET YOU TAKE THEM, NATASHA!

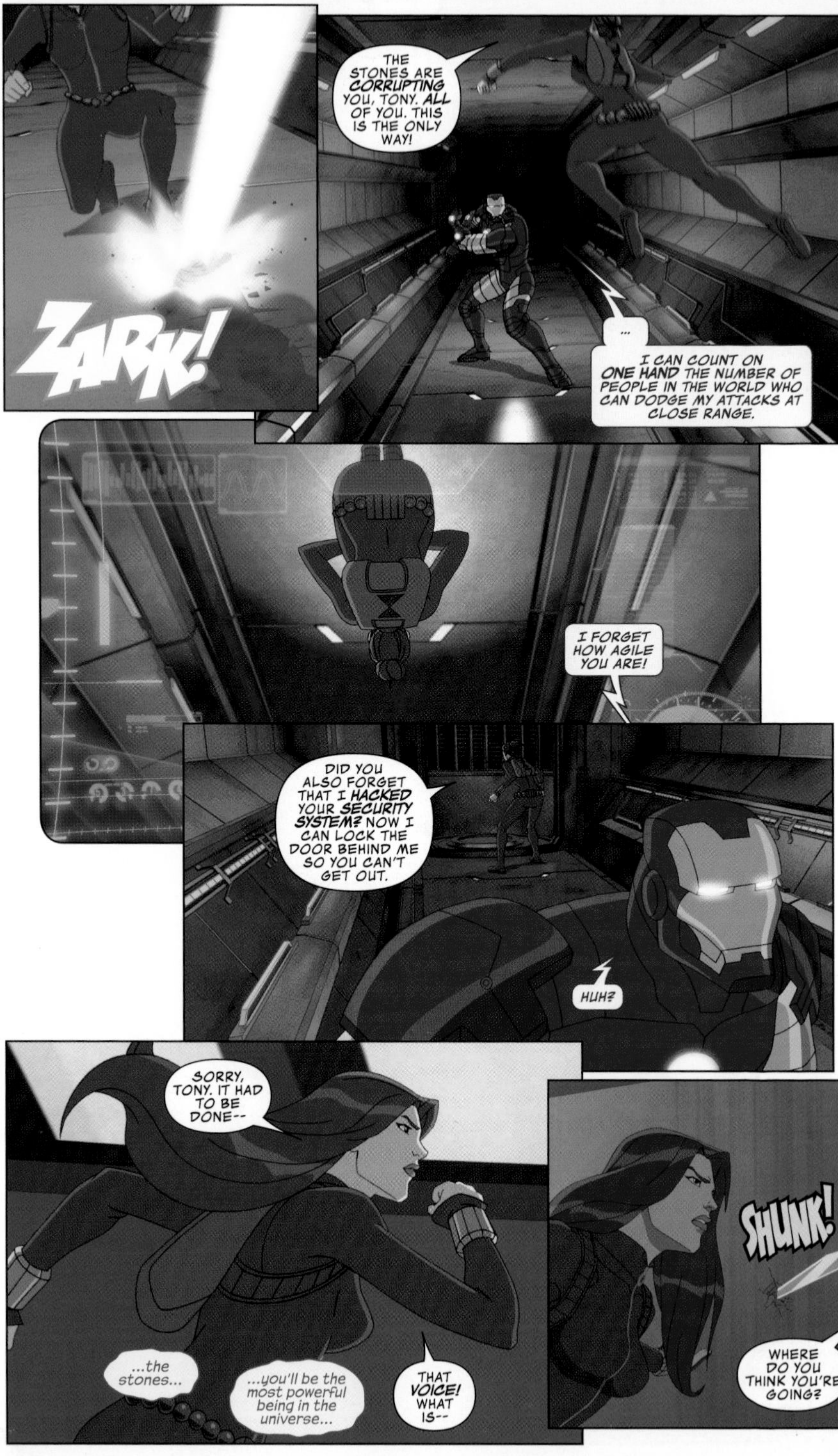
ZARK!
THE STONES ARE CORRUPTING YOU, TONY. ALL OF YOU. THIS IS THE ONLY WAY!
...
I CAN COUNT ON ONE HAND THE NUMBER OF PEOPLE IN THE WORLD WHO CAN DODGE MY ATTACKS AT CLOSE RANGE.
I FORGET HOW AGILE YOU ARE!
DID YOU ALSO FORGET THAT I HACKED YOUR SECURITY SYSTEM? NOW I CAN LOCK THE DOOR BEHIND ME SO YOU CAN'T GET OUT.
HUH?
SORRY, TONY. IT HAD TO BE DONE--
...the stones...
...you'll be the most powerful being in the universe...
THAT VOICE! WHAT IS--
SHUNK!
WHERE DO YOU THINK YOU'RE GOING?

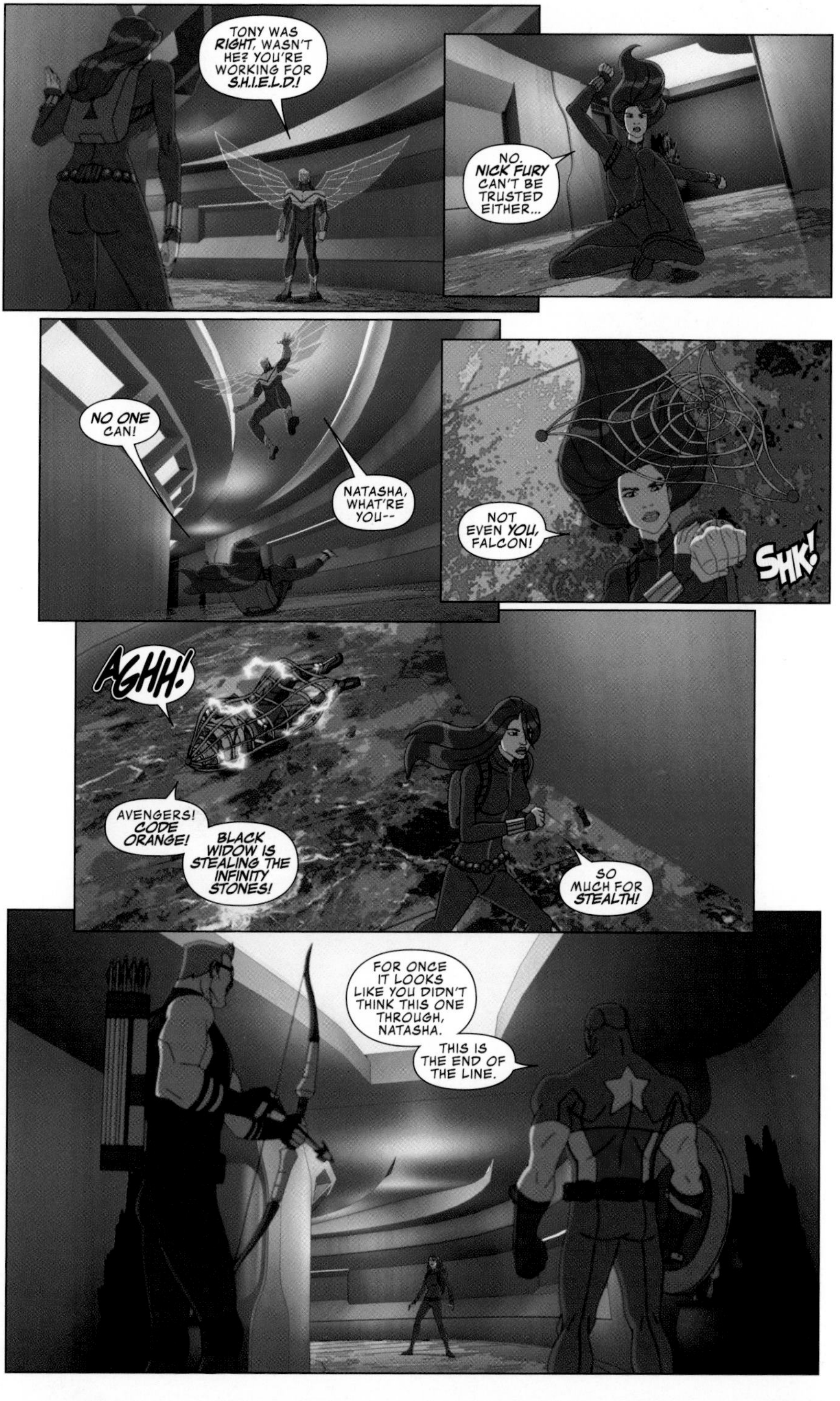
TONY WAS RIGHT, WASN'T HE? YOU'RE WORKING FOR S.H.I.E.L.D.!
NO. NICK FURY CAN'T BE TRUSTED EITHER...
NO ONE CAN!
NATASHA, WHAT'RE YOU--
NOT EVEN YOU, FALCON!
SHK!
AGHH!
AVENGERS! CODE ORANGE!
BLACK WIDOW IS STEALING THE INFINITY STONES!
SO MUCH FOR STEALTH!
FOR ONCE IT LOOKS LIKE YOU DIDN'T THINK THIS ONE THROUGH, NATASHA.
THIS IS THE END OF THE LINE.

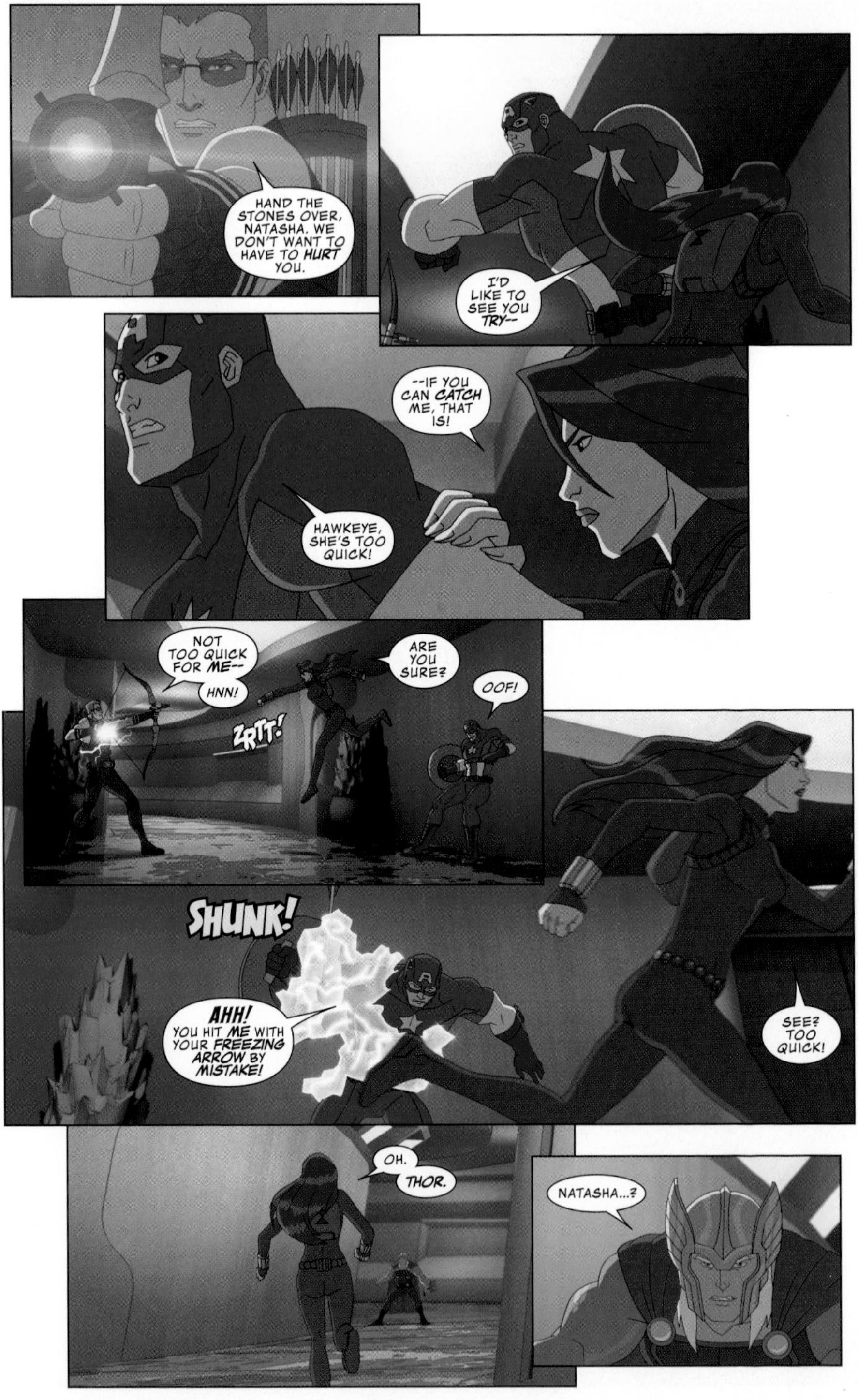
HAND THE STONES OVER, NATASHA. WE DON'T WANT TO HAVE TO HURT YOU.
I'D LIKE TO SEE YOU TRY--
--IF YOU CAN CATCH ME, THAT IS!
HAWKEYE, SHE'S TOO QUICK!
NOT TOO QUICK FOR ME--
HNN!
ARE YOU SURE?
OOF!
ZRTT!
SHUNK!
AHH! YOU HIT ME WITH YOUR FREEZING ARROW BY MISTAKE!
SEE? TOO QUICK!
OH.
THOR.
NATASHA...?

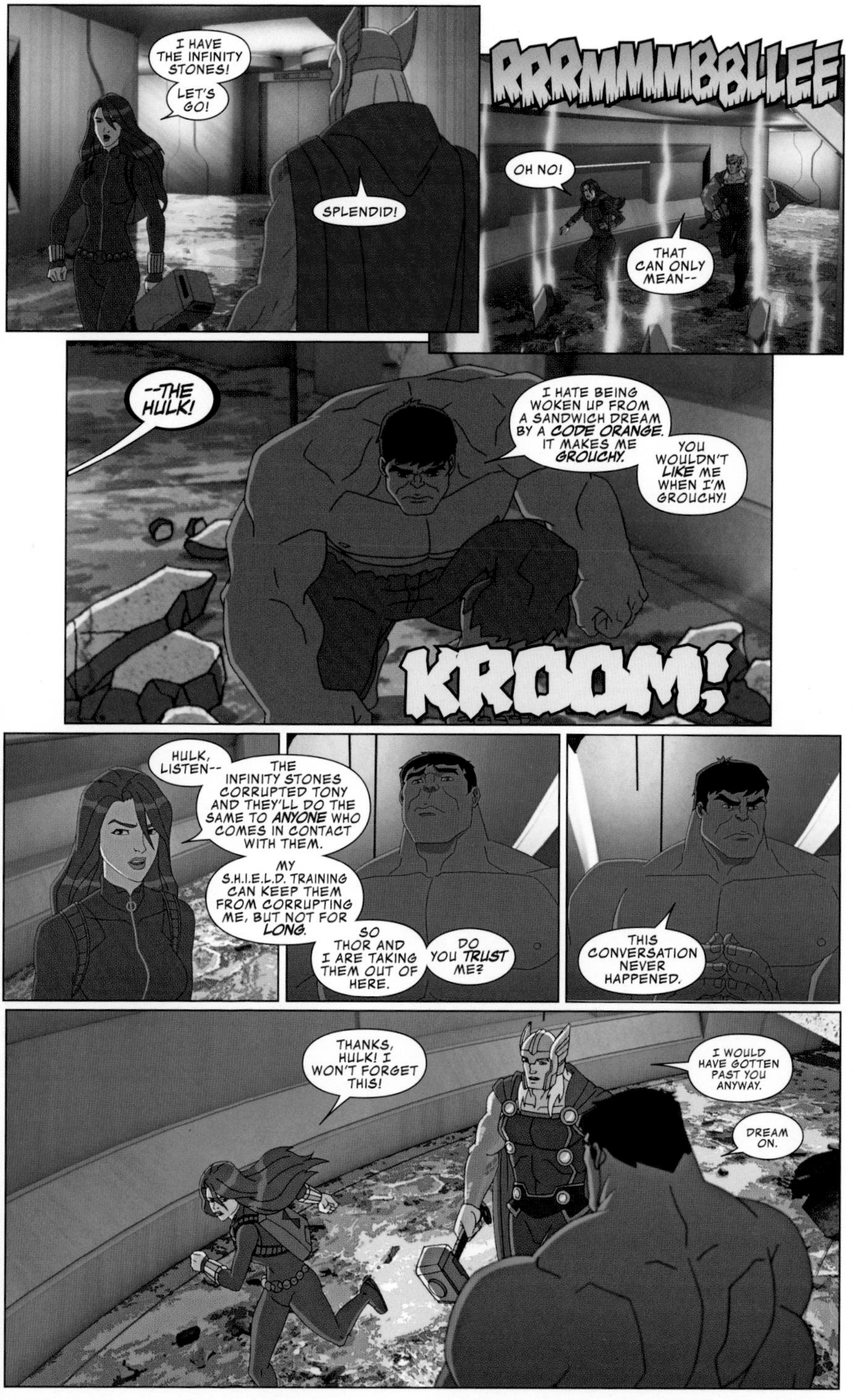
I HAVE THE INFINITY STONES!
LET'S GO!
SPLENDID!
RRRMMMMBBLLEE
OH NO!
THAT CAN ONLY MEAN--
--THE HULK!
I HATE BEING WOKEN UP FROM A SANDWICH DREAM BY A CODE ORANGE. IT MAKES ME GROUCHY.
YOU WOULDN'T LIKE ME WHEN I'M GROUCHY!
KROOM!
HULK, LISTEN--
THE INFINITY STONES CORRUPTED TONY AND THEY'LL DO THE SAME TO ANYONE WHO COMES IN CONTACT WITH THEM.
MY S.H.I.E.L.D. TRAINING CAN KEEP THEM FROM CORRUPTING ME, BUT NOT FOR LONG.
SO THOR AND I ARE TAKING THEM OUT OF HERE.
DO YOU TRUST ME?
THIS CONVERSATION NEVER HAPPENED.
THANKS, HULK! I WON'T FORGET THIS!
I WOULD HAVE GOTTEN PAST YOU ANYWAY.
DREAM ON.

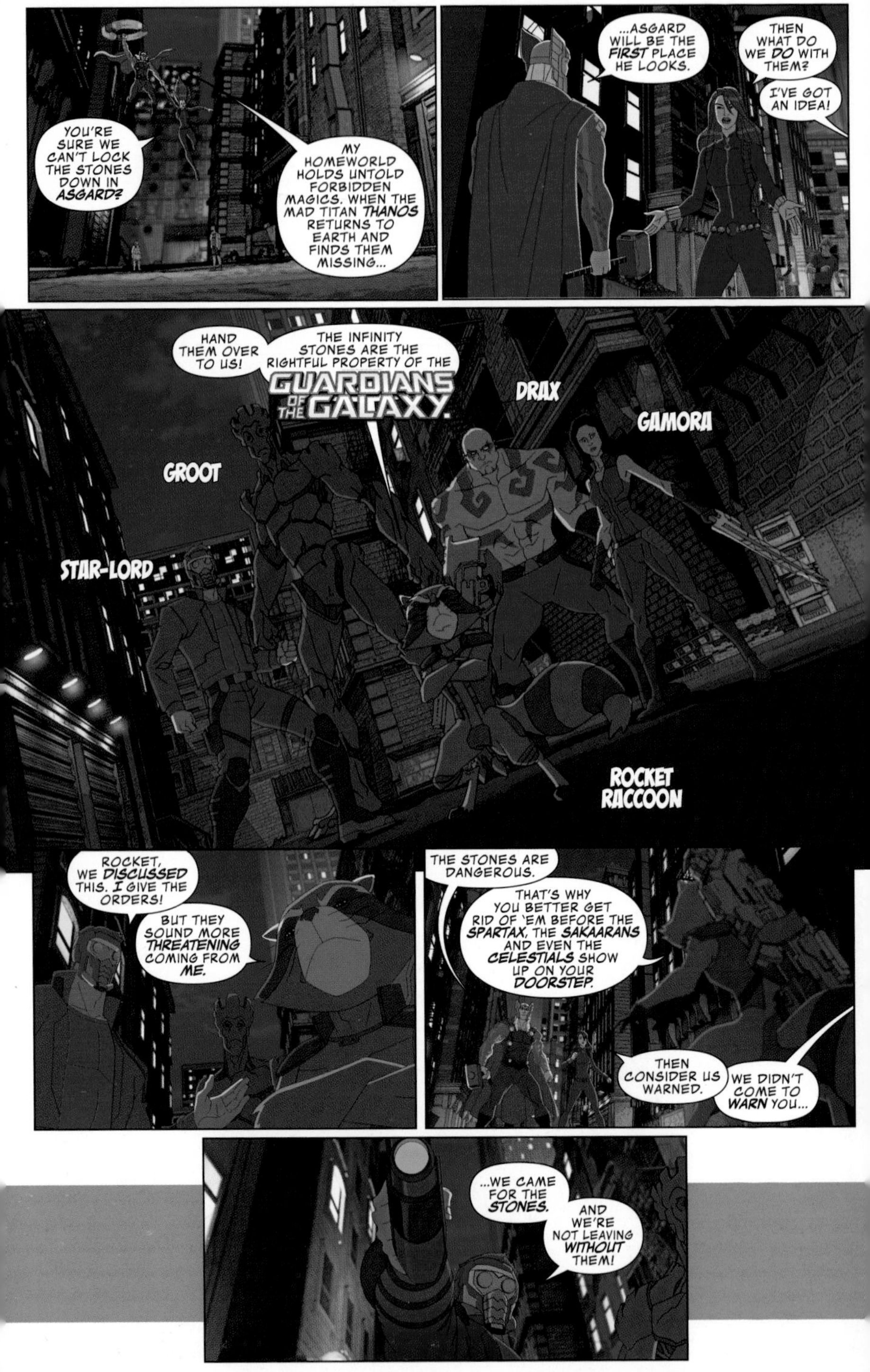
YOU'RE SURE WE CAN'T LOCK THE STONES DOWN IN ASGARD?
MY HOMEWORLD HOLDS UNTOLD FORBIDDEN MAGICS. WHEN THE MAD TITAN THANOS RETURNS TO EARTH AND FINDS THEM MISSING...
...ASGARD WILL BE THE FIRST PLACE HE LOOKS.
THEN WHAT DO WE DO WITH THEM?
I'VE GOT AN IDEA!
HAND THEM OVER TO US!
THE INFINITY STONES ARE THE RIGHTFUL PROPERTY OF THE
GUARDIANS OF THE GALAXY.
DRAX
GAMORA
GROOT
STAR-LORD
ROCKET RACCOON
ROCKET, WE DISCUSSED THIS. I GIVE THE ORDERS!
BUT THEY SOUND MORE THREATENING COMING FROM ME.
THE STONES ARE DANGEROUS.
THAT'S WHY YOU BETTER GET RID OF 'EM BEFORE THE SPARTAX, THE SAKAARANS AND EVEN THE CELESTIALS SHOW UP ON YOUR DOORSTEP.
THEN CONSIDER US WARNED.
WE DIDN'T COME TO WARN YOU...
...WE CAME FOR THE STONES.
AND WE'RE NOT LEAVING WITHOUT THEM!

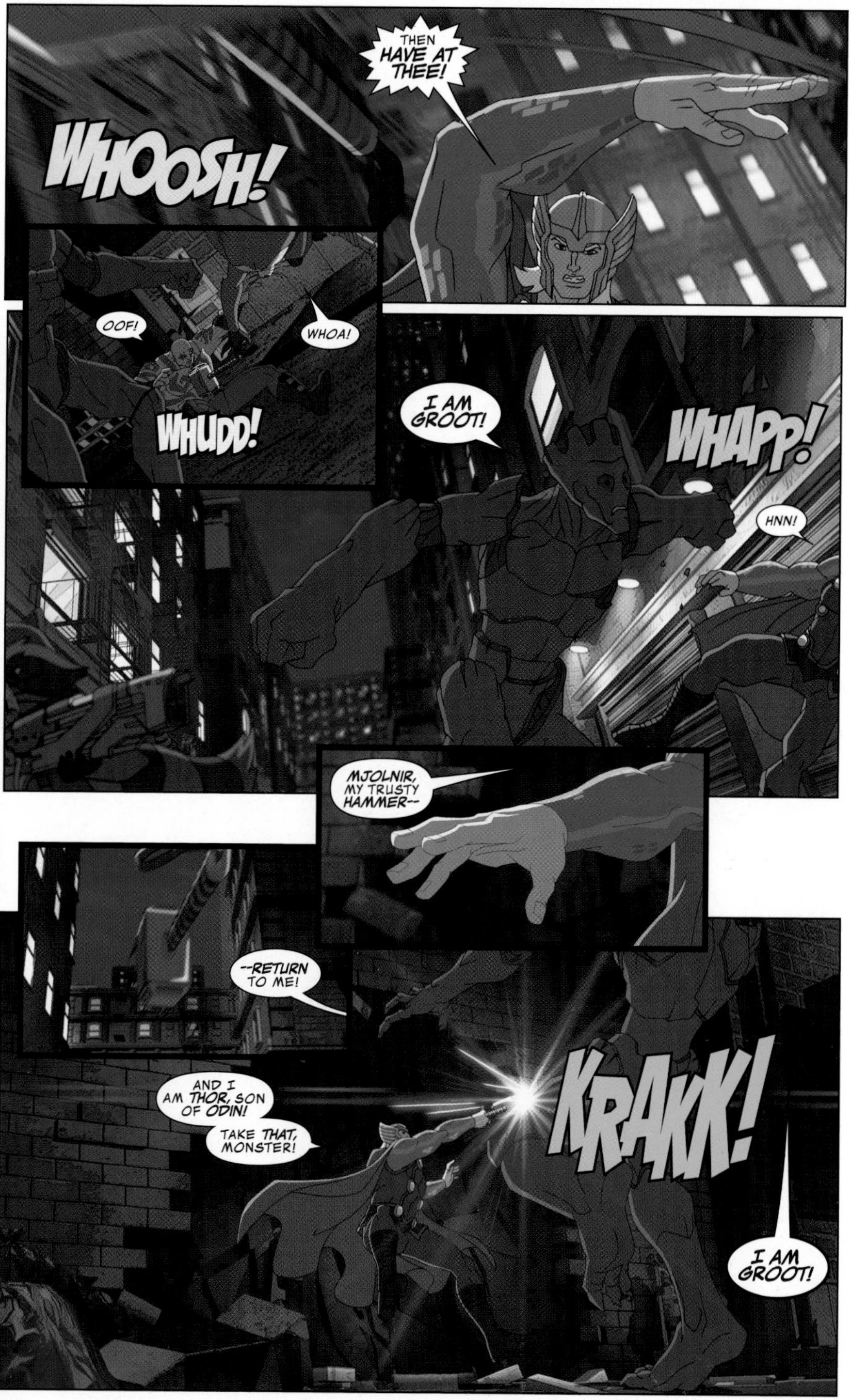

THEN HAVE AT THEE!
WHOOSH!
OOF!
WHOA!
WHUDD!
I AM GROOT!
WHAPP!
HNN!
MJOLNIR, MY TRUSTY HAMMER--
--RETURN TO ME!
AND I AM THOR, SON OF ODIN!
TAKE THAT, MONSTER!
KRAKK!
I AM GROOT!

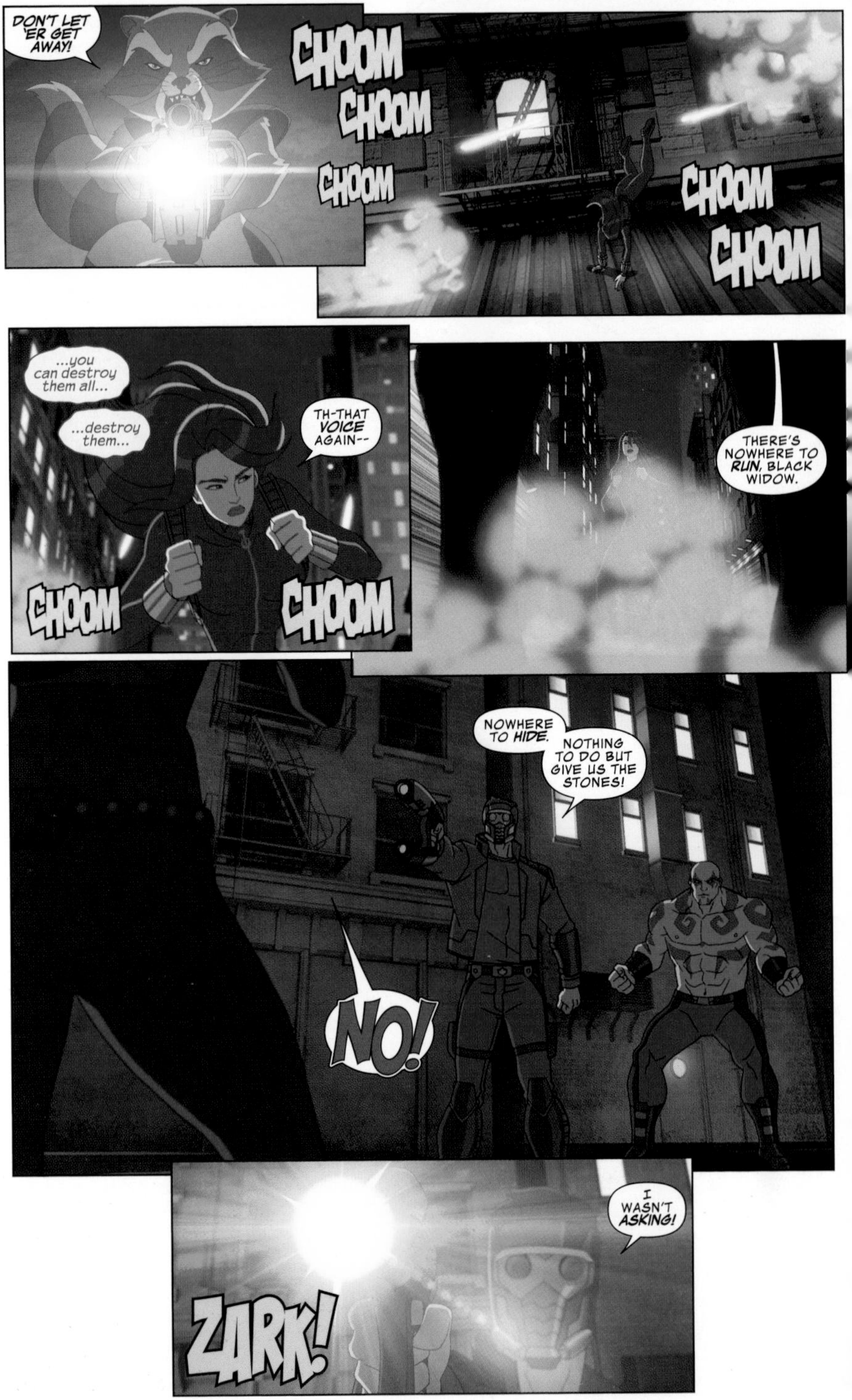
DON'T LET 'ER GET AWAY!
CHOOM
CHOOM
CHOOM
CHOOM
CHOOM
...you can destroy them all...
...destroy them...
TH-THAT VOICE AGAIN--
CHOOM
CHOOM
THERE'S NOWHERE TO RUN, BLACK WIDOW.
NOWHERE TO HIDE.
NOTHING TO DO BUT GIVE US THE STONES!
NO!
I WASN'T ASKING!
ZARK!

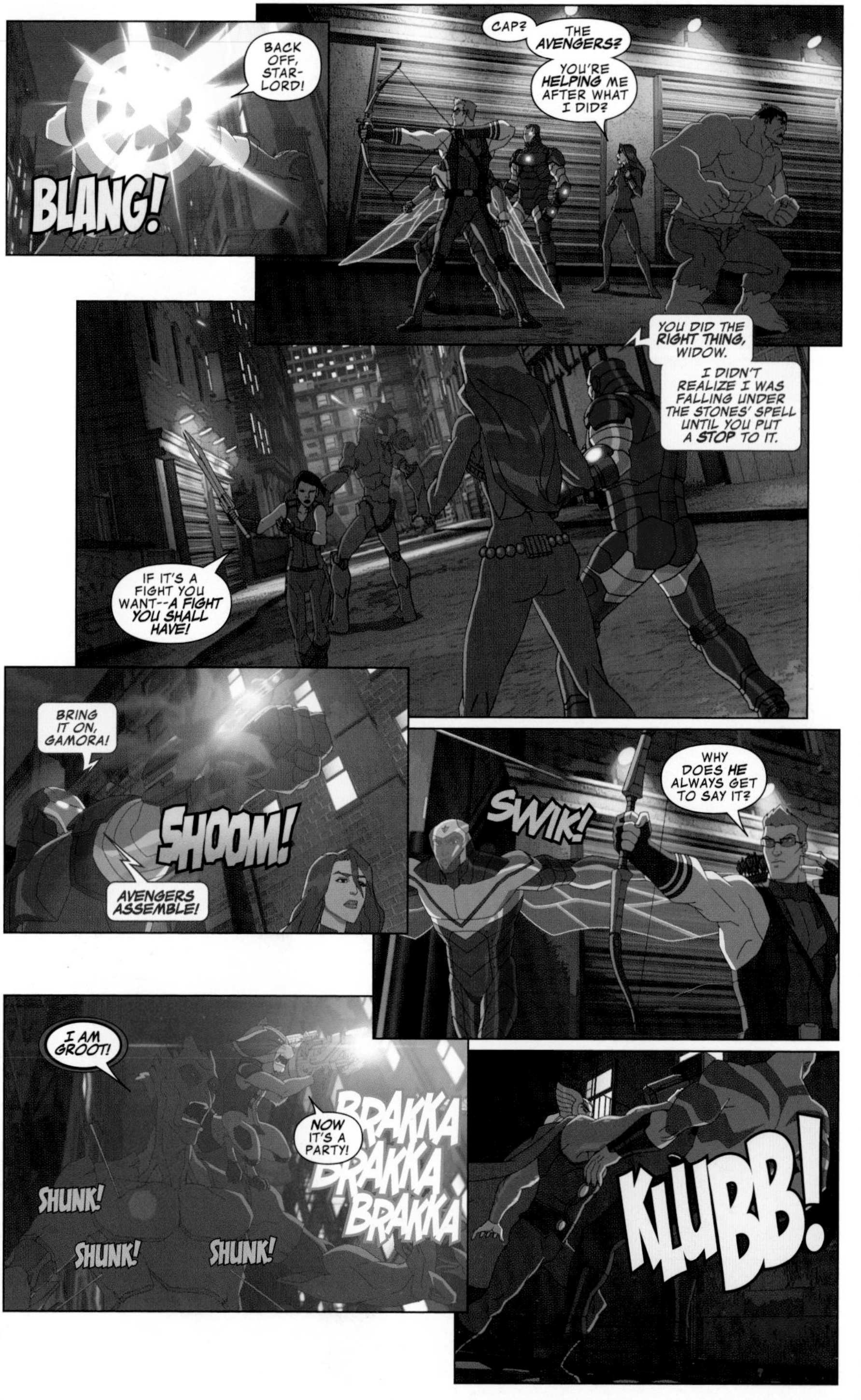
BACK OFF, STAR-LORD!
BLANG!
CAP?
THE AVENGERS?
YOU'RE HELPING ME AFTER WHAT I DID?
YOU DID THE RIGHT THING, WIDOW.
I DIDN'T REALIZE I WAS FALLING UNDER THE STONES' SPELL UNTIL YOU PUT A STOP TO IT.
IF IT'S A FIGHT YOU WANT--A FIGHT YOU SHALL HAVE!
BRING IT ON, GAMORA!
SHOOM!
AVENGERS ASSEMBLE!
WHY DOES HE ALWAYS GET TO SAY IT?
SWIK!
I AM GROOT!
NOW IT'S A PARTY!
BRAKKA BRAKKA BRAKKA
SHUNK!
SHUNK!
SHUNK!
KLUBB!

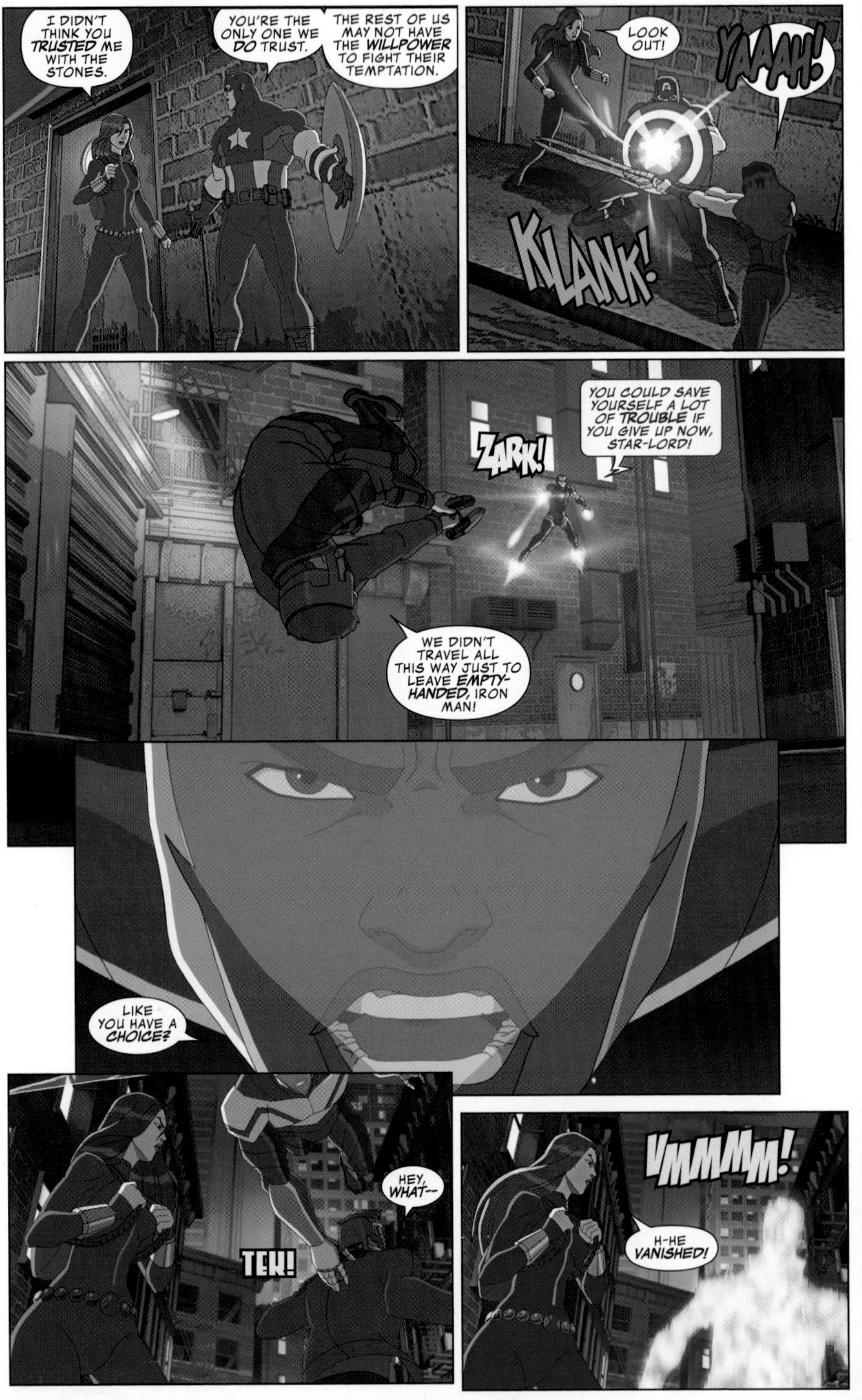
I DIDN'T THINK YOU TRUSTED ME WITH THE STONES.
YOU'RE THE ONLY ONE WE DO TRUST.
THE REST OF US MAY NOT HAVE THE WILLPOWER TO FIGHT THEIR TEMPTATION.
LOOK OUT!
YAAAH!
KLANK!
ZARK!
YOU COULD SAVE YOURSELF A LOT OF TROUBLE IF YOU GIVE UP NOW, STAR-LORD!
WE DIDN'T TRAVEL ALL THIS WAY JUST TO LEAVE EMPTY-HANDED, IRON MAN!
LIKE YOU HAVE A CHOICE?
HEY, WHAT--
TEK!
VMMMM!
H-HE VANISHED!

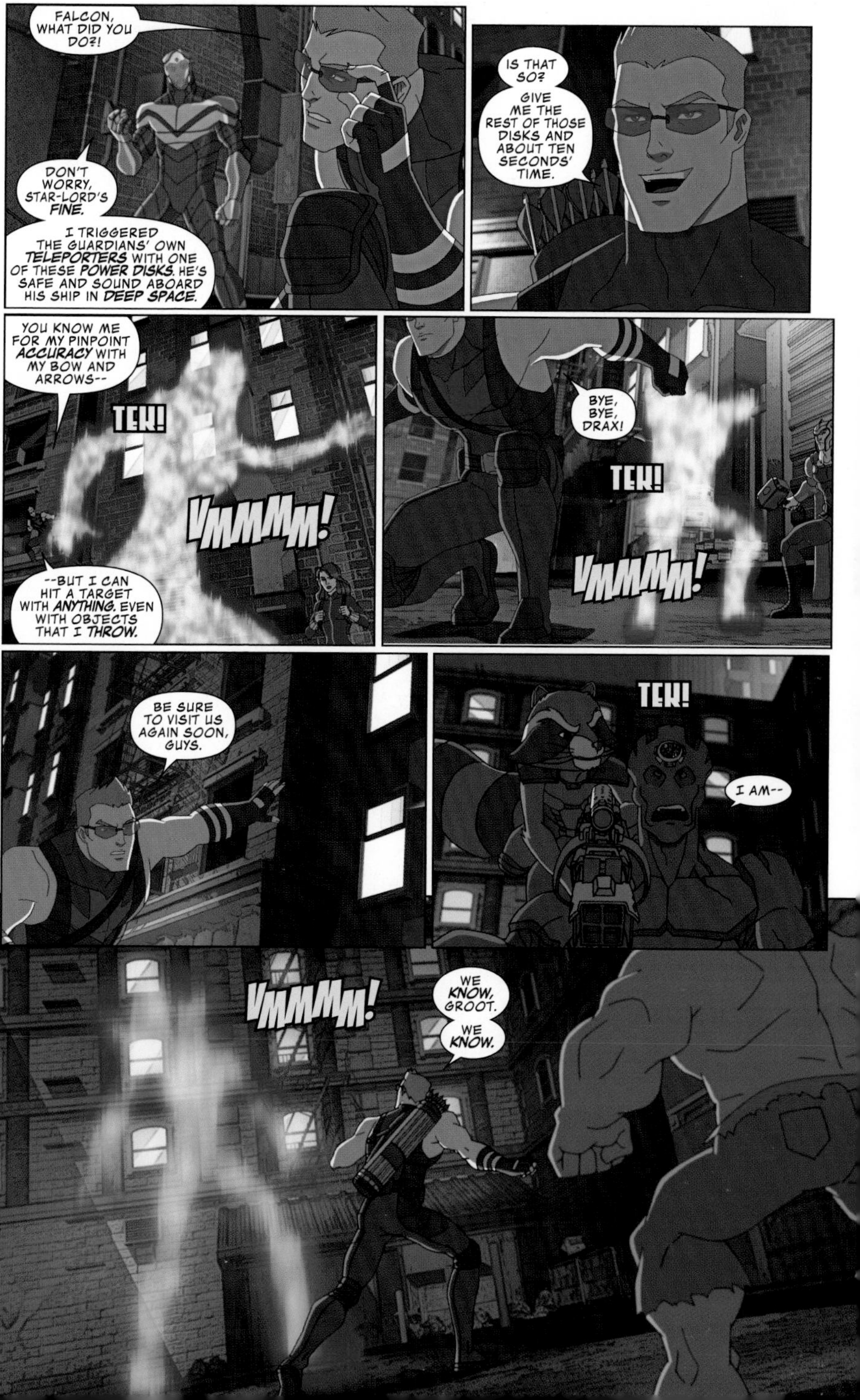
FALCON, WHAT DID YOU DO?!
DON'T WORRY, STAR-LORD'S FINE.
I TRIGGERED THE GUARDIANS' OWN TELEPORTERS WITH ONE OF THESE POWER DISKS. HE'S SAFE AND SOUND ABOARD HIS SHIP IN DEEP SPACE.
IS THAT SO?
GIVE ME THE REST OF THOSE DISKS AND ABOUT TEN SECONDS' TIME.
YOU KNOW ME FOR MY PINPOINT ACCURACY WITH MY BOW AND ARROWS--
TEK!
VMMMM!
--BUT I CAN HIT A TARGET WITH ANYTHING. EVEN WITH OBJECTS THAT I THROW.
BYE, BYE, DRAX!
TEK!
VMMMM!
BE SURE TO VISIT US AGAIN SOON, GUYS.
TEK!
I AM--
VMMMM!
WE KNOW, GROOT.
WE KNOW.

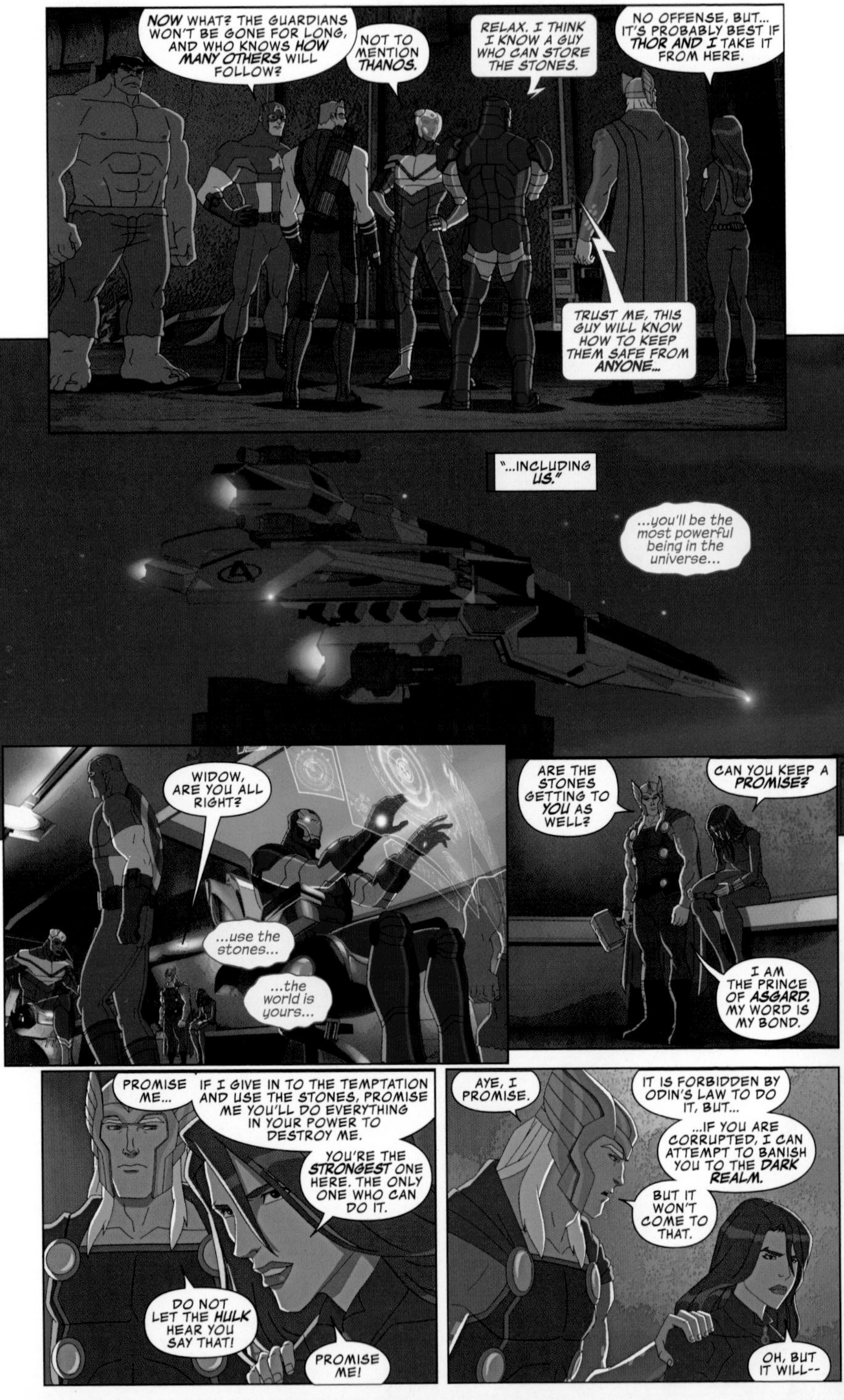
NOW WHAT? THE GUARDIANS WON'T BE GONE FOR LONG, AND WHO KNOWS HOW MANY OTHERS WILL FOLLOW?
NOT TO MENTION THANOS.
RELAX. I THINK I KNOW A GUY WHO CAN STORE THE STONES.
NO OFFENSE, BUT... IT'S PROBABLY BEST IF THOR AND I TAKE IT FROM HERE.
TRUST ME, THIS GUY WILL KNOW HOW TO KEEP THEM SAFE FROM ANYONE...
"...INCLUDING US."
...you'll be the most powerful being in the universe...
WIDOW, ARE YOU ALL RIGHT?
...use the stones...
...the world is yours...
ARE THE STONES GETTING TO YOU AS WELL?
CAN YOU KEEP A PROMISE?
I AM THE PRINCE OF ASGARD. MY WORD IS MY BOND.
PROMISE ME...
IF I GIVE IN TO THE TEMPTATION AND USE THE STONES, PROMISE ME YOU'LL DO EVERYTHING IN YOUR POWER TO DESTROY ME.
YOU'RE THE STRONGEST ONE HERE. THE ONLY ONE WHO CAN DO IT.
DO NOT LET THE HULK HEAR YOU SAY THAT!
PROMISE ME!
AYE, I PROMISE.
IT IS FORBIDDEN BY ODIN'S LAW TO DO IT, BUT...
...IF YOU ARE CORRUPTED, I CAN ATTEMPT TO BANISH YOU TO THE DARK REALM.
BUT IT WON'T COME TO THAT.
OH, BUT IT WILL--

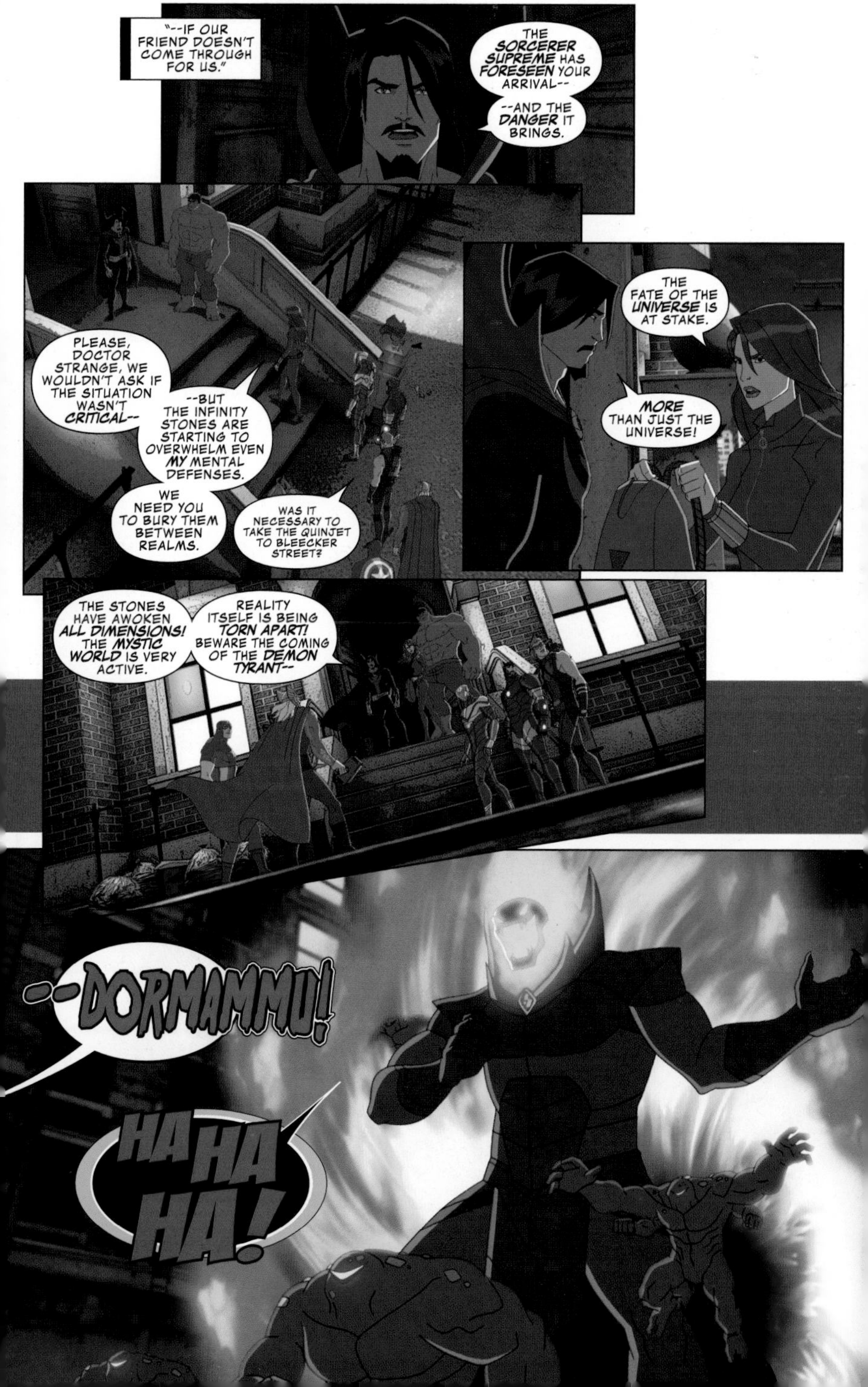
"--IF OUR FRIEND DOESN'T COME THROUGH FOR US."
THE SORCERER SUPREME HAS FORESEEN YOUR ARRIVAL--
--AND THE DANGER IT BRINGS.
PLEASE, DOCTOR STRANGE, WE WOULDN'T ASK IF THE SITUATION WASN'T CRITICAL--
--BUT THE INFINITY STONES ARE STARTING TO OVERWHELM EVEN MY MENTAL DEFENSES.
WE NEED YOU TO BURY THEM BETWEEN REALMS.
WAS IT NECESSARY TO TAKE THE QUINJET TO BLEECKER STREET?
THE FATE OF THE UNIVERSE IS AT STAKE.
MORE THAN JUST THE UNIVERSE!
THE STONES HAVE AWOKEN ALL DIMENSIONS! THE MYSTIC WORLD IS VERY ACTIVE.
REALITY ITSELF IS BEING TORN APART! BEWARE THE COMING OF THE DEMON TYRANT--
--DORMAMMU!
HA HA HA!

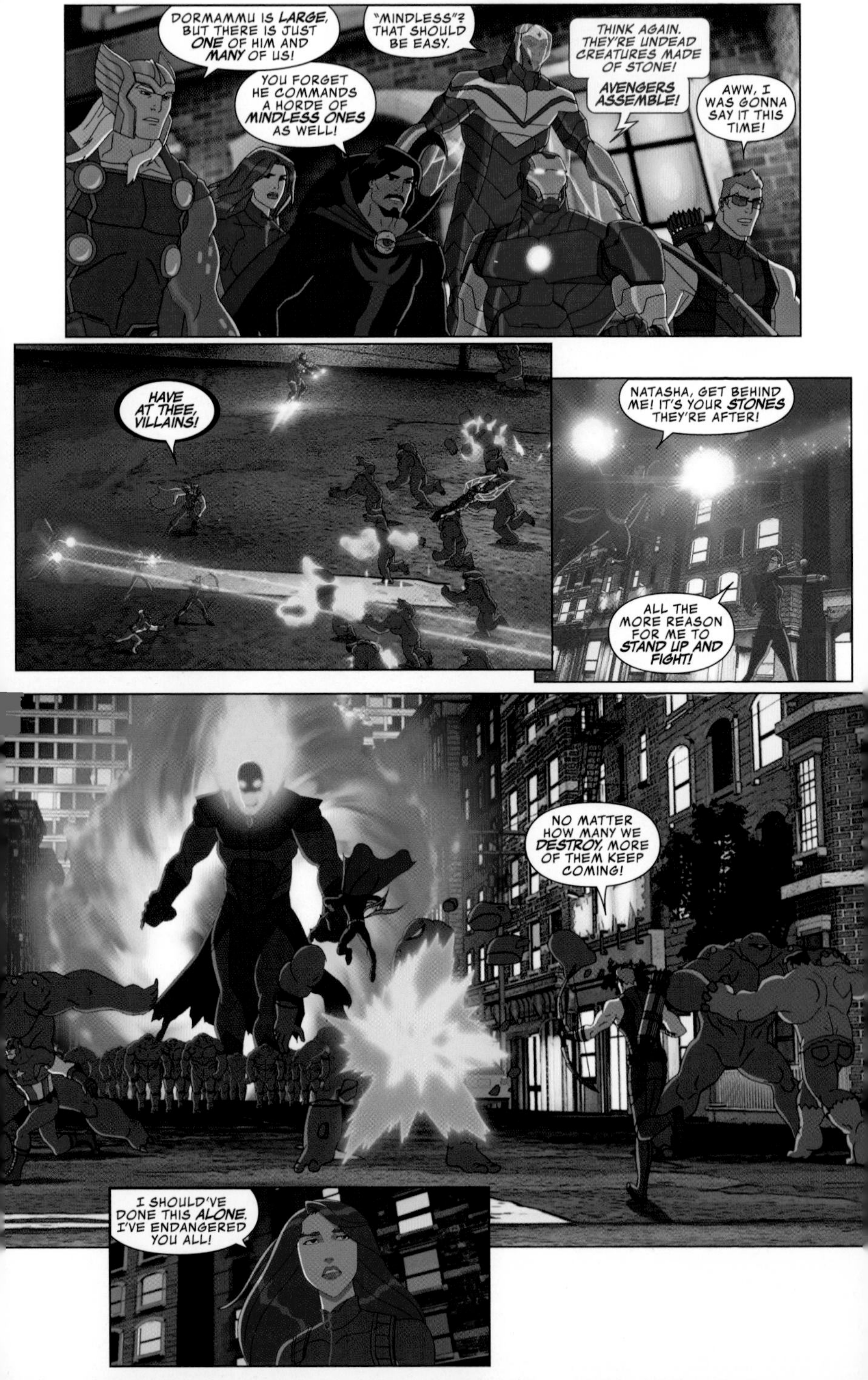
DORMAMMU IS LARGE, BUT THERE IS JUST ONE OF HIM AND MANY OF US!
YOU FORGET HE COMMANDS A HORDE OF MINDLESS ONES AS WELL!
"MINDLESS"? THAT SHOULD BE EASY.
THINK AGAIN. THEY'RE UNDEAD CREATURES MADE OF STONE!
AVENGERS ASSEMBLE!
AWW, I WAS GONNA SAY IT THIS TIME!
HAVE AT THEE, VILLAINS!
NATASHA, GET BEHIND ME! IT'S YOUR STONES THEY'RE AFTER!
ALL THE MORE REASON FOR ME TO STAND UP AND FIGHT!
NO MATTER HOW MANY WE DESTROY, MORE OF THEM KEEP COMING!
I SHOULD'VE DONE THIS ALONE. I'VE ENDANGERED YOU ALL!

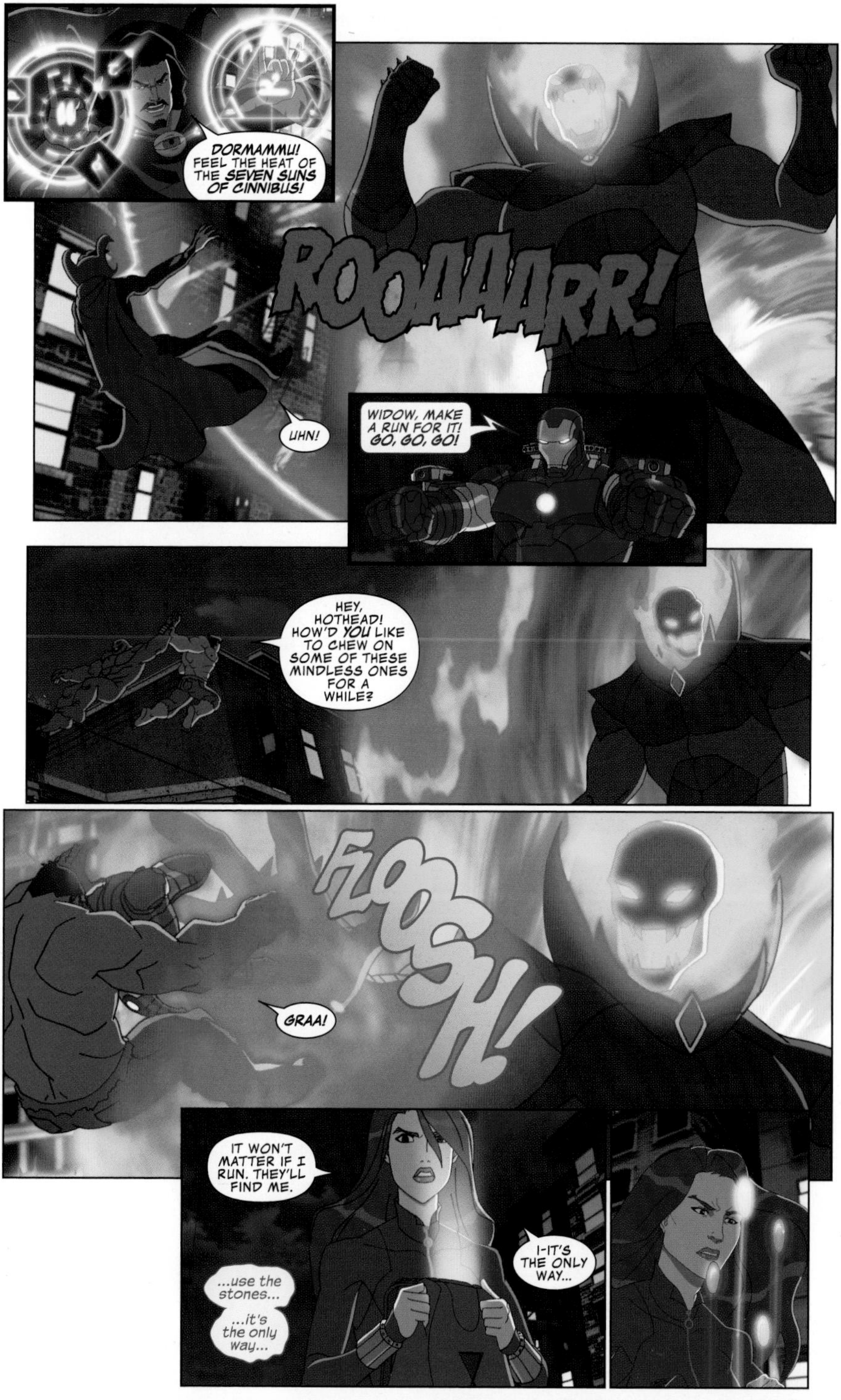
DORMAMMU! FEEL THE HEAT OF THE SEVEN SUNS OF CINNIBUS!
ROOAAARR!
UHN!
WIDOW, MAKE A RUN FOR IT! GO, GO, GO!
HEY, HOTHEAD! HOW'D YOU LIKE TO CHEW ON SOME OF THESE MINDLESS ONES FOR A WHILE?
FLOOSH!
GRAA!
IT WON'T MATTER IF I RUN. THEY'LL FIND ME.
...use the stones...
...it's the only way...
I-IT'S THE ONLY WAY...

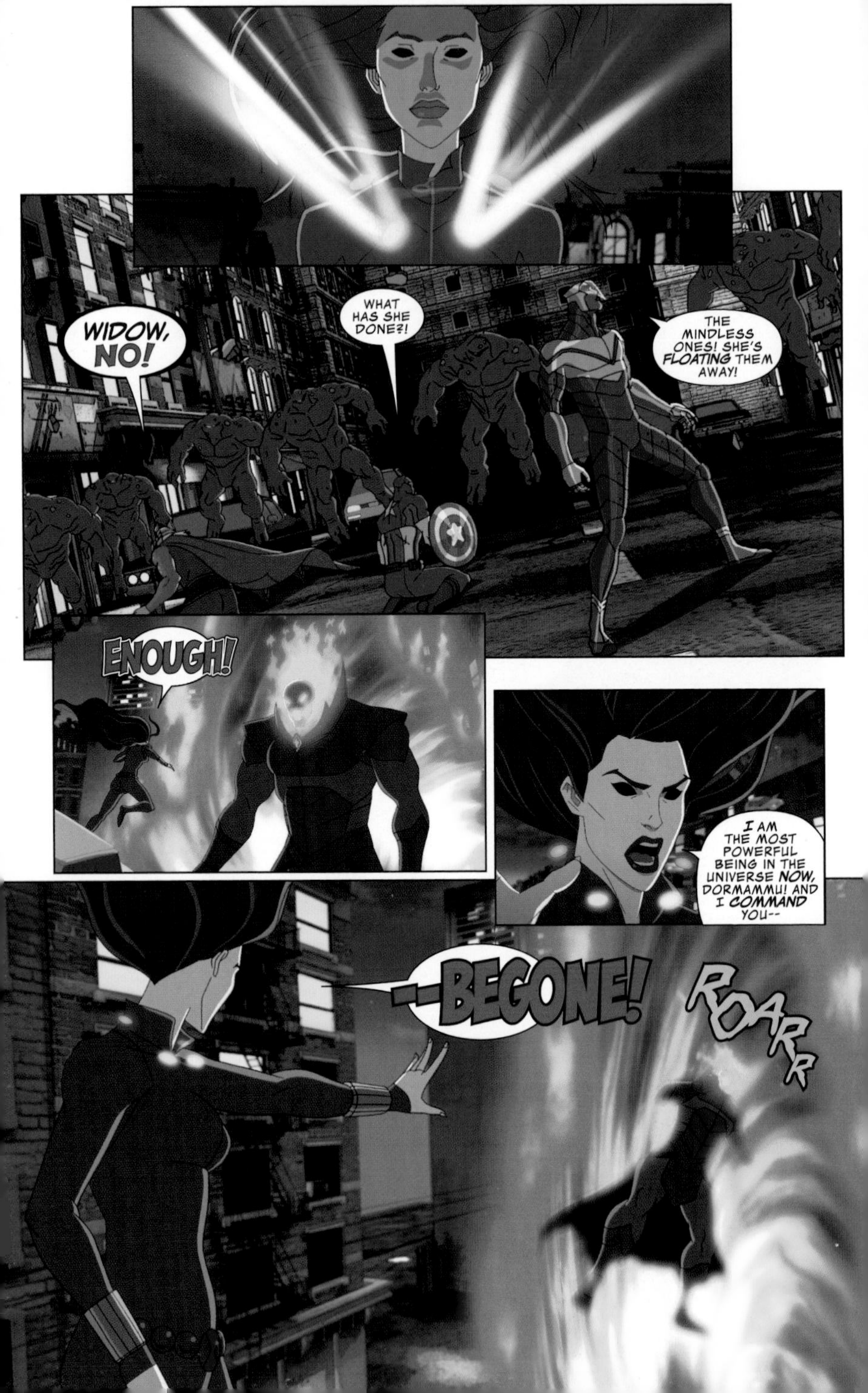
WIDOW, NO!
WHAT HAS SHE DONE?!
THE MINDLESS ONES! SHE'S FLOATING THEM AWAY!
ENOUGH!
I AM THE MOST POWERFUL BEING IN THE UNIVERSE NOW, DORMAMMU! AND I COMMAND YOU--
--BEGONE!
ROARR

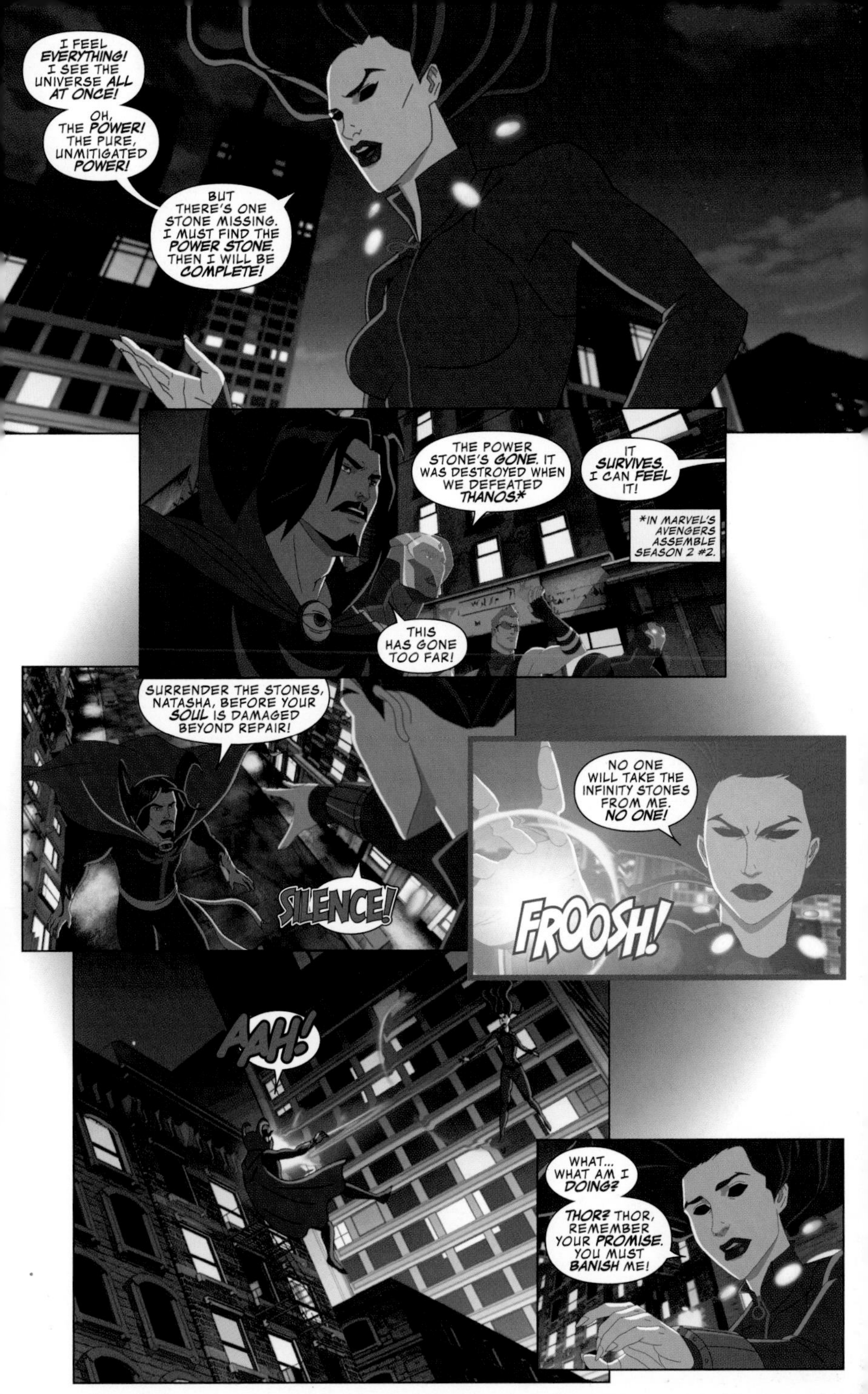
I FEEL EVERYTHING! I SEE THE UNIVERSE ALL AT ONCE!
OH, THE POWER! THE PURE, UNMITIGATED POWER!
BUT THERE'S ONE STONE MISSING. I MUST FIND THE POWER STONE. THEN I WILL BE COMPLETE!
THE POWER STONE'S GONE. IT WAS DESTROYED WHEN WE DEFEATED THANOS.*
IT SURVIVES. I CAN FEEL IT!
*IN MARVEL'S AVENGERS ASSEMBLE SEASON 2 #2.
THIS HAS GONE TOO FAR!
SURRENDER THE STONES, NATASHA, BEFORE YOUR SOUL IS DAMAGED BEYOND REPAIR!
SILENCE!
NO ONE WILL TAKE THE INFINITY STONES FROM ME. NO ONE!
FROOSH!
AAH!
WHAT... WHAT AM I DOING?
THOR? THOR, REMEMBER YOUR PROMISE. YOU MUST BANISH ME!

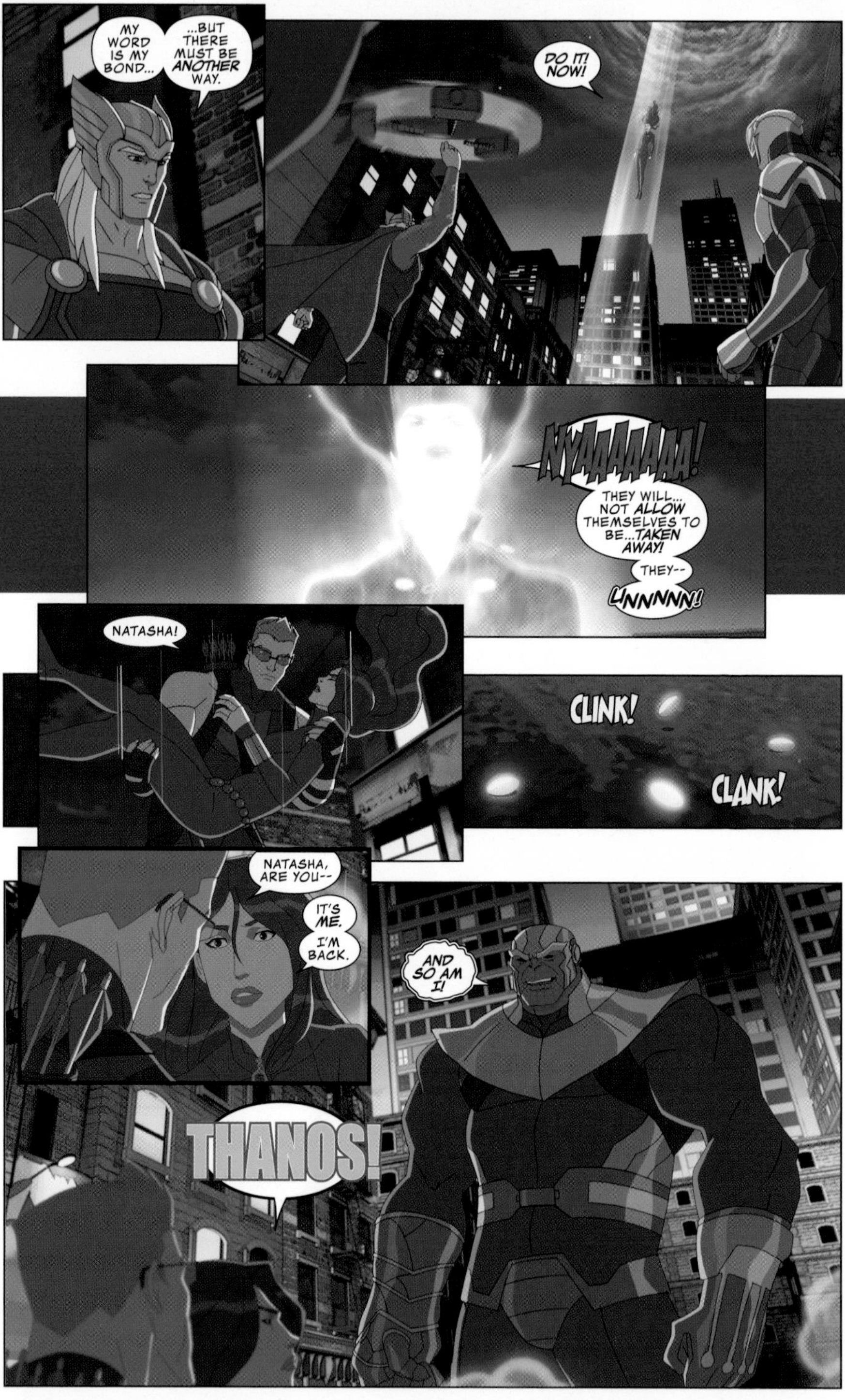
MY WORD IS MY BOND...
...BUT THERE MUST BE ANOTHER WAY.
DO IT! NOW!
NYAAAAAAA!
THEY WILL... NOT ALLOW THEMSELVES TO BE...TAKEN AWAY!
THEY--
UNNNNN!
NATASHA!
CLINK!
CLANK!
NATASHA, ARE YOU--
IT'S ME.
I'M BACK.
AND SO AM I!
THANOS!

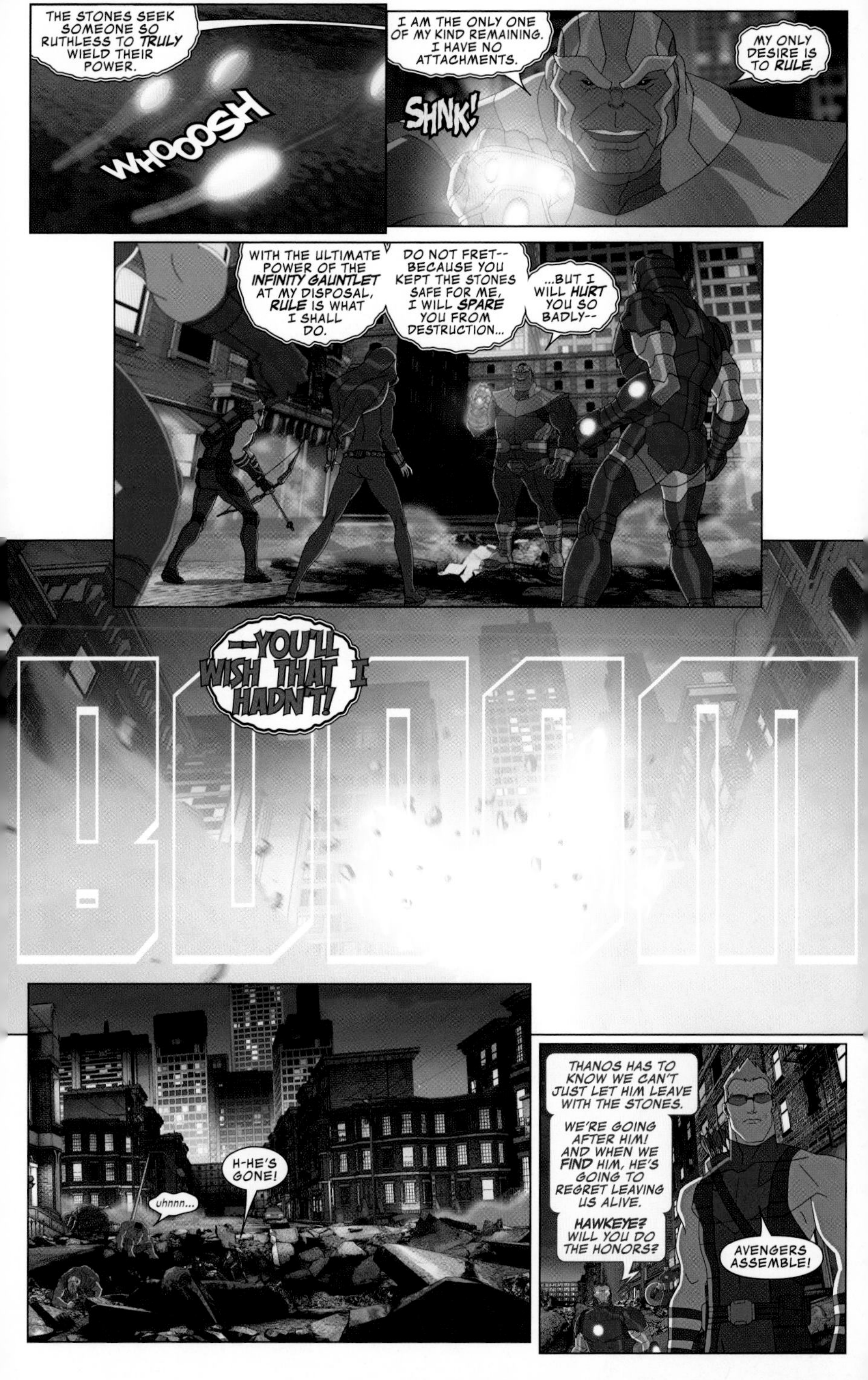
THE STONES SEEK SOMEONE SO RUTHLESS TO TRULY WIELD THEIR POWER.
WHOOOSH
I AM THE ONLY ONE OF MY KIND REMAINING. I HAVE NO ATTACHMENTS.
SHNK!
MY ONLY DESIRE IS TO RULE.
WITH THE ULTIMATE POWER OF THE INFINITY GAUNTLET AT MY DISPOSAL, RULE IS WHAT I SHALL DO.
DO NOT FRET-- BECAUSE YOU KEPT THE STONES SAFE FOR ME, I WILL SPARE YOU FROM DESTRUCTION...
...BUT I WILL HURT YOU SO BADLY--
--YOU'LL WISH THAT I HADN'T!
BOOOM!
uhnnn...
H-HE'S GONE!
THANOS HAS TO KNOW WE CAN'T JUST LET HIM LEAVE WITH THE STONES.
WE'RE GOING AFTER HIM! AND WHEN WE FIND HIM, HE'S GOING TO REGRET LEAVING US ALIVE.
HAWKEYE? WILL YOU DO THE HONORS?
AVENGERS ASSEMBLE!

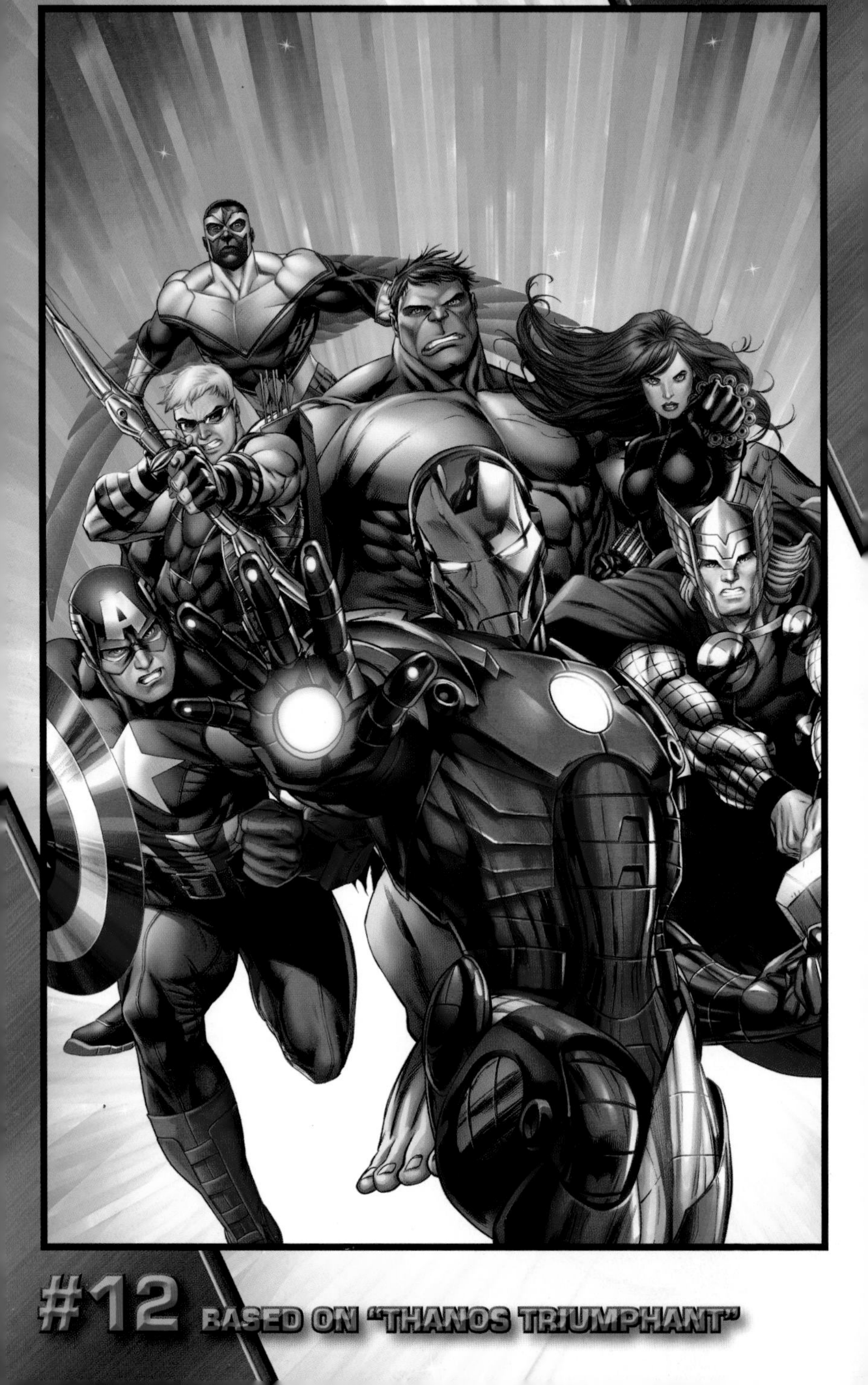

#12 BASED ON "THANOS TRIUMPHANT"

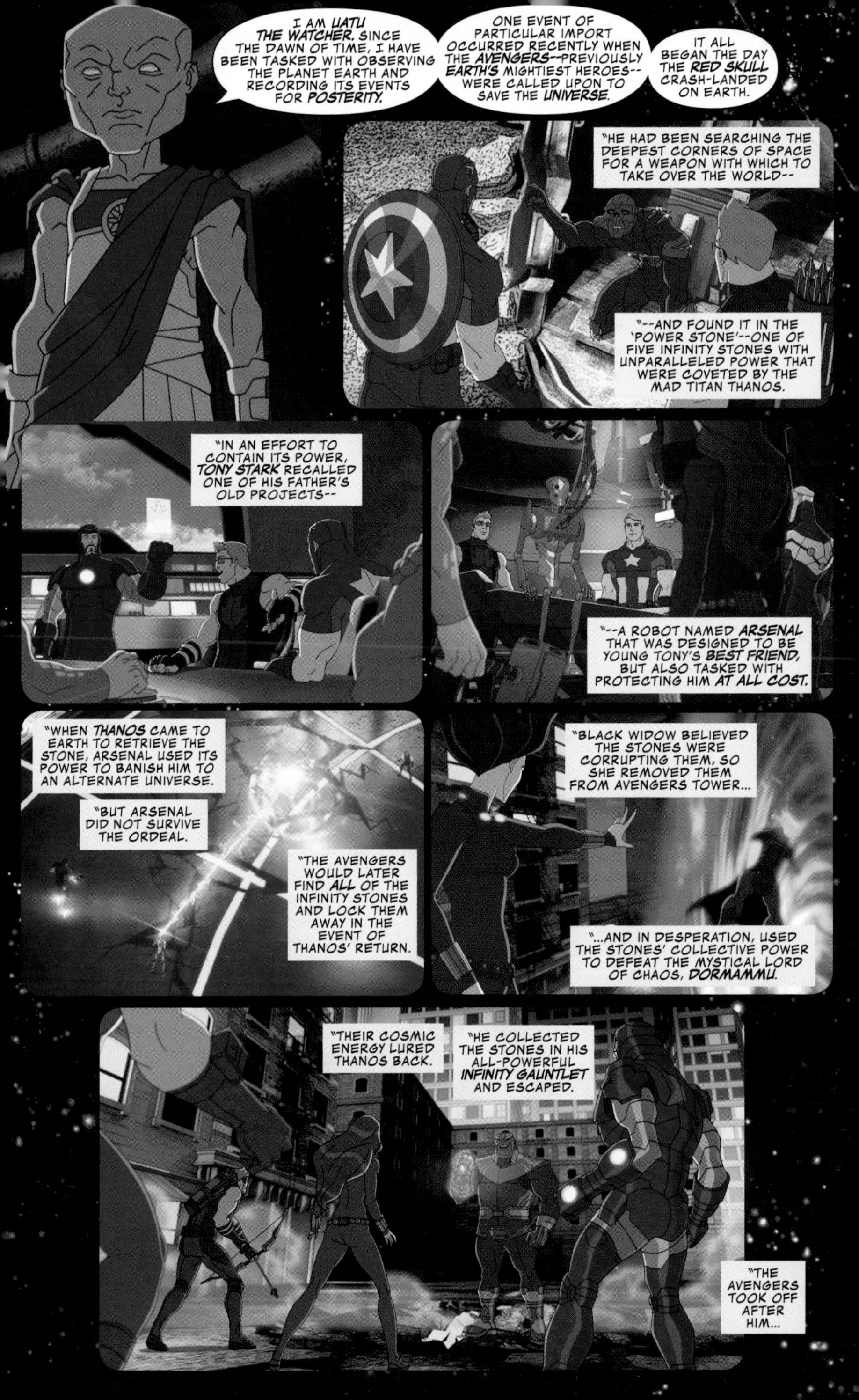
I AM UATU THE WATCHER. SINCE THE DAWN OF TIME, I HAVE BEEN TASKED WITH OBSERVING THE PLANET EARTH AND RECORDING ITS EVENTS FOR POSTERITY.
ONE EVENT OF PARTICULAR IMPORT OCCURRED RECENTLY WHEN THE AVENGERS--PREVIOUSLY EARTH'S MIGHTIEST HEROES--WERE CALLED UPON TO SAVE THE UNIVERSE.
IT ALL BEGAN THE DAY THE RED SKULL CRASH-LANDED ON EARTH.
"HE HAD BEEN SEARCHING THE DEEPEST CORNERS OF SPACE FOR A WEAPON WITH WHICH TO TAKE OVER THE WORLD--
"--AND FOUND IT IN THE 'POWER STONE'--ONE OF FIVE INFINITY STONES WITH UNPARALLELED POWER THAT WERE COVETED BY THE MAD TITAN THANOS.
"IN AN EFFORT TO CONTAIN ITS POWER, TONY STARK RECALLED ONE OF HIS FATHER'S OLD PROJECTS--
"--A ROBOT NAMED ARSENAL THAT WAS DESIGNED TO BE YOUNG TONY'S BEST FRIEND, BUT ALSO TASKED WITH PROTECTING HIM AT ALL COST.
"WHEN THANOS CAME TO EARTH TO RETRIEVE THE STONE, ARSENAL USED ITS POWER TO BANISH HIM TO AN ALTERNATE UNIVERSE.
"BUT ARSENAL DID NOT SURVIVE THE ORDEAL.
"THE AVENGERS WOULD LATER FIND ALL OF THE INFINITY STONES AND LOCK THEM AWAY IN THE EVENT OF THANOS' RETURN.
"BLACK WIDOW BELIEVED THE STONES WERE CORRUPTING THEM, SO SHE REMOVED THEM FROM AVENGERS TOWER...
"...AND IN DESPERATION, USED THE STONES' COLLECTIVE POWER TO DEFEAT THE MYSTICAL LORD OF CHAOS, DORMAMMU.
"THEIR COSMIC ENERGY LURED THANOS BACK.
"HE COLLECTED THE STONES IN HIS ALL-POWERFUL INFINITY GAUNTLET AND ESCAPED.
"THE AVENGERS TOOK OFF AFTER HIM...

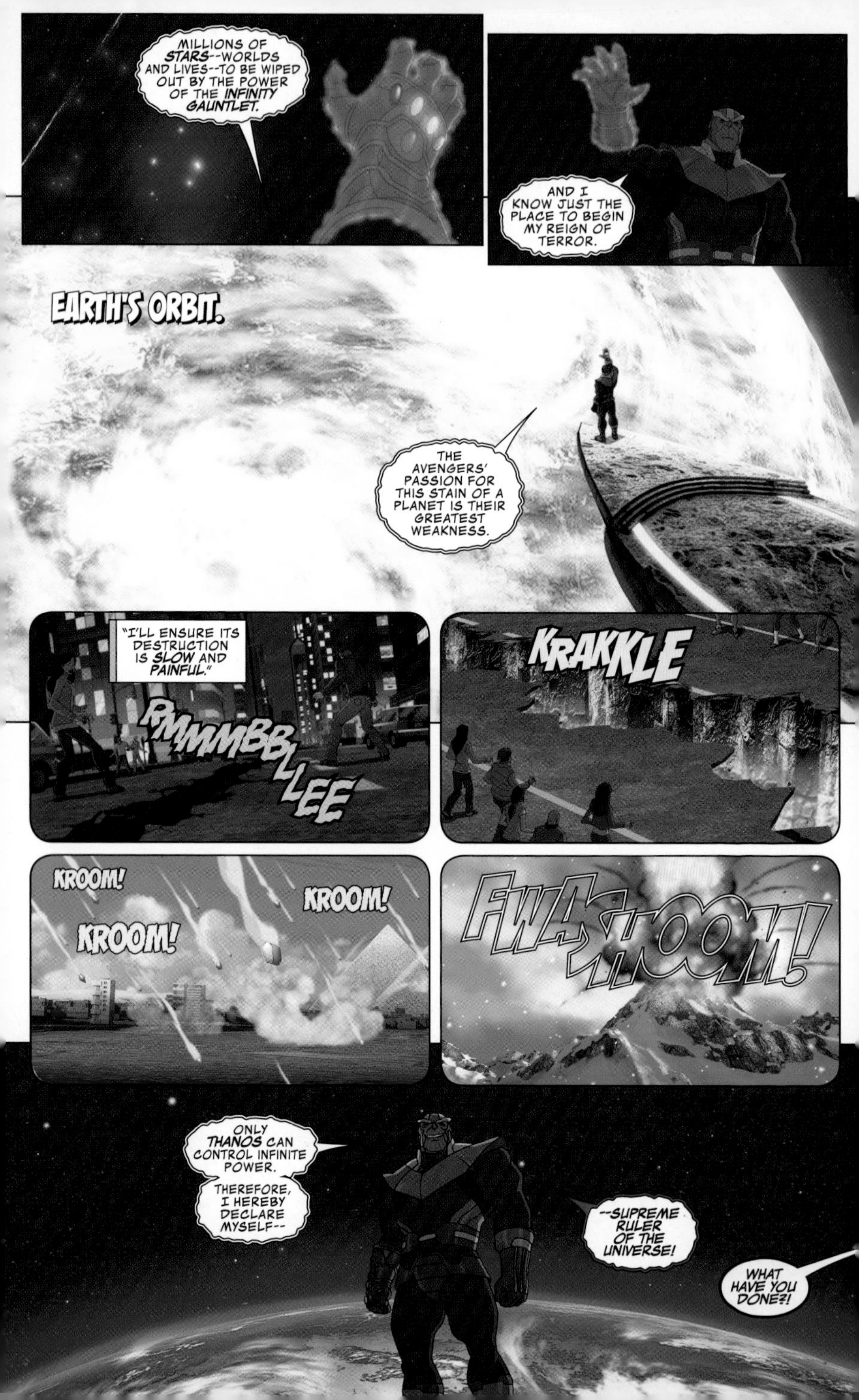

MILLIONS OF STARS--WORLDS AND LIVES--TO BE WIPED OUT BY THE POWER OF THE INFINITY GAUNTLET.
AND I KNOW JUST THE PLACE TO BEGIN MY REIGN OF TERROR.
EARTH'S ORBIT.
THE AVENGERS' PASSION FOR THIS STAIN OF A PLANET IS THEIR GREATEST WEAKNESS.
"I'LL ENSURE ITS DESTRUCTION IS SLOW AND PAINFUL."
RMMMBBLLEE
KRAKKLE
KROOM!
KROOM!
KROOM!
FWASHOOM!
ONLY THANOS CAN CONTROL INFINITE POWER.
THEREFORE, I HEREBY DECLARE MYSELF--
--SUPREME RULER OF THE UNIVERSE!
WHAT HAVE YOU DONE?!

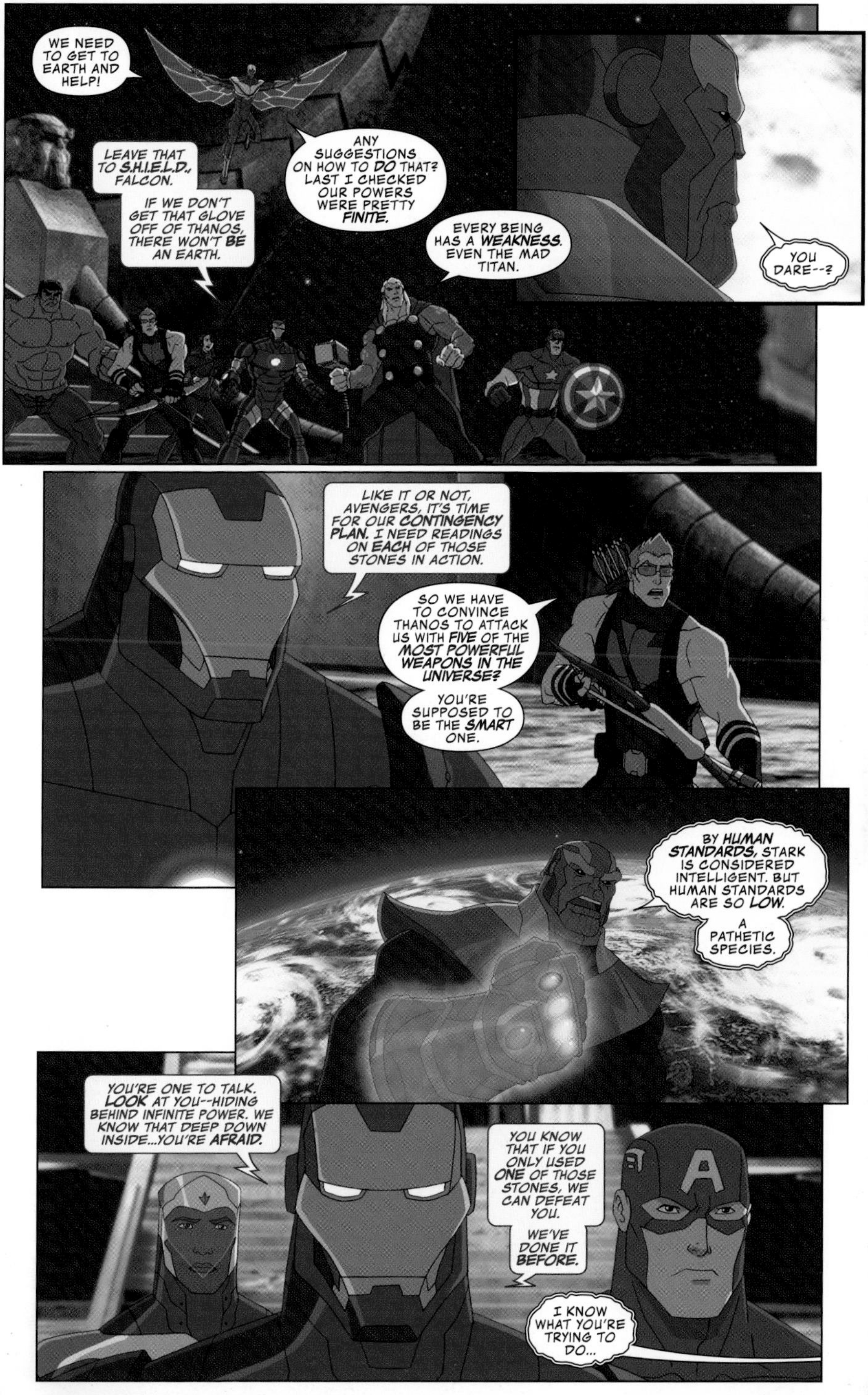
WE NEED TO GET TO EARTH AND HELP!
LEAVE THAT TO S.H.I.E.L.D., FALCON.
IF WE DON'T GET THAT GLOVE OFF OF THANOS, THERE WON'T BE AN EARTH.
ANY SUGGESTIONS ON HOW TO DO THAT? LAST I CHECKED OUR POWERS WERE PRETTY FINITE.
EVERY BEING HAS A WEAKNESS. EVEN THE MAD TITAN.
YOU DARE--?
LIKE IT OR NOT, AVENGERS, IT'S TIME FOR OUR CONTINGENCY PLAN. I NEED READINGS ON EACH OF THOSE STONES IN ACTION.
SO WE HAVE TO CONVINCE THANOS TO ATTACK US WITH FIVE OF THE MOST POWERFUL WEAPONS IN THE UNIVERSE?
YOU'RE SUPPOSED TO BE THE SMART ONE.
BY HUMAN STANDARDS, STARK IS CONSIDERED INTELLIGENT. BUT HUMAN STANDARDS ARE SO LOW.
A PATHETIC SPECIES.
YOU'RE ONE TO TALK. LOOK AT YOU--HIDING BEHIND INFINITE POWER. WE KNOW THAT DEEP DOWN INSIDE...YOU'RE AFRAID.
YOU KNOW THAT IF YOU ONLY USED ONE OF THOSE STONES, WE CAN DEFEAT YOU.
WE'VE DONE IT BEFORE.
I KNOW WHAT YOU'RE TRYING TO DO...

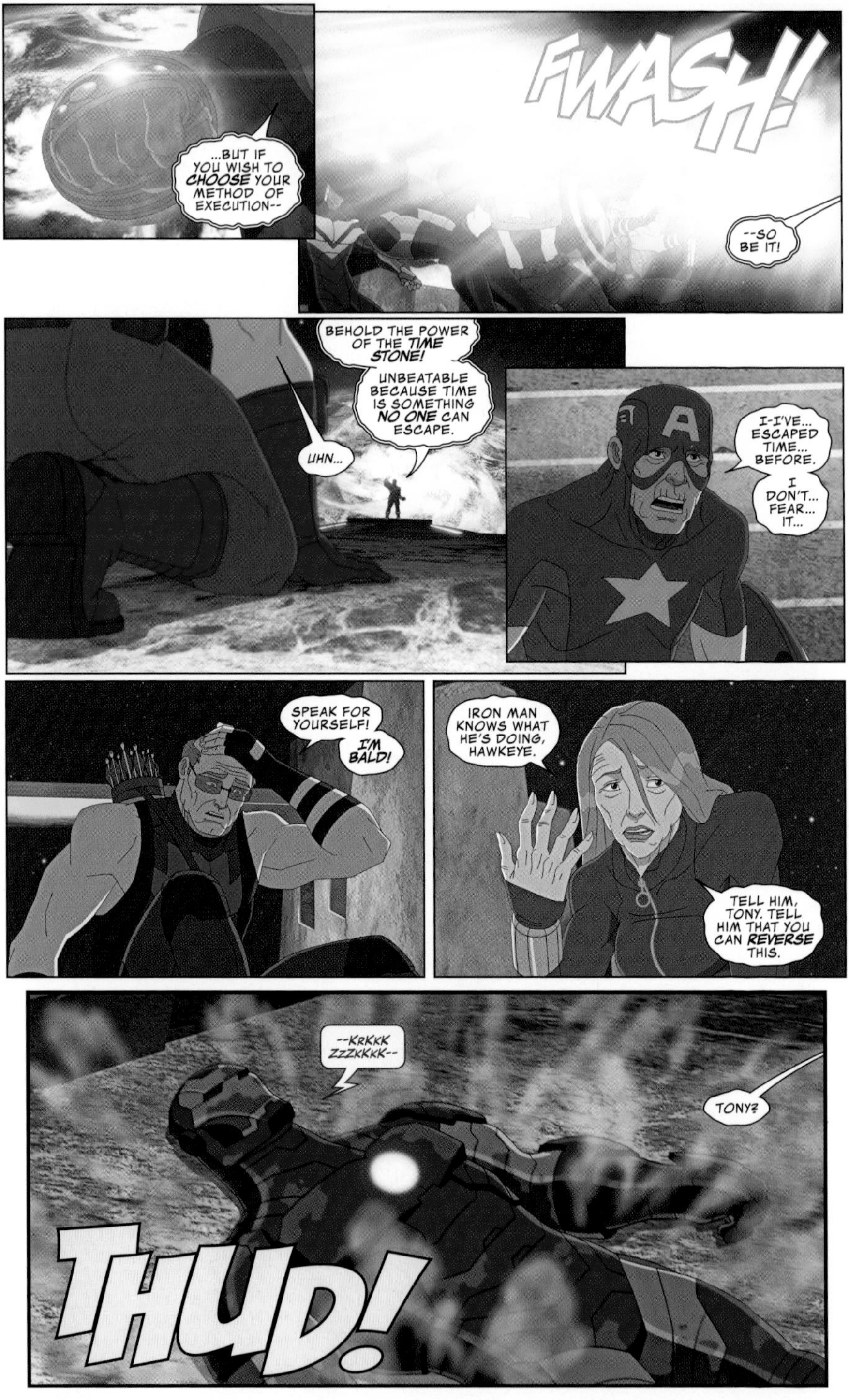
...BUT IF YOU WISH TO CHOOSE YOUR METHOD OF EXECUTION--
FWASH!
--SO BE IT!
BEHOLD THE POWER OF THE TIME STONE!
UNBEATABLE BECAUSE TIME IS SOMETHING NO ONE CAN ESCAPE.
UHN...
I-I'VE... ESCAPED TIME... BEFORE.
I DON'T... FEAR... IT...
SPEAK FOR YOURSELF! I'M BALD!
IRON MAN KNOWS WHAT HE'S DOING, HAWKEYE.
TELL HIM, TONY. TELL HIM THAT YOU CAN REVERSE THIS.
--KRKKK ZZZKKKK--
TONY?
THUD!

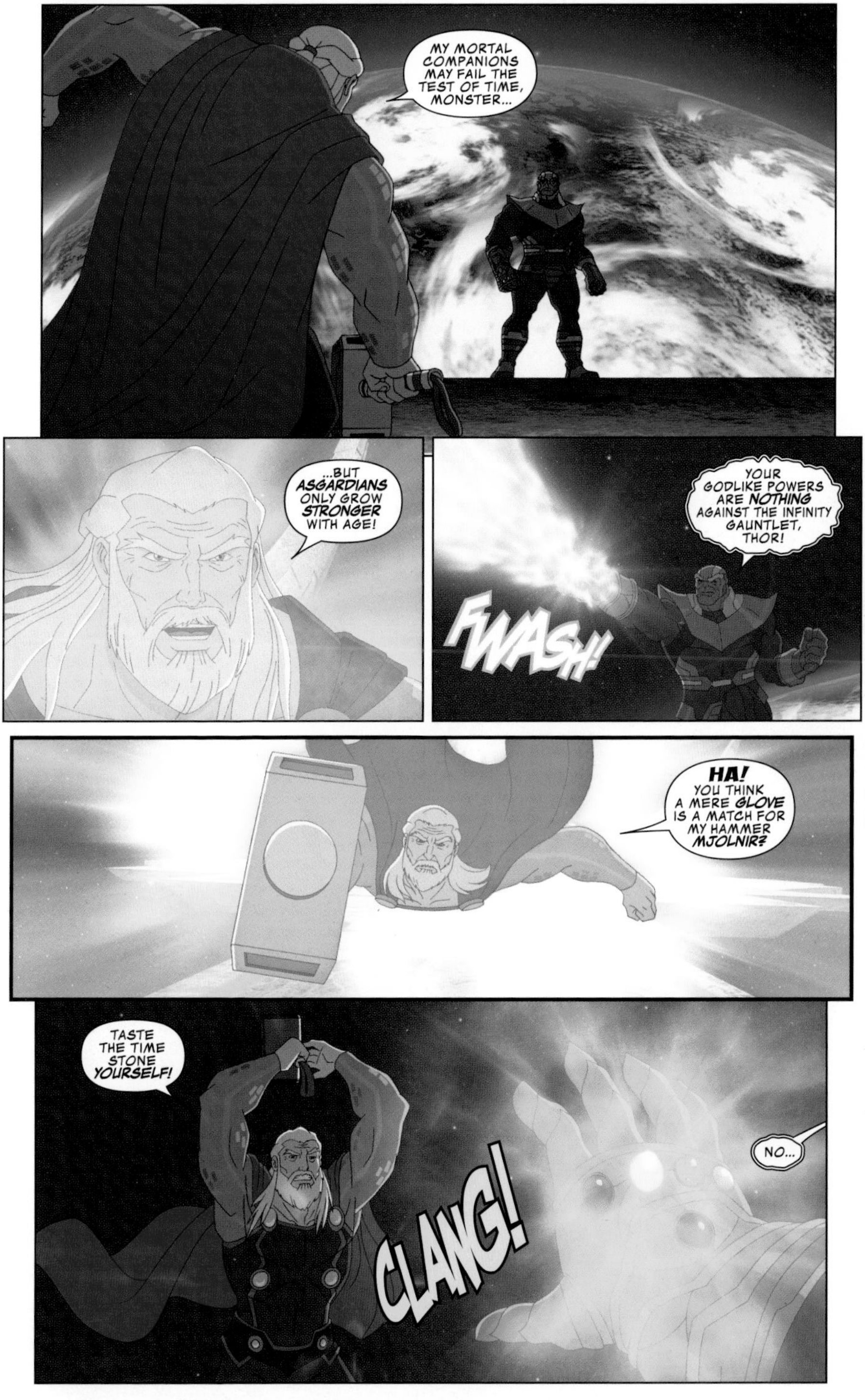
MY MORTAL COMPANIONS MAY FAIL THE TEST OF TIME, MONSTER...
...BUT ASGARDIANS ONLY GROW STRONGER WITH AGE!
YOUR GODLIKE POWERS ARE NOTHING AGAINST THE INFINITY GAUNTLET, THOR!
FWASH!
HA! YOU THINK A MERE GLOVE IS A MATCH FOR MY HAMMER MJOLNIR?
TASTE THE TIME STONE YOURSELF!
CLANG!
NO...

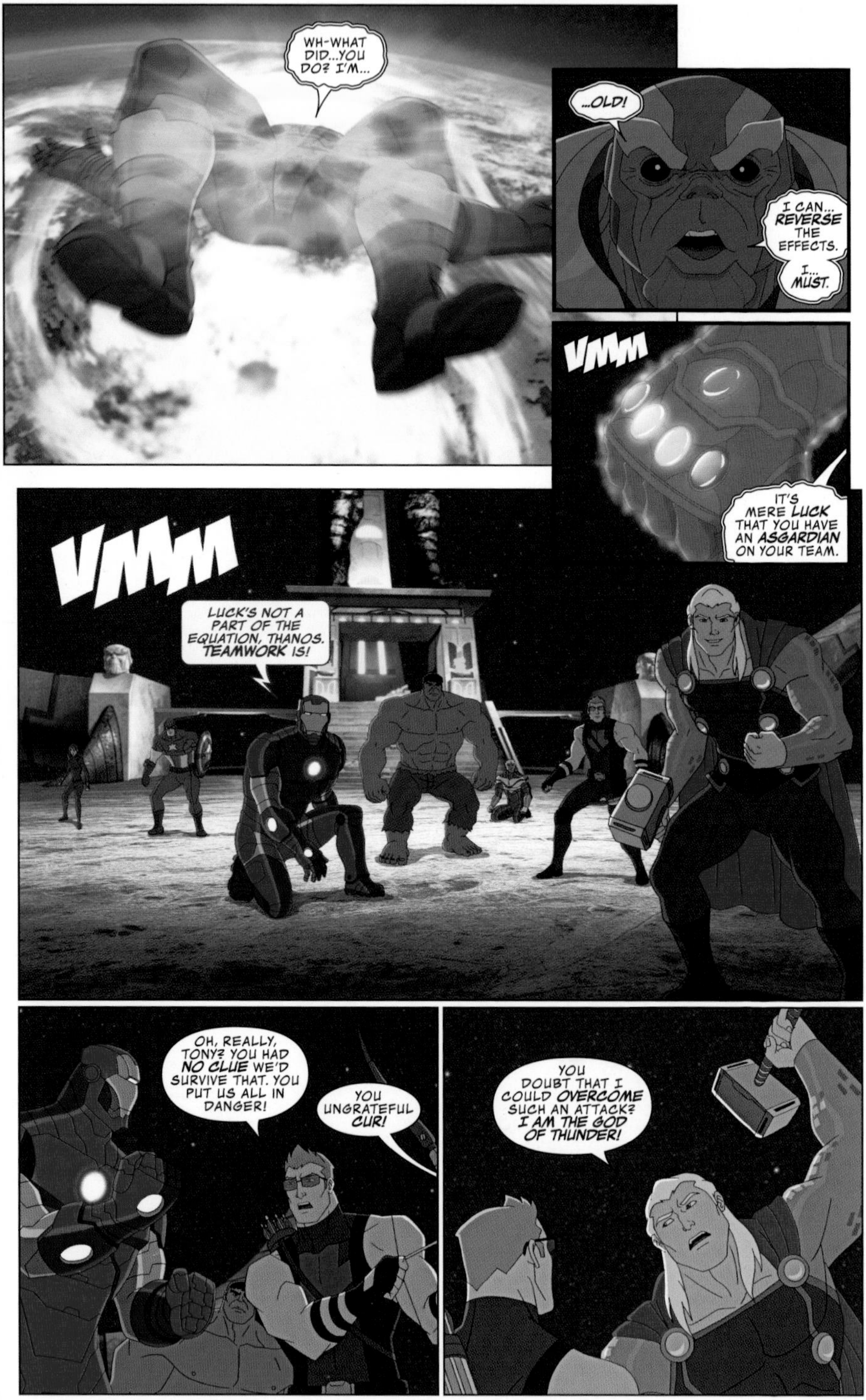
WH-WHAT DID...YOU DO? I'M...
...OLD!
I CAN... REVERSE THE EFFECTS.
I... MUST.
VMM
IT'S MERE LUCK THAT YOU HAVE AN ASGARDIAN ON YOUR TEAM.
VMM
LUCK'S NOT A PART OF THE EQUATION, THANOS. TEAMWORK IS!
OH, REALLY, TONY? YOU HAD NO CLUE WE'D SURVIVE THAT. YOU PUT US ALL IN DANGER!
YOU UNGRATEFUL CUR!
YOU DOUBT THAT I COULD OVERCOME SUCH AN ATTACK? I AM THE GOD OF THUNDER!

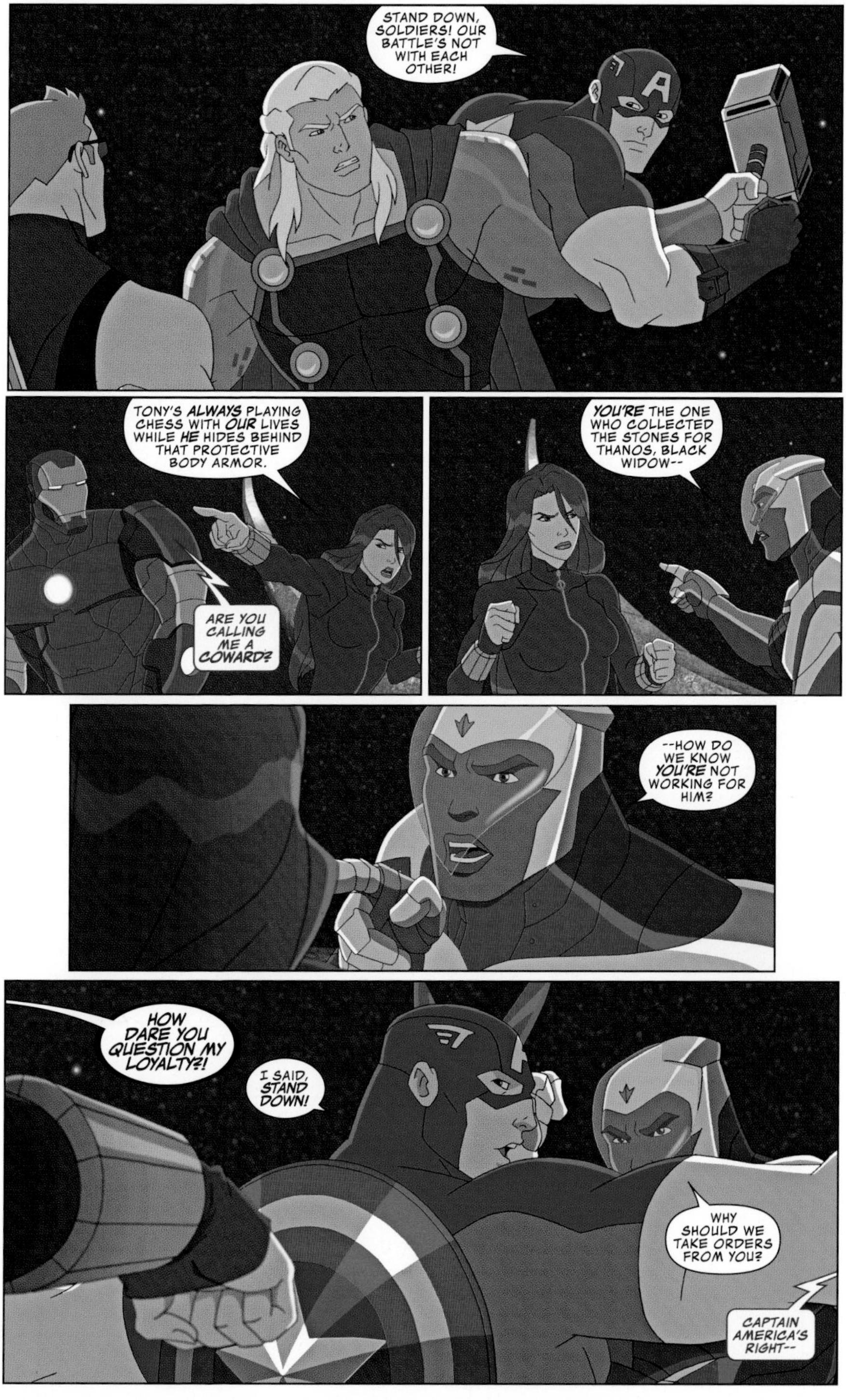
STAND DOWN, SOLDIERS! OUR BATTLE'S NOT WITH EACH OTHER!
TONY'S ALWAYS PLAYING CHESS WITH OUR LIVES WHILE HE HIDES BEHIND THAT PROTECTIVE BODY ARMOR.
ARE YOU CALLING ME A COWARD?
YOU'RE THE ONE WHO COLLECTED THE STONES FOR THANOS, BLACK WIDOW--
--HOW DO WE KNOW YOU'RE NOT WORKING FOR HIM?
HOW DARE YOU QUESTION MY LOYALTY?!
I SAID, STAND DOWN!
WHY SHOULD WE TAKE ORDERS FROM YOU?
CAPTAIN AMERICA'S RIGHT--

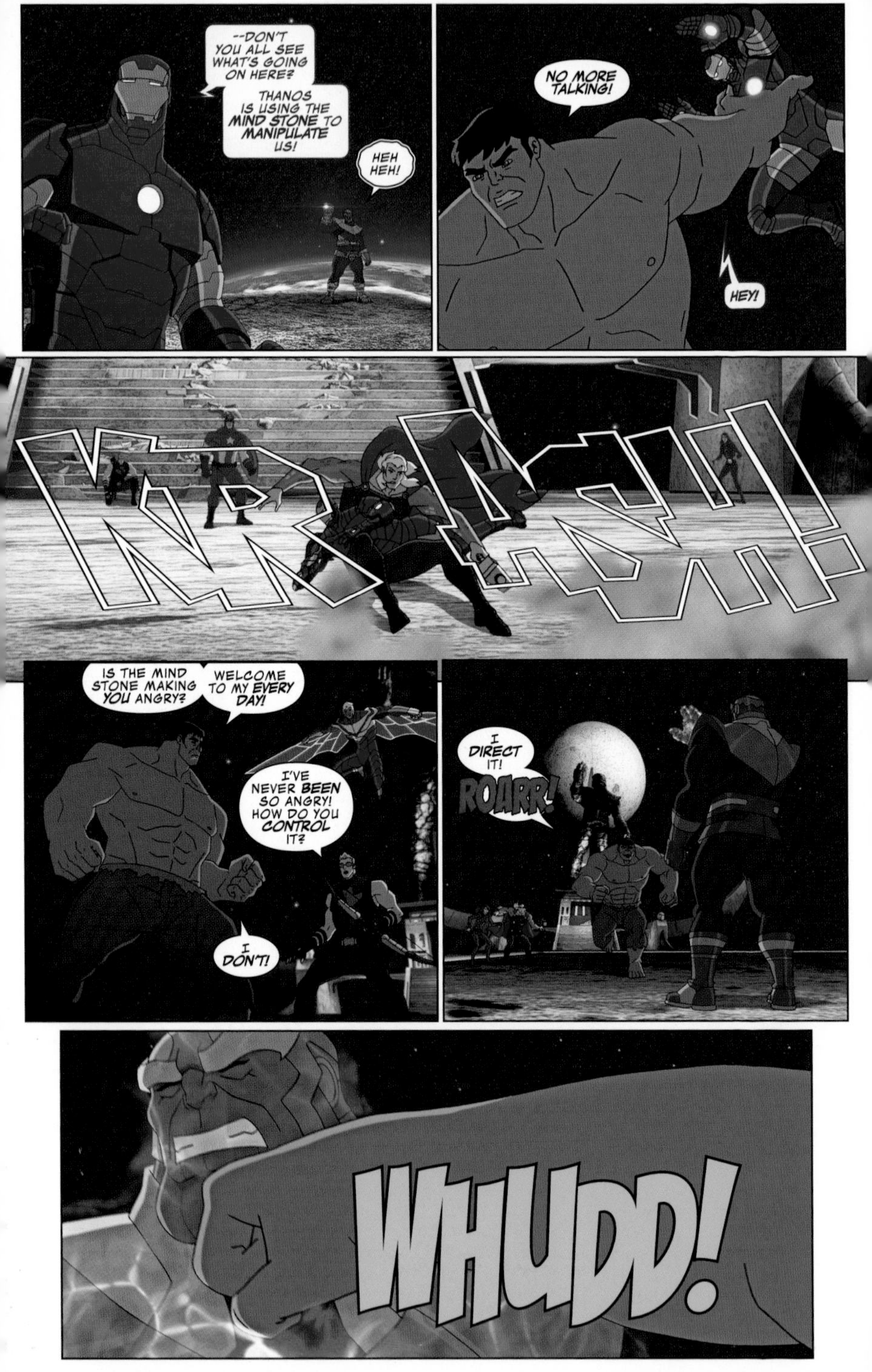
--DON'T YOU ALL SEE WHAT'S GOING ON HERE?
THANOS IS USING THE MIND STONE TO MANIPULATE US!
HEH HEH!
NO MORE TALKING!
HEY!
IS THE MIND STONE MAKING YOU ANGRY?
WELCOME TO MY EVERY DAY!
I'VE NEVER BEEN SO ANGRY! HOW DO YOU CONTROL IT?
I DON'T!
I DIRECT IT!
ROARR!
WHUDD!

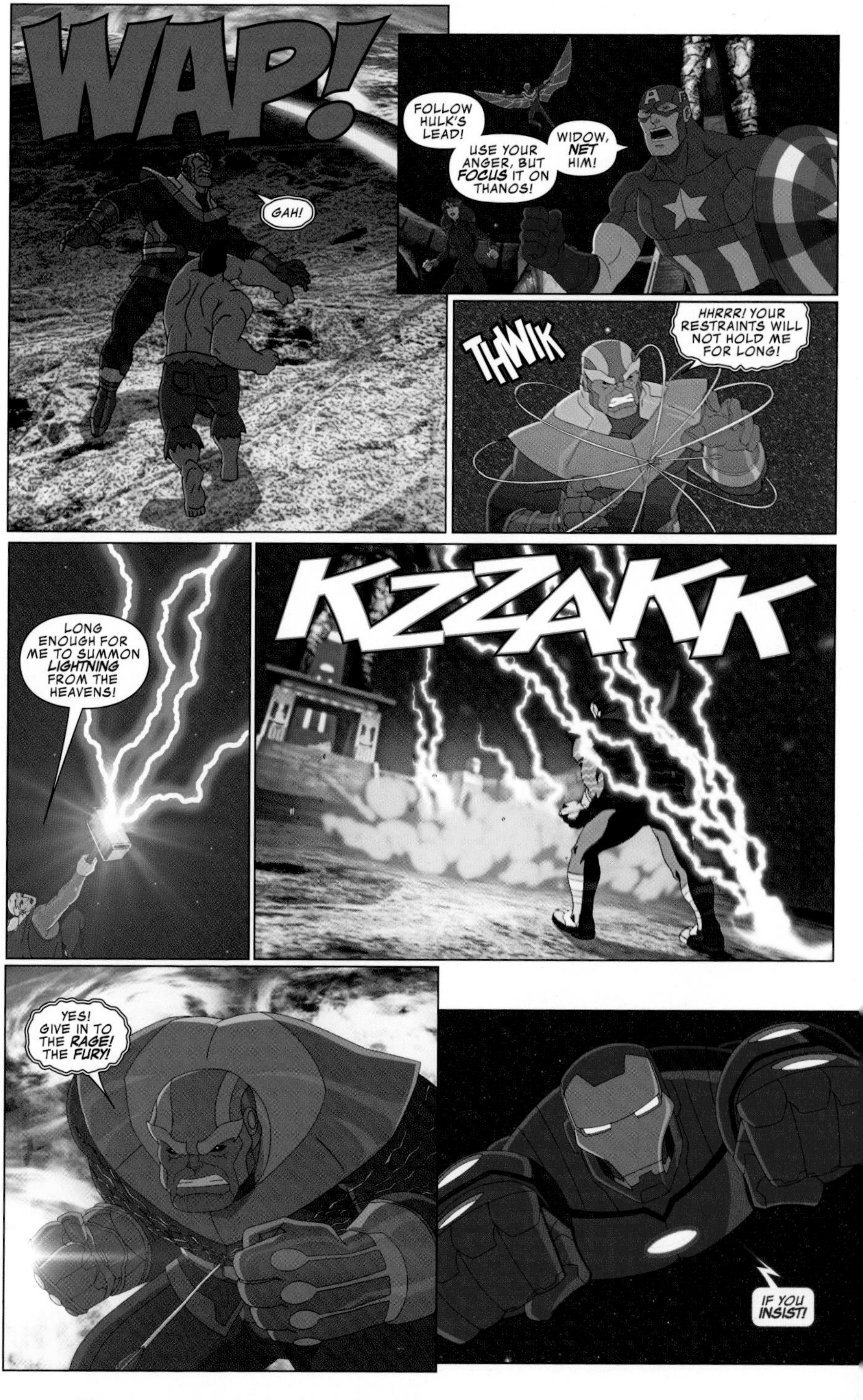
WAP!
GAH!
FOLLOW HULK'S LEAD!
USE YOUR ANGER, BUT FOCUS IT ON THANOS!
WIDOW, NET HIM!
THWIK
HHRRR! YOUR RESTRAINTS WILL NOT HOLD ME FOR LONG!
LONG ENOUGH FOR ME TO SUMMON LIGHTNING FROM THE HEAVENS!
KZZAKK
YES! GIVE IN TO THE RAGE! THE FURY!
IF YOU INSIST!

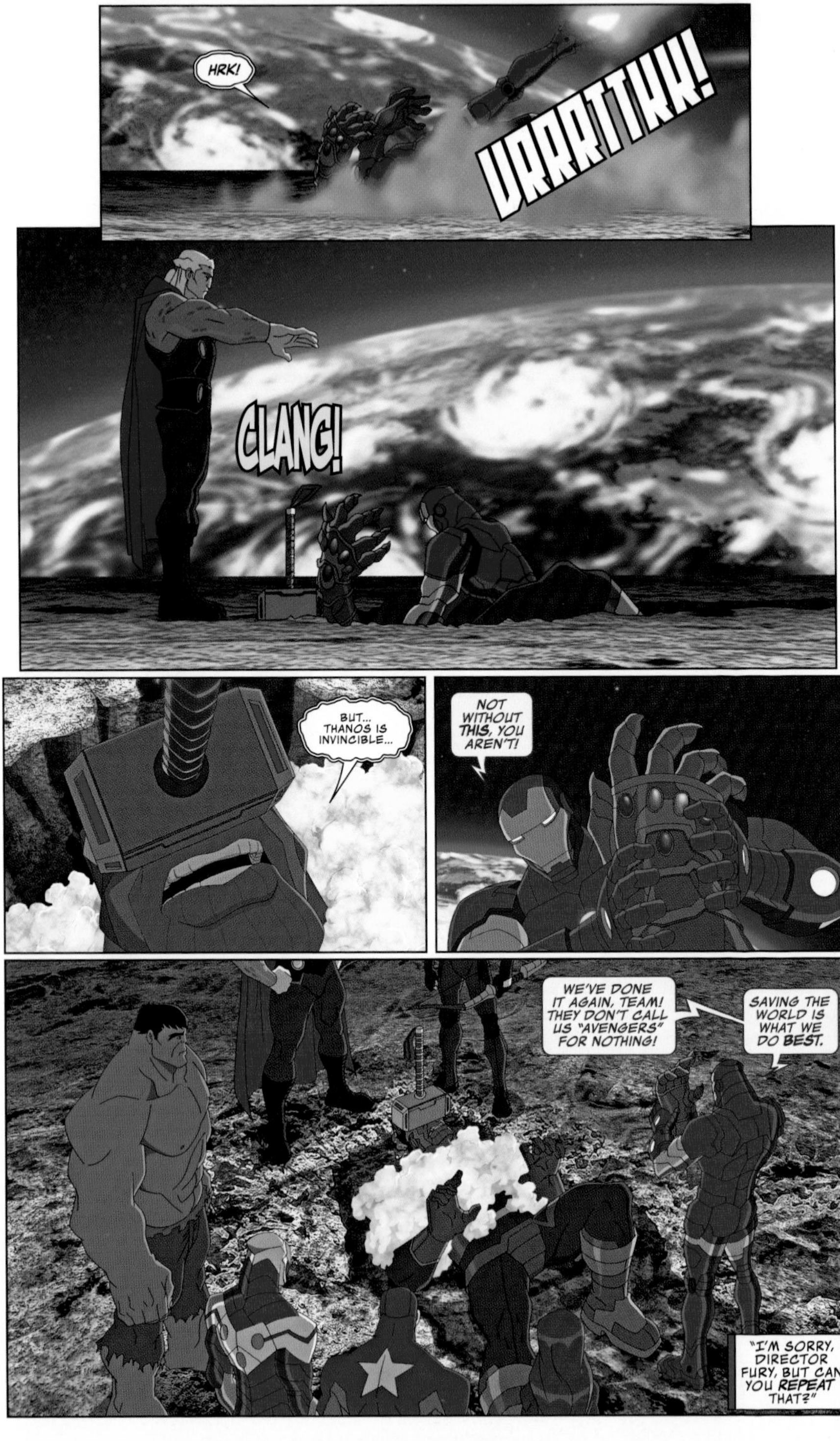
HRK!
VRRRTTKK!
CLANG!
BUT... THANOS IS INVINCIBLE...
NOT WITHOUT THIS, YOU AREN'T!
WE'VE DONE IT AGAIN, TEAM! THEY DON'T CALL US "AVENGERS" FOR NOTHING!
SAVING THE WORLD IS WHAT WE DO BEST.
"I'M SORRY, DIRECTOR FURY, BUT CAN YOU REPEAT THAT?"

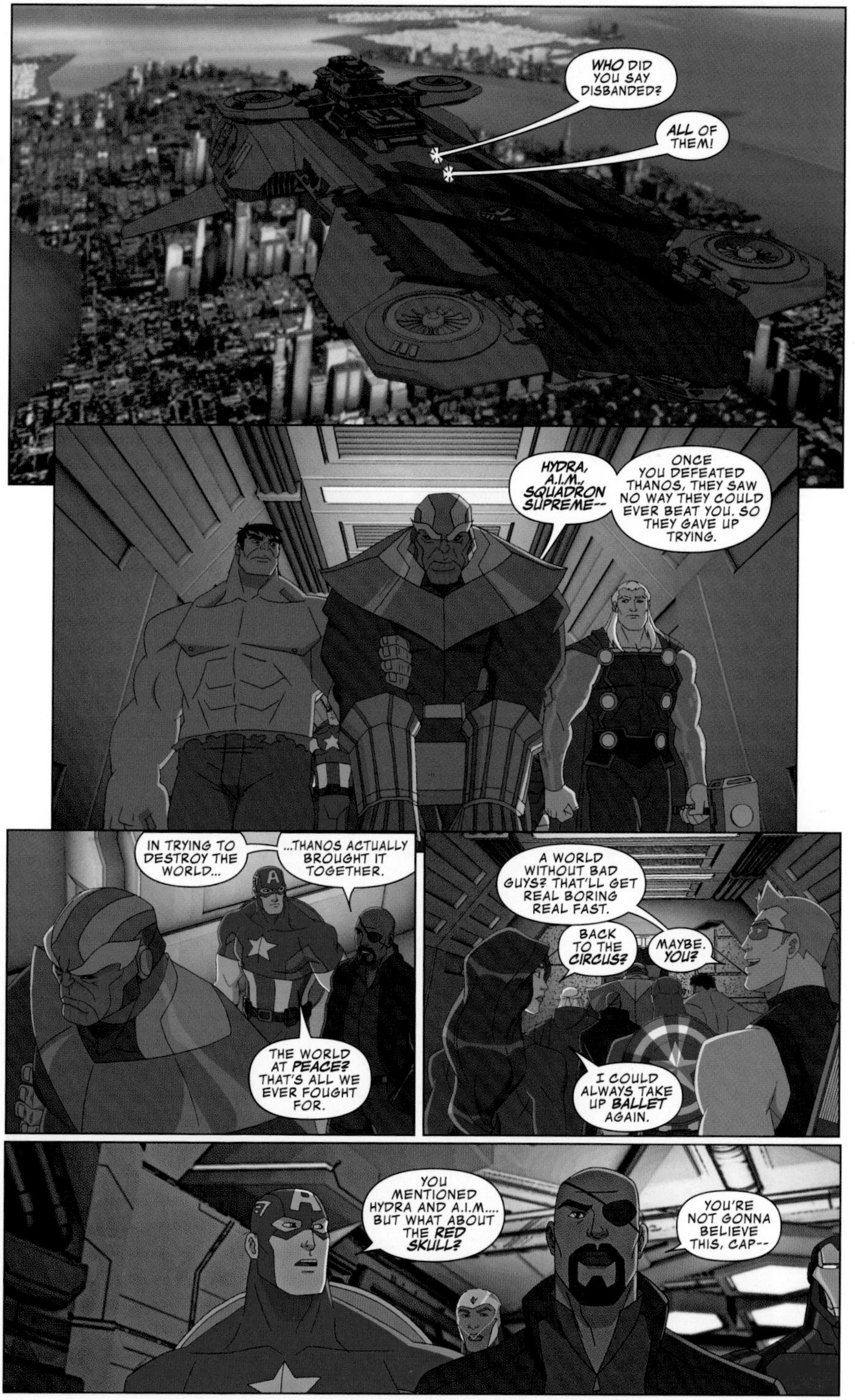
WHO DID YOU SAY DISBANDED?
ALL OF THEM!
HYDRA, A.I.M., SQUADRON SUPREME--
ONCE YOU DEFEATED THANOS, THEY SAW NO WAY THEY COULD EVER BEAT YOU. SO THEY GAVE UP TRYING.
IN TRYING TO DESTROY THE WORLD...
...THANOS ACTUALLY BROUGHT IT TOGETHER.
THE WORLD AT PEACE? THAT'S ALL WE EVER FOUGHT FOR.
A WORLD WITHOUT BAD GUYS? THAT'LL GET REAL BORING REAL FAST.
BACK TO THE CIRCUS?
MAYBE. YOU?
I COULD ALWAYS TAKE UP BALLET AGAIN.
YOU MENTIONED HYDRA AND A.I.M.... BUT WHAT ABOUT THE RED SKULL?
YOU'RE NOT GONNA BELIEVE THIS, CAP--

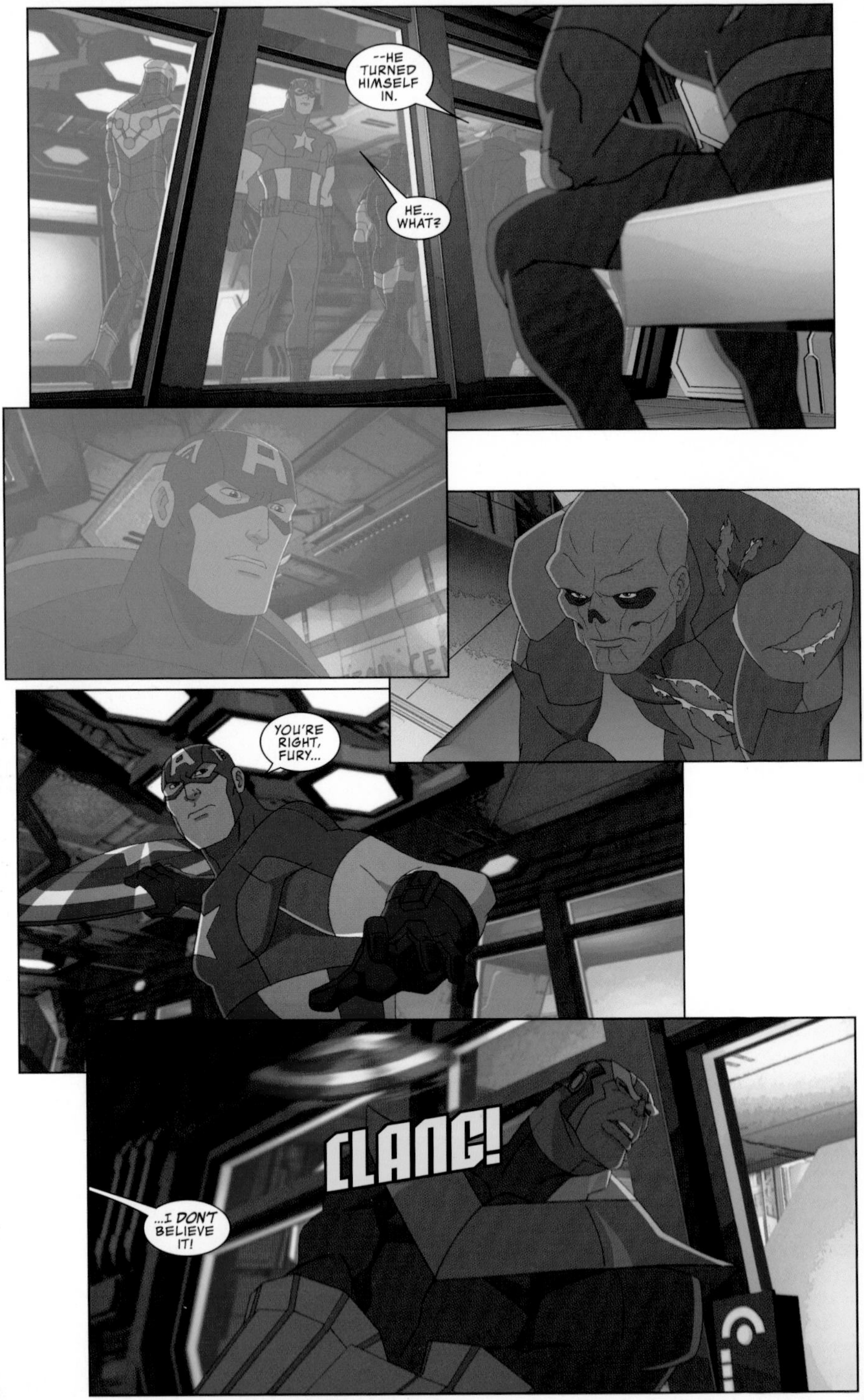
--HE TURNED HIMSELF IN.
HE... WHAT?
YOU'RE RIGHT, FURY...
CLANG!
...I DON'T BELIEVE IT!

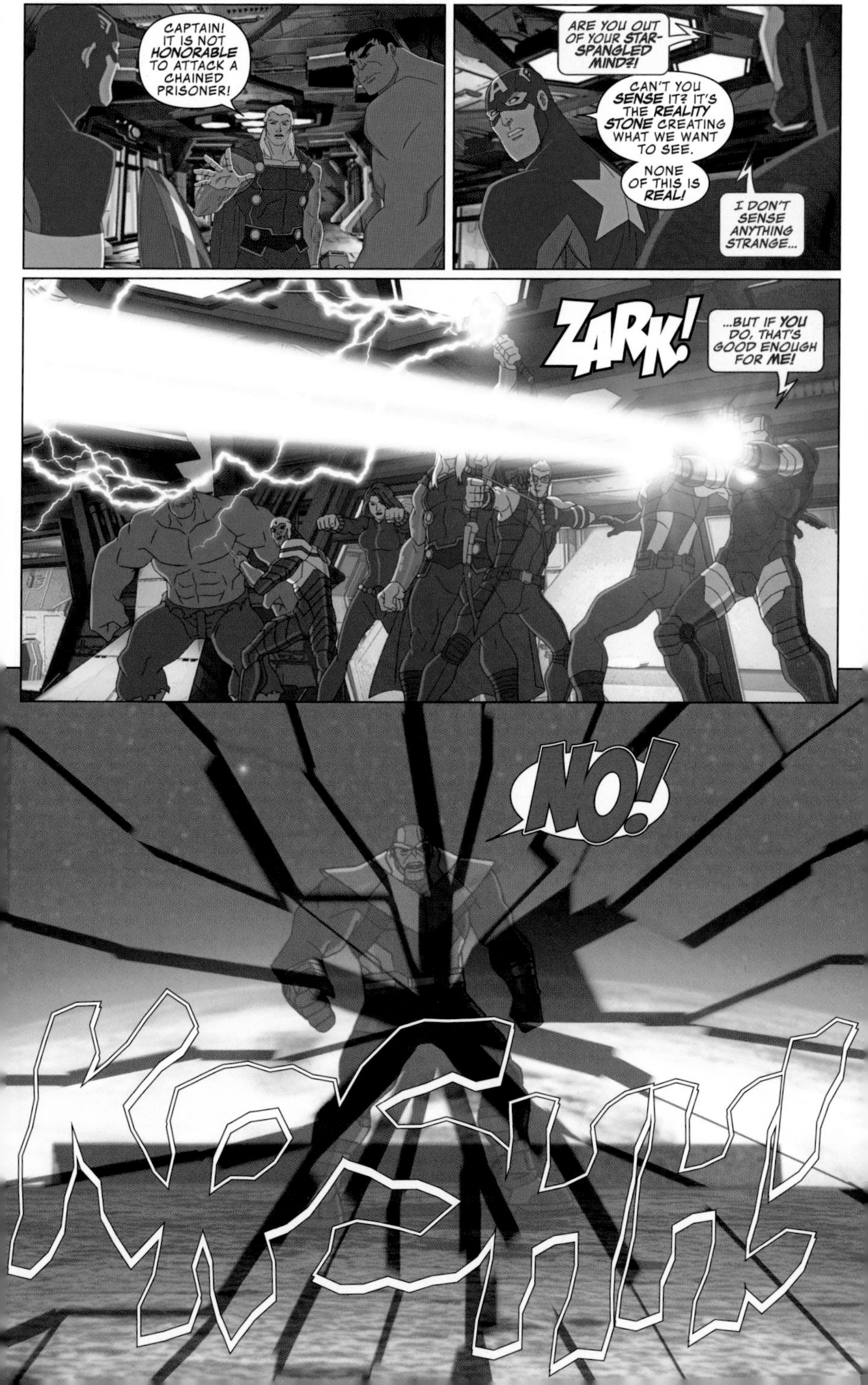
CAPTAIN! IT IS NOT HONORABLE TO ATTACK A CHAINED PRISONER!
ARE YOU OUT OF YOUR STAR-SPANGLED MIND?!
CAN'T YOU SENSE IT? IT'S THE REALITY STONE CREATING WHAT WE WANT TO SEE.
NONE OF THIS IS REAL!
I DON'T SENSE ANYTHING STRANGE...
ZARK!
...BUT IF YOU DO, THAT'S GOOD ENOUGH FOR ME!
NO!

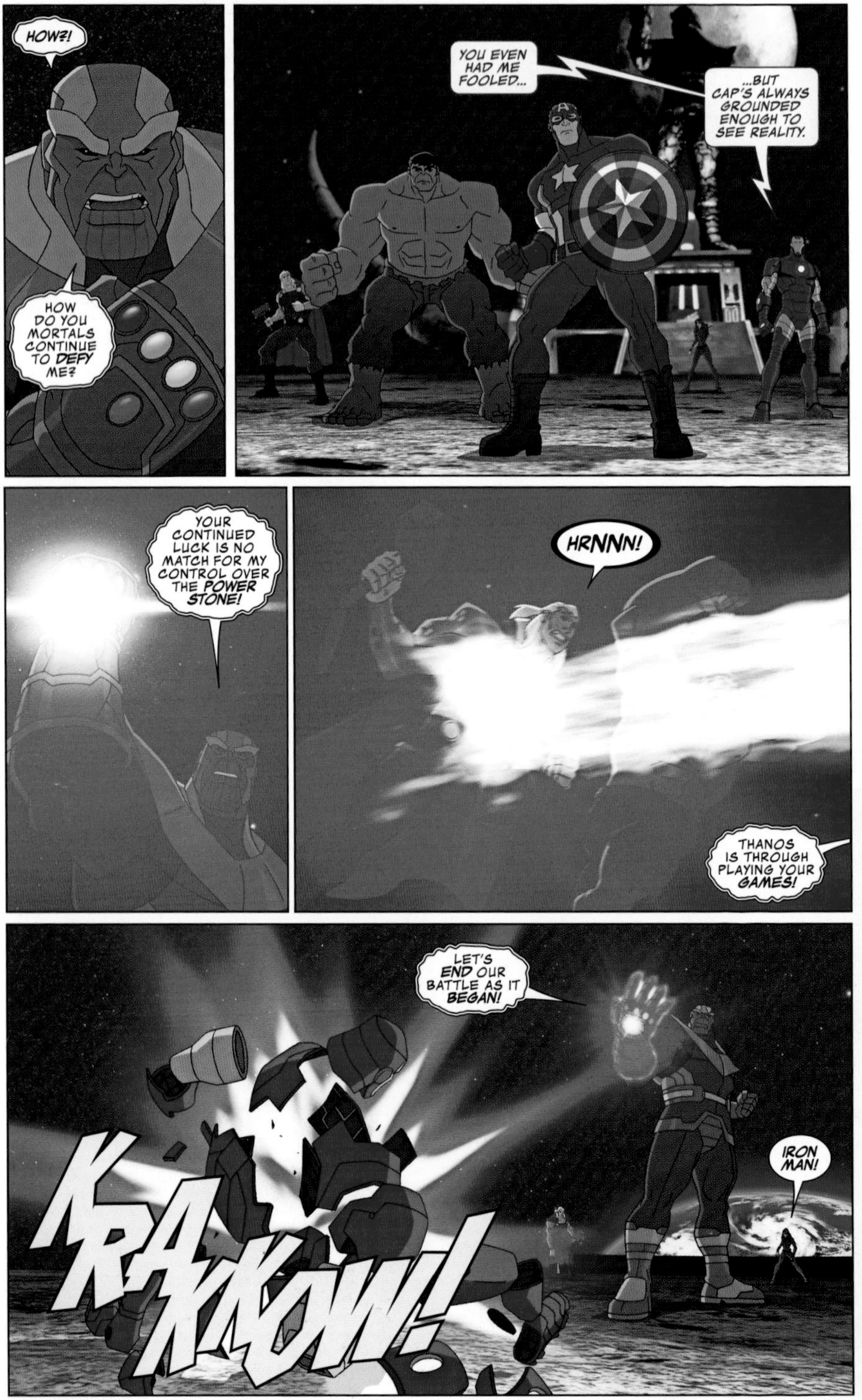
HOW?!
HOW DO YOU MORTALS CONTINUE TO DEFY ME?
YOU EVEN HAD ME FOOLED...
...BUT CAP'S ALWAYS GROUNDED ENOUGH TO SEE REALITY.
YOUR CONTINUED LUCK IS NO MATCH FOR MY CONTROL OVER THE POWER STONE!
HRNNN!
THANOS IS THROUGH PLAYING YOUR GAMES!
LET'S END OUR BATTLE AS IT BEGAN!
KRAKKOW!
IRON MAN!

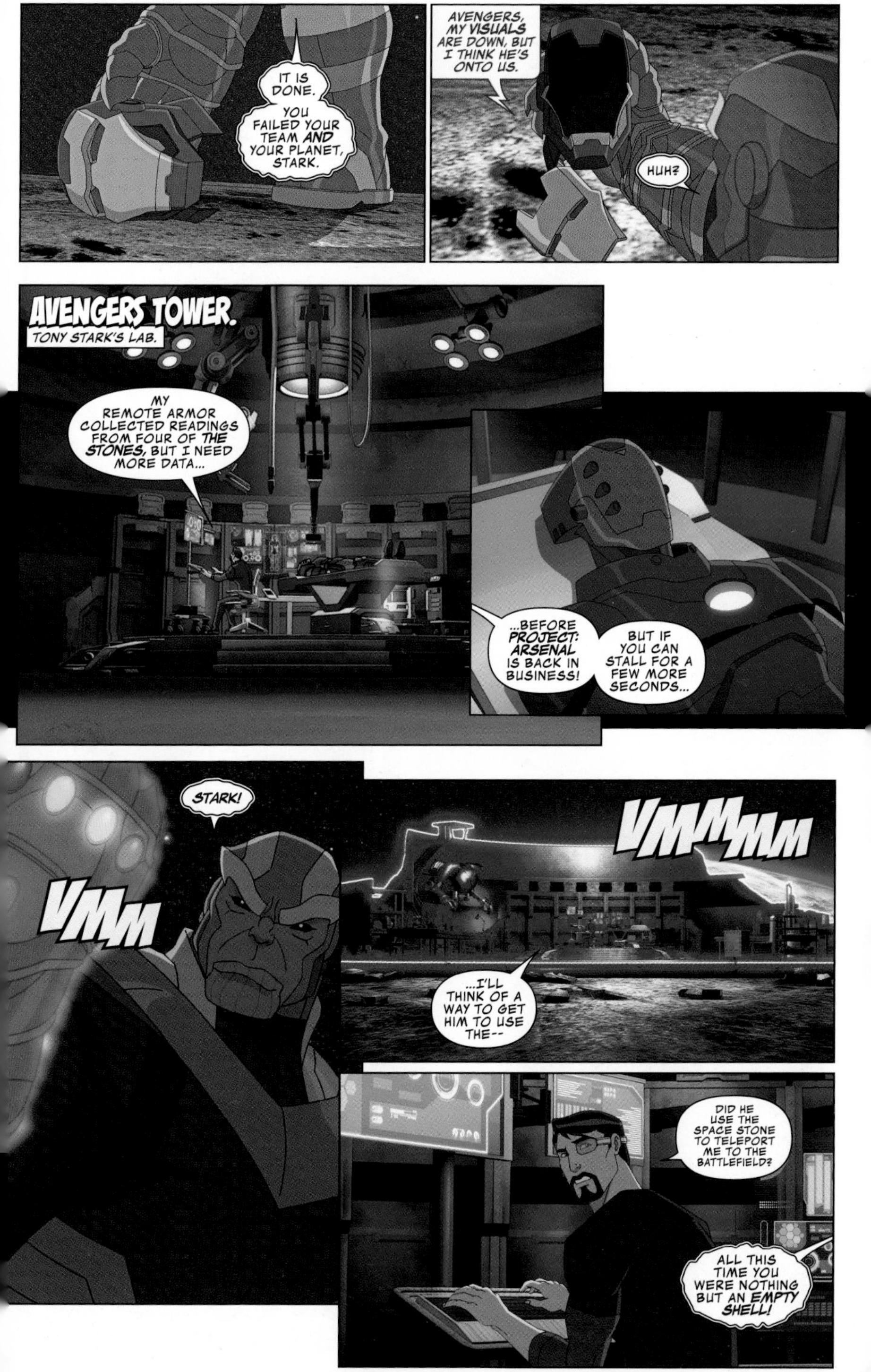
IT IS DONE.
YOU FAILED YOUR TEAM AND YOUR PLANET, STARK.
AVENGERS, MY VISUALS ARE DOWN, BUT I THINK HE'S ONTO US.
HUH?
AVENGERS TOWER.
TONY STARK'S LAB.
MY REMOTE ARMOR COLLECTED READINGS FROM FOUR OF THE STONES, BUT I NEED MORE DATA...
...BEFORE PROJECT: ARSENAL IS BACK IN BUSINESS!
BUT IF YOU CAN STALL FOR A FEW MORE SECONDS...
STARK!
VMM
VMMMMM
...I'LL THINK OF A WAY TO GET HIM TO USE THE--
DID HE USE THE SPACE STONE TO TELEPORT ME TO THE BATTLEFIELD?
ALL THIS TIME YOU WERE NOTHING BUT AN EMPTY SHELL!

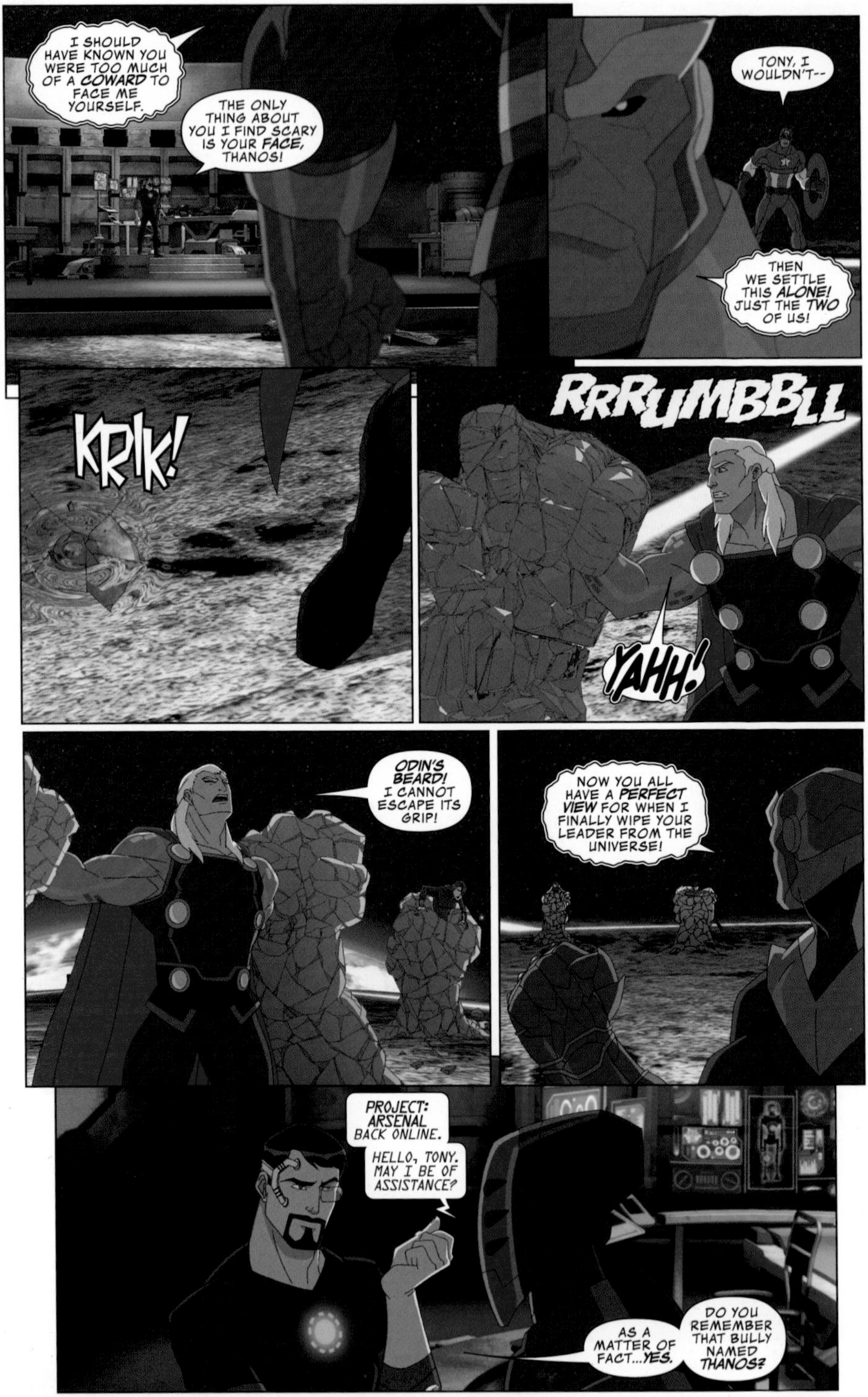
I SHOULD HAVE KNOWN YOU WERE TOO MUCH OF A COWARD TO FACE ME YOURSELF.
THE ONLY THING ABOUT YOU I FIND SCARY IS YOUR FACE, THANOS!
TONY, I WOULDN'T--
THEN WE SETTLE THIS ALONE! JUST THE TWO OF US!
KRIK!
RRRUMBBLL
YAHH!
ODIN'S BEARD! I CANNOT ESCAPE ITS GRIP!
NOW YOU ALL HAVE A PERFECT VIEW FOR WHEN I FINALLY WIPE YOUR LEADER FROM THE UNIVERSE!
PROJECT: ARSENAL BACK ONLINE.
HELLO, TONY. MAY I BE OF ASSISTANCE?
DO YOU REMEMBER THAT BULLY NAMED THANOS?
AS A MATTER OF FACT...YES.

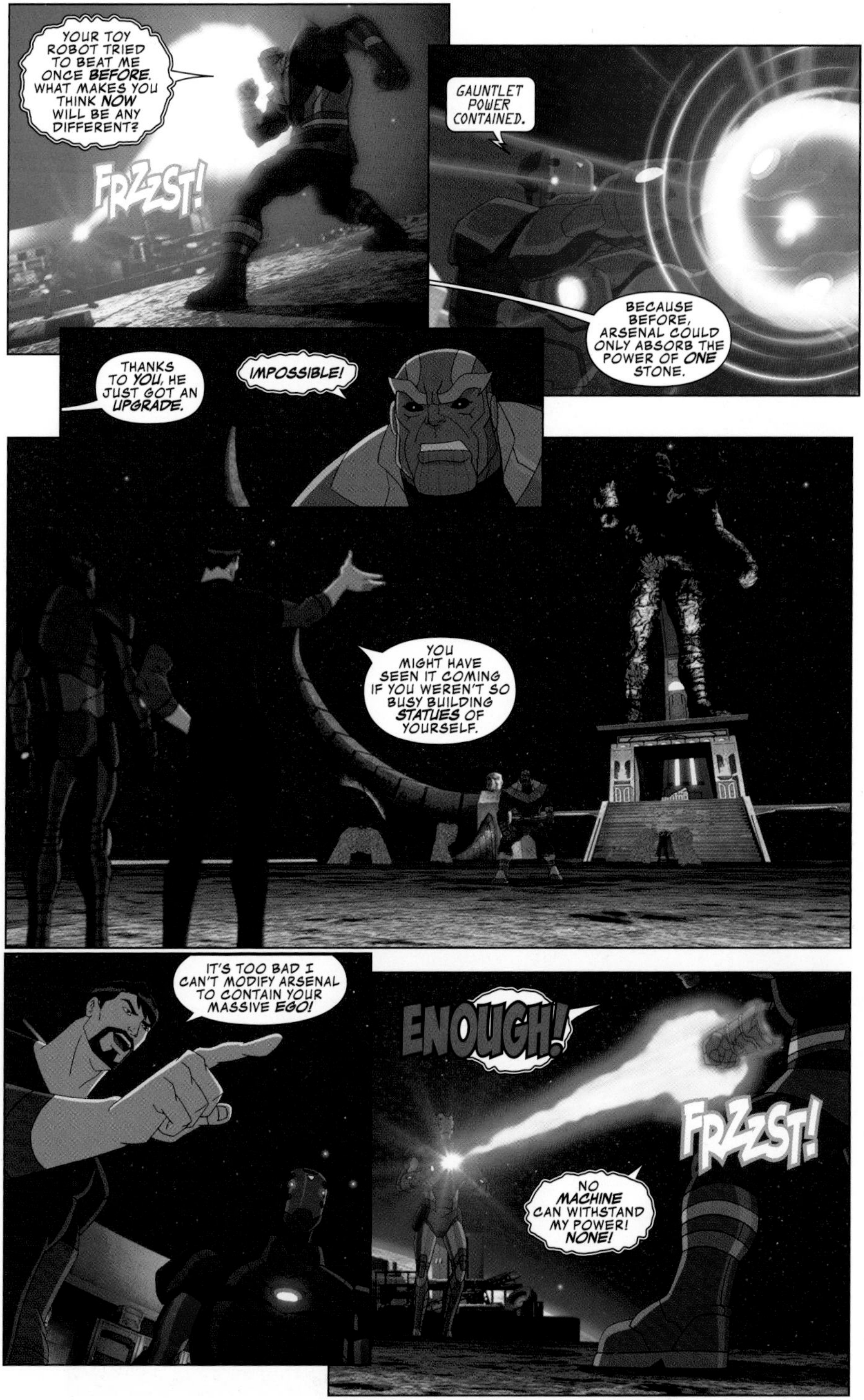
YOUR TOY ROBOT TRIED TO BEAT ME ONCE BEFORE. WHAT MAKES YOU THINK NOW WILL BE ANY DIFFERENT?
FRZZST!
GAUNTLET POWER CONTAINED.
BECAUSE BEFORE, ARSENAL COULD ONLY ABSORB THE POWER OF ONE STONE.
THANKS TO YOU, HE JUST GOT AN UPGRADE.
IMPOSSIBLE!
YOU MIGHT HAVE SEEN IT COMING IF YOU WEREN'T SO BUSY BUILDING STATUES OF YOURSELF.
IT'S TOO BAD I CAN'T MODIFY ARSENAL TO CONTAIN YOUR MASSIVE EGO!
ENOUGH!
FRZZST!
NO MACHINE CAN WITHSTAND MY POWER! NONE!

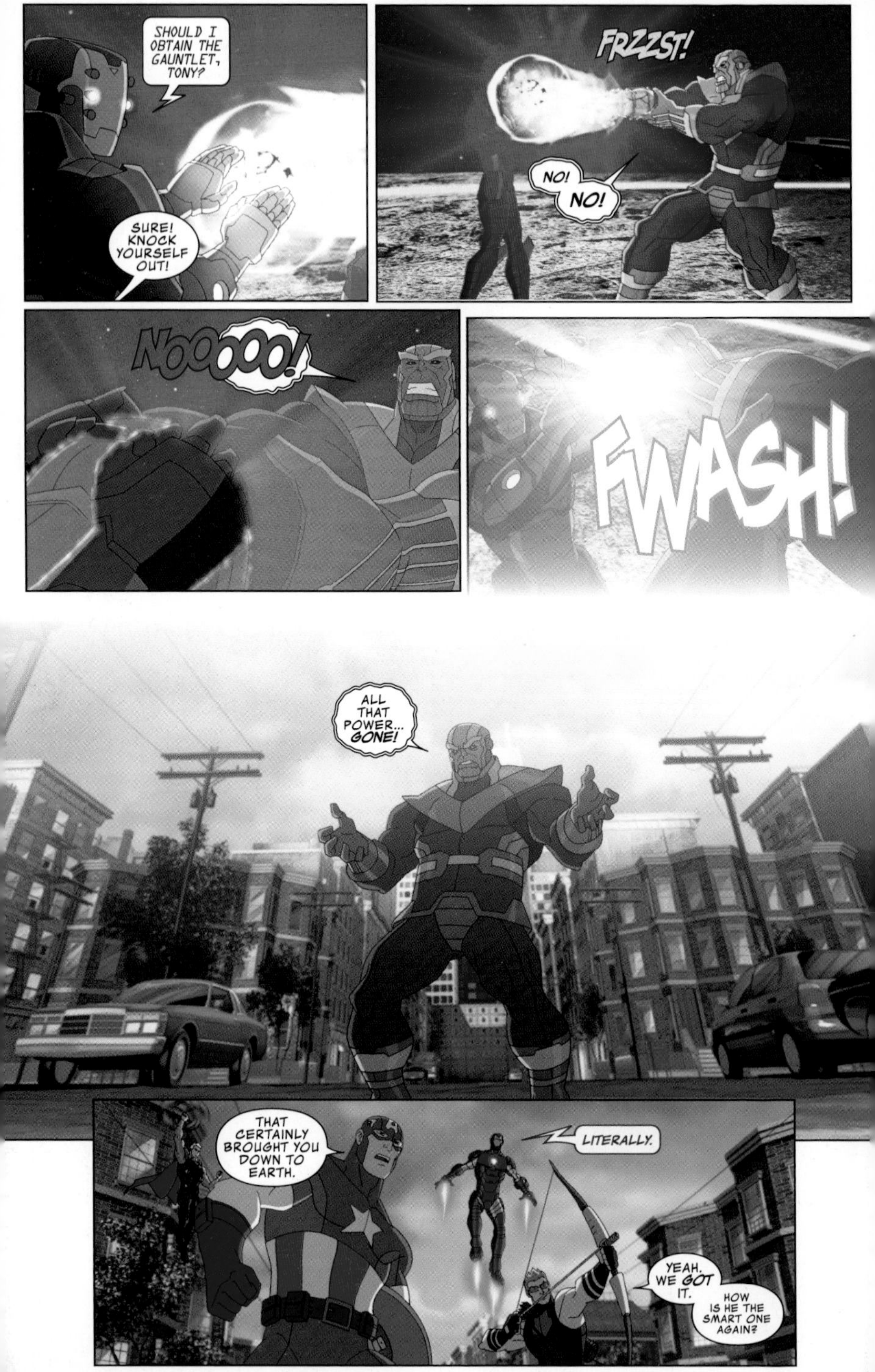
SHOULD I OBTAIN THE GAUNTLET, TONY?
SURE! KNOCK YOURSELF OUT!
FRZZST!
NO! NO!
NOOOOO!
FWASH!
ALL THAT POWER... GONE!
THAT CERTAINLY BROUGHT YOU DOWN TO EARTH.
LITERALLY.
YEAH. WE GOT IT.
HOW IS HE THE SMART ONE AGAIN?

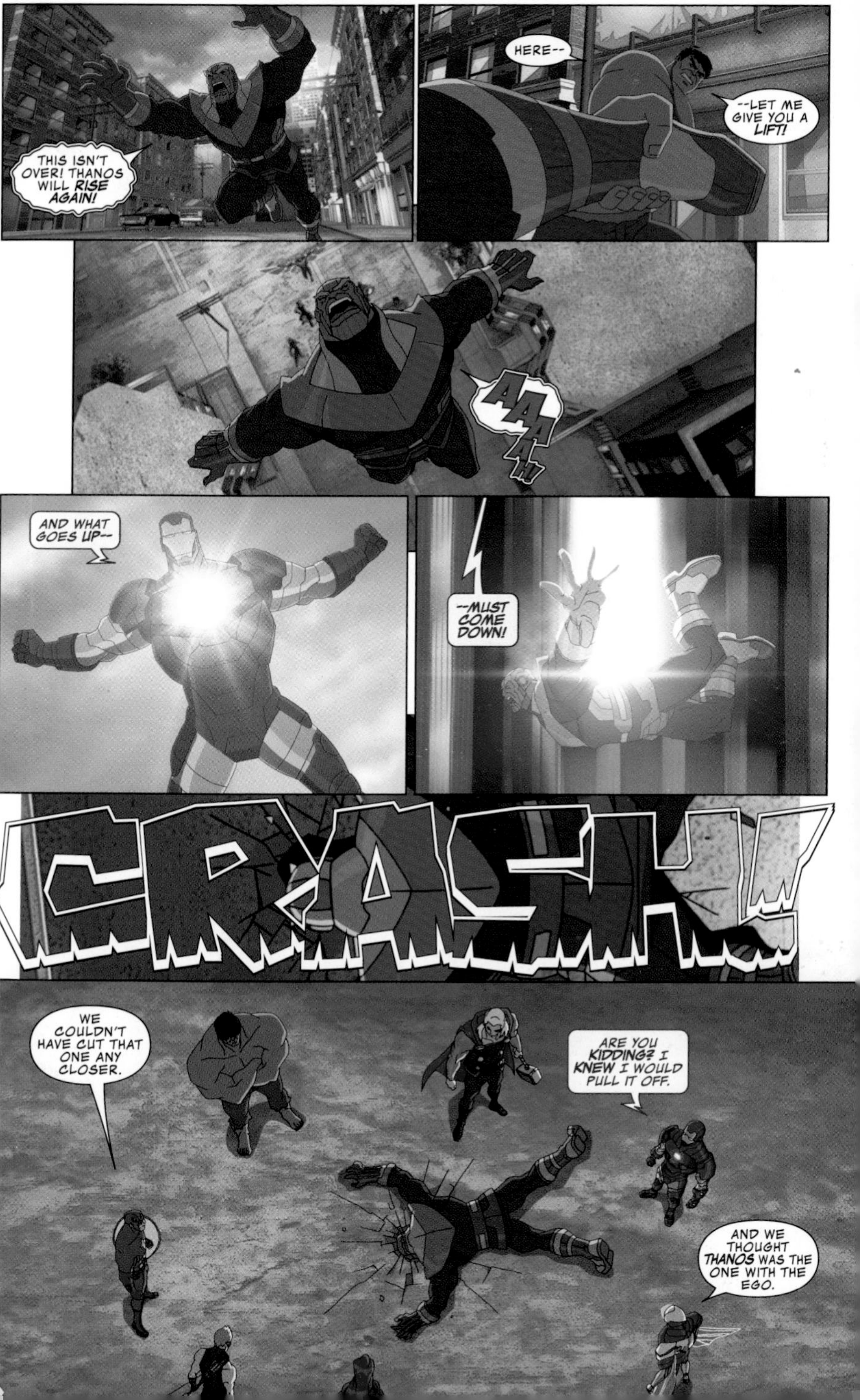
THIS ISN'T OVER! THANOS WILL RISE AGAIN!
HERE--
--LET ME GIVE YOU A LIFT!
AAAAH!
AND WHAT GOES UP--
--MUST COME DOWN!
CRASH!
WE COULDN'T HAVE CUT THAT ONE ANY CLOSER.
ARE YOU KIDDING? I KNEW I WOULD PULL IT OFF.
AND WE THOUGHT THANOS WAS THE ONE WITH THE EGO.

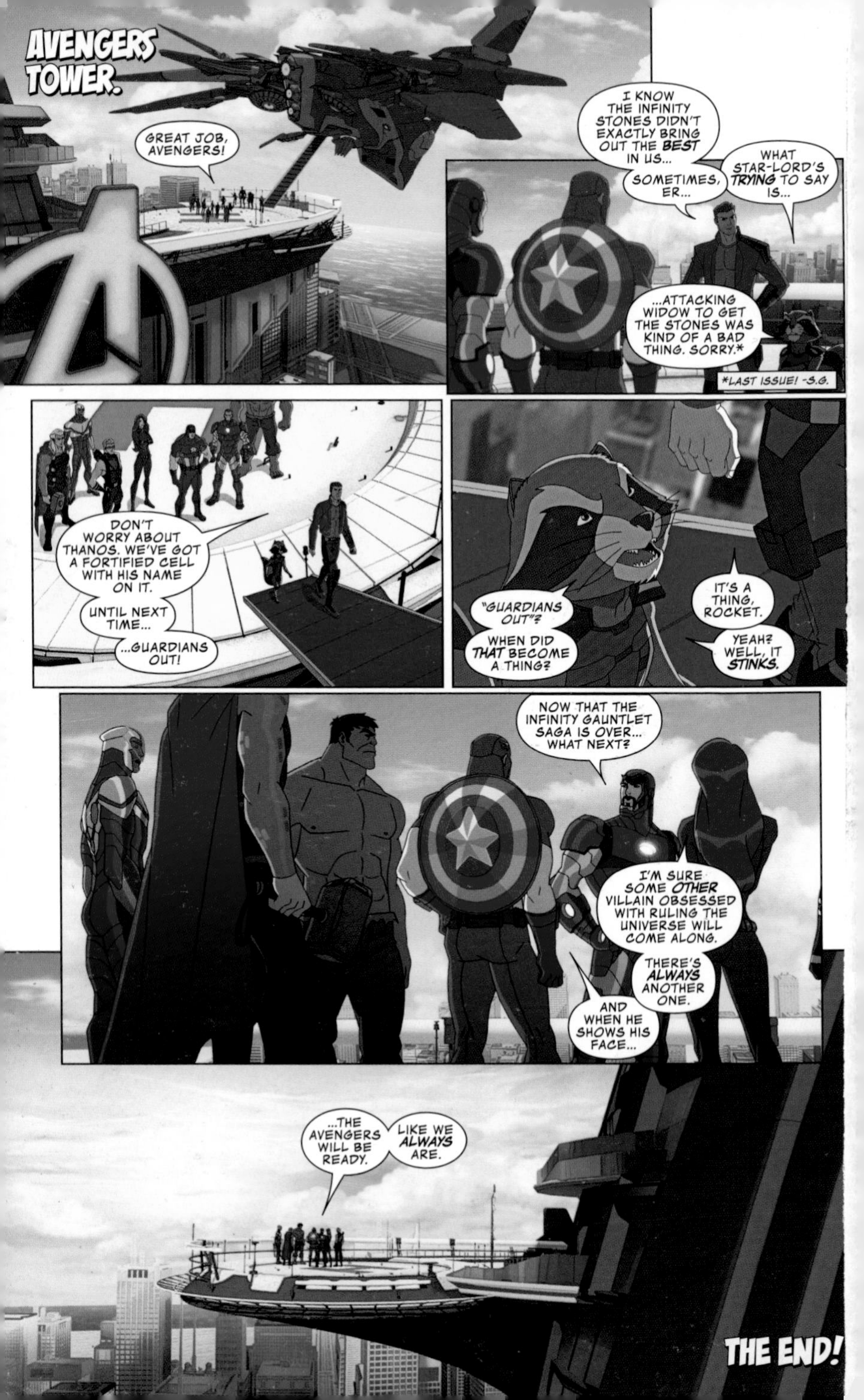
AVENGERS TOWER.
GREAT JOB, AVENGERS!
I KNOW THE INFINITY STONES DIDN'T EXACTLY BRING OUT THE BEST IN US...
SOMETIMES, ER...
WHAT STAR-LORD'S TRYING TO SAY IS...
...ATTACKING WIDOW TO GET THE STONES WAS KIND OF A BAD THING. SORRY.*
*LAST ISSUE! -S.G.
DON'T WORRY ABOUT THANOS. WE'VE GOT A FORTIFIED CELL WITH HIS NAME ON IT.
UNTIL NEXT TIME...
...GUARDIANS OUT!
"GUARDIANS OUT"?
WHEN DID THAT BECOME A THING?
IT'S A THING, ROCKET.
YEAH? WELL, IT STINKS.
NOW THAT THE INFINITY GAUNTLET SAGA IS OVER... WHAT NEXT?
I'M SURE SOME OTHER VILLAIN OBSESSED WITH RULING THE UNIVERSE WILL COME ALONG.
THERE'S ALWAYS ANOTHER ONE.
AND WHEN HE SHOWS HIS FACE...
...THE AVENGERS WILL BE READY.
LIKE WE ALWAYS ARE.
THE END!